THE TRIUNE MAN

THE TRIUNE MAN

Richard A. Lupoff

Published by
BERKLEY PUBLISHING CORPORATION
Distributed by
G.P. PUTNAM'S SONS, NEW YORK

SBN: 399-11680-X

Library of Congress Catalog
Card Number: 75-26867

PRINTED IN THE UNITED STATES OF AMERICA

1. Sravasti

THEY came for him in the violent ward.

He lay writhing on the padded floor, thrashing in fury against his restraints. His arms were immobilized in a canvas camisole. His hair, drenched with sweat, whipped with each jerk of contorted neck muscles.

His chin was flecked with foam.

Between incoherent grunts and moans he shouted fearfully. "Project . . . engineering specs . . . performance bond . . . someone. . . ." He hunched himself to a seated posture, propped against the wall. His eyes blazed furiously as he cast his gaze around the padded room, but he seemed, nonetheless, to grow slightly calmer with the passage of the raging spasm.

A fresh torrent of words tumbled dispiritedly from his lips. "You could have . . . not like other . . . Satvan you could have. . . ." His head flopped onto his shoulder, sudden exhaustion overcoming him. His blond hair hung flaccidly before his eyes as they began slowly to glaze. His breathing, previously a series of ragged, nearly explosive gasps, grew slower.

He moaned once loudly and slid to the floor. A blackness fell before his eyes, a rushing filled his ears and in some small surviving corner of his mind sanity told him that it was happening again. He fought to retain control, forced his fingers to knot into fists inside the tapering canvas sleeves, commanded his eyelids to snap open, to return to him vision and contact with his surroundings.

But the blackness advanced inexorably until he felt himself fading into a tiny, impotent point of semiawareness only vaguely able to perceive his actions, quite incapable of controlling his body or his speech.

He rose from submersion in the black mind-sea where he

had floated since his last period of dominance, possessing the memories of the period between, expecting the hateful feel of the canvas restraining jacket and the softness of the floor of his hospital room.

Instead he found himself standing on a circular platform surrounded by strange devices, light sources and rods, conduits and oddly shaped panels covered with indicators that made no sense whatever to him. The plate upon which he stood seemed bitterly cold to his feet, which he realized with a start were bare. He swung his hands around freely, looked down and discovered that he was naked.

Startled, he swayed dizzily, found himself steadied by unexpected helpers, led unsteadily from the platform across a hard floor to some sort of chair. The room he was in was lighted oddly, as if for eyes attuned to a different spectrum from that in which he had grown up.

Strange shadows and unfamiliar forms seemed to materialize and fade before him. There were sounds, but they came from all directions. They seemed to contain words, but he was not able to tell what they were.

He raised his hands to his brow, suddenly trembling. He looked around. An incoherent gargling sound escaped from his throat. He started to speak. "I . . . I. . . ." He gathered his strength and managed to blurt the sentence.

"I—they were right after all! I've gone crackers!"

He examined himself, studying his nude body. Paunchy, soft, with a roll of excess flesh around his middle that stopped well short of grossness. He raised his eyes, trying to pierce the shadows around him.

"Who's there? Hello! Hey, what's happening?"

Whispers and uncertain cracklings.

"Hey, where is this place? What's going on?"

He jumped to his feet. No one, nothing tried to interfere with him. He swayed momentarily and again there was support from the vague forms that appeared and disappeared around him.

"Is this some new treatment?"

Hisses, something with a sound somewhere between a hiss and a moan, something with a sound somewhere between a moan and a grunt.

"Oh, I can't be—" He doubled over with wracking laughter. "I'm not dead! Oh, no, that's too freaky! Nossir, I won't believe that! Who's there?"

He leaned forward, peered deeply into the almost tangible murk that seemed to hang in the air like swamp gas over a stagnant pond. Amazingly, a face materialized before him, peered back into his own eyes. Black, vague, a wavering oval with features visible only as differently textured blurs against the vague background.

"Yeah, that's better. This is old Buddy here. I'm grateful you got me out of there, but where is *here*? Who are you?"

More faces, forming and fading behind the first. That one rising and growing nearer to him. A voice, a sound something like a voice.

"Old Buddy?"

Liquid burblings. Humming.

"Yeah, it's me all right!"

He felt perspiration beginning to form on his face. It ran from his armpits down his naked sides despite the chill of the . . . room. "You're not—" He cracked a smile, held his voice jocular despite a quaver halfway through. "You're not working for the despicable Doctor Anubis? Because if you are, ah—"

"Doctor Anubis?"

"Yeah. No, you're not. I could always tell that."

"We are not . . . Doctor Anubis. You are . . . ?"

"Yeah, yeah, right." He nodded twice, too quickly. Dizziness threatened to return. He clutched the arms that offered themselves.

"You are?"

"Yeah, I'm old Buddy all right. Buddy Satvan. You know, I do *Diamond Sutro.*" He looked around, trying to find faces in the gloom, trying to find acceptance and understanding of his statement.

The hiss.

"You are Diamond Sutro? You are Buddy Satvan?"

"Uh, no . . . and yes. I'm Buddy Satvan and I draw *Diamond Sutro.*"

"And Doctor Anubis, the despicable Doctor Anubis? You are also he?"

"Uh, no, I—"

"You had best come with us. You appear addled."

Strong hands guiding him, not roughly but not leaving any question that he would comply.

"Uh, okay. You did, uh. . . ." He allowed himself to be led farther away from the platform where he had first found himself, away from the seat he had used when he had left the platform.

They passed—Buddy and his guides—through a portal of some vague sort. Buddy felt himself beginning to slip away as he struggled to stand upright, keep his legs working properly. His vision grew faint, the murky room grew even darker, the rushing came to his ears again.

He cried out. "This isn't right! I haven't had my turn! I was only here a few minutes. Dang-crack you, who's coming? Let me—leave me—let me. . . ."

Darkness became complete. Buddy felt his control of his body lapse, thought he heard the voices of strangers, muffled and incomprehensible. Then he was gone.

Strong arms carried the portly blond man onward, reaching a raised pallet of some smooth material, cold as the platform he had stood upon, gray and dull. They lowered him onto it and vague figures clustered, conferring, raising dim faces to cast dismal looks upon the man lying, breathing heavily, naked upon the pallet.

Suddenly the figure rose upward from the waist. He swung his legs off the edge of the pallet and sat upright, balancing himself with his hands on the edge of the gray slab. With one hand he swept his hair back from his brow and then spoke sharply.

"Thank you, my friends. You have freed your leader from the imprisonment into which he was betrayed. Now we will proceed."

A dark figure loomed near him. "Are you—well?"

"Well? Your concern is appreciated. I will need some appropriate garments. At once. Have you a uniform or other suitable clothing?"

The figures conferred. One spoke. "You must. . . ." The voice faded out and in, nuances lost in the rushings of sonic vagaries. ". . . . our understanding . . . data available to us. Are you Old Buddy?"

"The name of the leader is Roland L. K. Washburn." He slid his thighs over the edge of the pallet and stood on the floor facing the dark forms. "Don't you know what clothing is?"

He peered at them, straining pale eyes against the darkness and the murk that filled the place. "Trousers. Tunic. Boots." He indicated the parts of his body where each garment would be used, gesturing with pudgy hands.

"Don't you—?" He reached out to grasp the nearest figure by the shirtfront. His hand encountered a vague, cool springiness.

He drew back, shocked. He held his hand against his chest with his other hand. He looked down at it, flexed his fingers, saw that no injury had been done.

He fixed the nearest dark form with a commanding glare that took in the others as well. "Identify yourself," he ordered.

They bent together, swaying and flowing in alien communion. Washburn heard sounds, fragments of unfamiliar syllables, unidentifiable interjections.

The central figure loomed forward again, features visible by their texture that contrasted with the rest of each being. Rush and gurgle of fluids, a distorted voice speaking. "We are . . . tell you . . . help understand . . . Yakshis [some word like Yakshis]. . . help us . . . save us . . . save you. . . ."

The sound subsided gradually rather than reaching a definite end.

"You are incoherent," Washburn snapped. "I require clothing. Look here! This floor is cold! It is entirely inappropriate for the leader to stand around naked on a cold floor!"

Heads together, the figures swayed.

Washburn pantomimed the act of donning clothes, slowly calling out the name of each garment as he mimed adjusting it in place.

"Ah . . ." sigh, ". . . ouh. . . ."

A shadow detached itself from the cluster, flitted into the murk. Washburn heard rustling sounds, thought he might be seeing vague movements in the darkness. The shadow returned carrying shards of some formless stuff. It held it toward Washburn, touched him with it.

Washburn recoiled from its touch. It was as if the vague figures had pressed a nothingness onto his naked flesh. The texture was a nontexture, the temperature a nontemperature. He peered at the stuff: even its color was a kind of characterless lack rather than a positive attribute.

Still, his eyes interpreted it as a dark, dull gray.

The . . . Yakshi . . . moved in a circle around Washburn, pressing the gray, flaccid stuff against him. It conformed itself loosely to the shape of his body, forming into baggy shirt and trousers. Washburn raised one foot and felt the stuff become a crude heavy-soled shoe.

"That's better," he grunted. "Now, let's get down to the matter at hand. Which of you is commander of this group?"

The shadows clustered, flitted, seemed almost to swoop. From them came the cold voice Washburn had heard before.

"We are . . . Yakshis are. . . ." Fade-out, watery rushing. "Welcome you here leader Roland L. K. Washburn . . . urgent assistance . . . all benefit or. . . ."

The voice faded out.

Washburn stepped forward toward the vague . . . Yakshis. They seemed to flitter away from his approach like dry leaves before a puff of wind.

"I want to know your names. You have names? And what is this organization? You are called Yakshis?"

"Yakshis . . . called, yes. You are Washburn."

"Dammit, yes!" Washburn clenched his fists, holding himself in rein. "Yes, I am. And I want to know your names. Each of you!"

He pointed angrily at the central figure confronting him.

"This Yakshi . . . yes, Washburn . . . called. . . ." The figure swayed, seemed to confer with another to either side, then resumed. "Called . . . Asoka. Washburn, Asoka."

"Good! And the others?"

"Yakshi. . . ." A sound like wind swishing through willow whips. "Nanda." A shadowy form rose, swooped forward and back.

"Yakshi . . . leader Washburn . . . Yakshi called . . . Kalinga."

They seemed to sigh together liquidly.

"All right, now we're getting somewhere. You in the middle, you seem to be the spokesman. Very well, ah, Asoka. You come with me and we can sort this out."

He strode past the vague shapes, headed for some edge of the room, some doorway to a place where he could command the situation beyond the murk and gloom that surrounded him. He turned back to see if Asoka was following him. The Yakshis stood still, wavering vaguely where they had been.

Washburn stamped back, tried to grab the central Yakshi by its shoulder. His hand jerked involuntarily away from the feel.

"Come on, then," he grunted. He gestured forcefully.

One of the Yakshis rose straight toward the indistinct dome above them, towered momentarily over Washburn as if it were going to swoop on him, but another spun and rose and interposed itself between the looming shadow and the man.

"Come along," Washburn repeated. The remaining Yakshi glided after him. Snorting, Washburn marched in a straight line, his hands held slightly before him to ward off any obstruction, his eyes straining to pierce the gloom and murk surrounding him.

"Washburn. . . ." The Yakshi's watery voice burbled.

He continued. His hands encountered an obstacle, a surface that felt strangely as if it were smooth as glass yet corrugated at the same time. He felt around, searching for some sign of a doorway or window. "Open up!" he commanded.

A section of the wall swung away.

Washburn took half a step through the portal before the blinding flash of sensory overload smote him. Dazzled, deafened, assailed by odors and flavors, the nerve endings of his skin set atingle. Up and down lost their meaning. He staggered backward, screaming "Betrayed!" and collapsed.

He lay on the floor crouching like a fetus, holding his head between his knees and his arms over his blond scalp. He moaned.

"Washburn. . . ." Asoka piped, "Not harm . . . allow . . . show. . . ."

Washburn let the Yakshi uncurl him carefully, aiding him

to his feet. In a few minutes he was upright, fighting down a roaring in his ears and a darkness that threatened momentarily to cut off even the strange dim murk of his surroundings. He clenched his teeth, gritted out words in a bitter hiss. "Not now, I won't let go now!"

Asoka guided Washburn, walking him confidently. Clearly the gloom of the environment provided no obstacle to his vision. Washburn held one hand out laterally, touching the strange smooth-rippled wall as he walked. After a while they came to a place where the murk seemed to grow thinner, the atmosphere marginally brighter.

The Yakshi stopped Washburn, guided him to a vaguely chair-shaped object, pressed him gently down upon it.

Washburn sat.

He was still shaken from the moment of total input. "What was that—that door I started through? I demand to know what this place is!"

"Yess . . . regret your . . . hurt . . . difficult . . . maintain . . . form . . . speech." The figure seemed to sink into itself momentarily, as if gathering strength to continue. "Washburn . . . permit. . . ." The figure writhed in some alien gesture. "Permit . . . demonstrate. . . ."

"All right!"

From the murk-covered floor beside the alien a pedestal rose to waist height. Washburn followed as closely as the diffused lighting permitted. The Yakshi moved, bent over the pedestal and manipulated small objects on its surface. He—or it—gave the impression of a machine operator setting controls.

Washburn's seat slid beneath him, stretching and distorting itself like a dentist's chair. Washburn clung to its sides, ready to leap up and make his escape.

The darkness above him cleared. Mist rolled away, leaving a clear view of the sky above. Washburn could not tell whether the chamber had opened to the sky or was covered by a perfectly transparent dome. He peered upward.

The sky was black with night, dotted with an array of bright points, swirls and clouds wholly unlike any Washburn had ever seen before. No familiar constellation showed itself, no recognizable object—only uncountable stars and unrecognizable distant galaxies.

In a far quadrant of the sky, surrounded by a glowing border of deep orange, an irregularly shaped blob of utter blackness writhed.

Washburn blinked. Against the blackness of the Yakshis, the dim murk of the chambers he had walked through, the blackness of the sky offered a still darker contrast. And against *that* blackness, the bright-edged blob—its shape had now become suggestive—was still blacker, an ultimate blackness that seemed to negate not merely material objects but even vacant volume.

The glowing orange edges writhed and curled. Washburn felt himself mimicking their movements with his body. He fought down a faint attack of the ear-roaring, the eye-dimming that he knew so well. He gazed at the black shape above him.

It resembled a great winged creature flapping angrily across the sky. It was a huge malevolent face peering down into the wickedness of the world. It was a hooded serpent prepared to devour the world, a monstrous famished maw ready to swallow all.

Washburn was falling upward into its yawning depths, clutching frantically at the edges of his couch, crying out to be saved.

He sat up, sweat pouring from him, holding a hand over his eyes to blot the horror from them. He scrambled off the seat and ran to Asoka. "Take it away! Cover it up!"

The Yakshi manipulated the controls on his console. Overhead the mists rolled back obliterating the sky. Washburn and Asoka stood and faced each other.

"Can you . . . we cannot . . . understand. . . ." The Yakshi gestured toward the section of roof above them where the orange-edged thing had appeared. Beside him the console had sunk back into the floor. Asoka and Washburn stood as they had earlier, shrouded in murk and gloom.

"You'll have to do better than that," Washburn glowered. He felt automatically of his new clothing, searching for a weapon of any sort.

There was none.

"Come then . . . leader Washburn." The Yakshi looked smaller, as if he had been drained of energy and of hope. "Understanding . . . is. . . ." A gurgle and rush. "One Yakshi, less Yakshi. . . ."

He took Washburn by the elbow, led him firmly through the murk. Washburn was unable to tell what course they followed. But shortly when Asoka stopped Washburn could sense the alien's companions, Nanda and Kalinga, swaying and fluttering in the gloom. Again they seemed to confer, almost to blend, swaying and nodding, indistinct susurrating sounds emerging from them.

They separated and moved to surround Washburn. He slid between them suspiciously, spun to face them again. "Watch it!" he commanded.

They moaned. "Not . . . will not . . . Washburn . . . afraid . . . hurt . . . will not harm. . . ."

He allowed them to shepherd him to another chamber, another seat. He crouched tentatively on the edge of it, watching the Yakshis. One of them—he guessed Asoka—lay back on a moving couch. The other Yakshi fetched a circlet of gloomily flashing metal and placed it on their companion's head.

Then they turned to Washburn, a similar circlet extended toward him. "No, you don't!" he shouted. He started to flee but was caught by one of the Yakshis and forced back onto his seat.

"Not . . . harm." Roar and sweep. "Not . . . hurt you . . . leader."

Gingerly, Washburn let the creature draw the circlet over his head.

2. Hollywood

"CHRIST, will you look at that crap in the sky! No wonder this place is called the smog capital of the world!"

Cantrowicz had the window seat so Burt Bahnson had to

lean over his shoulder to see out the window of the 747 circling LAX. All he could do was shake his head in appalled agreement.

"Well, here we go. You reset your watch yet?"

Burt looked at the dial of his electronic Seiko. "No. I'm still on New York time." He pulled out the stem and reset his readout for LA time, then slipped the watch back on his wrist.

"Better finish up, eh?" Burt tilted his drink, ran his tongue around the inside of the rim savoring the last woody burning of the whiskey, then lowered the plastic cup. He buckled himself into his seat belt in obedience to the letters that flashed across the overhead message board.

"Number one just better have that car waiting," Cantrowicz growled as the 747 banked into a long, thundering turn to make its final approach and landing. "Christ, if there's one thing I hate it's having to fight car rentals. Maybe we should have had somebody meet us instead."

"No, I thought we'd agreed. That is, I mean, it'll be more convenient for us to have a car for ourselves while we're here. To go to the hotel and all."

"Yeah, yeah, we did work it out. Okay, Burt. I'd as soon have settled this in New York, but you know these Hollywood types—hate to get off their own turf. I think they all have some kind of inadequacy syndrome. Work out their hangups on the screen instead of where they got 'em. If a weekend with a hot broad and a case of Scotch doesn't take care of 'em they ought to see a shrink, not drag us across the continent for one meeting!"

"You're right," Burt said. He picked up his empty glass and ran his tongue around the inside of the rim again.

The plane touched down heavily, its engines reversed to brake its momentum. It slowed and rolled to a stop.

Burt stood up and waited for Cantrowicz to thread his bulk out of the big first-class seat and lead their march to the exit. The smiling stewardess handed each of them his hat and Burt his briefcase—Arch Cantrowicz liked to travel light and Burt kept track of both their papers when Arch wasn't actually using them.

Hertz had a new LeMans ready for them and they threaded their way from LAX onto the freeway, keeping the AM radio on the airport's low-powered traffic control station until the signal disappeared into a roar of static.

"Nice car," Burt said. "Handles nicely."

He pulled the LeMans into the northbound lanes, found a niche in the off-hour traffic and began to watch for exit signs. They didn't have too far to go on the freeway. "Too bad Buddy Satvan couldn't come along. He'd really enjoy this trip. Kind of the star of the show, don't you think?"

Burt cast a glance at Arch Cantrowicz. Cantrowicz had bitten the tip off a cigar and spit it onto the floor of the LeMans. He leaned forward and punched the car's electric lighter. The only answer he offered Burt was a grunt. Burt wasn't sure whether that indicated agreement or disapproval.

"Well, maybe he'll pull out of it. Meanwhile Albertson is keeping up the strip. Buddy has this secretary, you know her? Tara something-or-other. Very nice person."

"Yeah," Arch growled around his cigar. "Gone with the wind."

Burt laughed nervously. "Uh, anyway, she goes down there to that hospital in Virginia where they have Buddy. They let her in for story conferences. Willy Albertson doesn't go. Buddy works with Tara, dictates into a cassette machine, you know. He does some sketches, too. Then Tara types up the cassettes and Willy draws from the script and Buddy's roughs."

Arch grunted.

Bahnson rotated a switch on the dashboard and the Pontiac's air conditioner whirred into action, sucking away the cigar smoke and replacing it with washed and filtered air. The pungent smell of the cigar gave way to an odor of exhaust fumes that managed somehow to triumph over the charcoal and fiber filters of the air conditioner.

Arch grunted and gestured with his cigar.

"Right," Burt responded, "here we go." He fought his way over to the exit lane and dropped from the freeway onto Pico. "Should I head for the hotel?" he asked. "Or would you rather—?" He looked at his watch.

"Studio," Cantrowicz said.

Burt maneuvered the LeMans through rows of local traffic on Pico, craning for sight of the studio sign on the left where his travel directions said it would be. "Aha!" He swept into the left-turn lane and pulled up at the traffic light in front of the studio. A minute later he was through the front gate and rolling the hardtop through the outer parking lot.

The studio road led past a row of turn-of-the-century storefronts and under the First Avenue El. "Will ya look at that!" Arch Cantrowicz laughed. "Christ, you'd think you were right back—I grew up in this neighborhood. Henry Street, Chatham Square. Isn't that incredible!" He laughed again.

Burt smiled, mirroring Arch's pleasure. If the mood continued it would make for a pleasanter time for him, he knew. He pulled the car to a stop in front of Tony Pastor's restaurant where a yellow-and-black barrier had been lowered from a guard's cabin. He turned and saw Arch gazing happily at the painted building fronts, then looked back at the uniformed man who'd stepped from the cabin and was peering in the car window.

"Ah, Mr. Sugarman is expecting us," Burt said. "Mr. Cantrowicz and Mr. Bahnson from, ah, New York? Mrs. Shapiro, Mr. Sugarman's, ah, secretary, said just to give our names?"

The guard stepped back inside his cabin and consulted a clipboard with a sheaf of pages attached to it. He picked up a phone and dialed, then mumbled a few words.

He stepped out of the cabin again and leaned into the car, pointing. "Just turn left at the beer garden," he said, "and park in the little lot about seventy-five yards inside."

Burt nodded.

"You'll see a red brick building, it's actually the back of Tony Pastor's. Go in the main entrance and you'll find a building map. Mr. Sugarman's office is three twenty-eight, that's third floor." The guard reached in his pocket and pulled a day-glo placard from it. He handed it to Burt. "Leave this on your windshield, sir, and please return it when you leave the studio."

He stepped back inside the cabin.

The barrier lifted and Burt pulled the car forward.

"You'd be amazed at how many greats started in places like that," Arch Cantrowicz reminisced. "Would you believe, when I was a kid I actually saw Al Jolson in this neighborhood? And

Fanny Brice? And Eddie Cantor and George Jessel and Jimmy Durante, every one of 'em! They all got their start around here." He gestured with his cigar. "They were all big *machers* by the time I saw them, but they all came back, every one of them! Every one!"

Stuart Sugarman stood up when Cantrowicz and Bahnson entered his office. He introduced them to the others already assembled, then asked if they'd eaten yet.

"Uh, yes, on the airplane, thanks," Burt said.

"Fine, fine. Now, if anybody gets hungry, Mrs. Shapiro can call down to the commissary and they'll make up a tray. Don't be shy, anything you want just ask, all right?" He grinned, flashing bright, Hollywood-perfect teeth. His hair was silvery white and thick, dropping to his velour shirt collar with just the hint of a flip to the ends.

"Let's see." Cantrowicz checked the hour. "I'm still on east coast time. Hah. Well, snacks are nice, but I didn't jet three thousand miles for corned beef. What do we have?"

Sugarman laughed and made a placating gesture. "I see you're a very blunt man, Archie. Good, I like directness. Okay. We like *Diamond Sutro* a lot. The network agrees." He inclined his silvery head toward Melody Warwick, a trim redhead wearing huge tinted glasses and a pale tan slack suit. Melody nodded agreement.

"The network is willing to put up some front money and we're willing to drop in some cash of our own." Sugarman leaned back in his chair, resting his elbows on its pale kid arms and spreading his manicured hands in the air. "Of course there are a few little hurdles to clear, but I'm sure we can handle them."

Cantrowicz grunted. "Ah-*ha.* How come *Diamond Sutro*? We have a lot of other strips. What about Big Pro?"

Melody Warwick leaned forward and spoke in a cool, polished voice. "Mr. Cantrowicz, we examined our ratings and trends for the past ten seasons and projected them for the next five. Personally I was doubtful of the value of going back that far or of projecting ahead that far, what with the volatility of our audience.

"But our statisticians were very eager to look for long-term trends and they got funded out of Seventh Avenue so we gave them their heads.

"Well, all for the best." She smiled. "They did pull some interesting cycles out of their computer printouts. And one thing that was very definitely indicated was that we're going to have a slot coming up for a good fantasy adventure. Everything converges, you see—we can spot five or six cycles with their curves moving up and down in different periodicities. Sometimes a couple of them coincide and reinforce each other. Sometimes three or even four of them coincide and you get a super hit."

She stopped and reached into a leatherette folder on her lap, pulled out a sheet of graph paper with multicolored lines running across it. "What our computer people found is a coming convergence of at least six cycles. And that means—jackpot!"

She laid the folder on Sugarman's desk. "If we know how to cash in on it, of course."

Cantrowicz leaned forward and examined the chart. After a minute he said, "What's this all mean?"

A black man in an ultaconservative business suit adjusted his narrow polka-dotted tie and cleared his throat. "I've been tapped as executive producer of the *Diamond Sutro* series. If we get to the series stage, of course."

Burt Bahnson watched his chief study the black man. Finally Cantrowicz said "Yes. Amos Elliott. I'm good at names. Never forget one."

"Very well," Elliott said. "Now then, what the network people worked out, and our own statisticians checked their conclusions and agree, is that the public is about ready for something that will combine fantasy with suspense and adventure. And with a touch of nostalgia."

He leaned forward, intense. "Maybe a tincture of camp as well. For comic relief, you see. A little sex appeal. Some hot special effects and extravagant costumes and sets." He sat nodding agreement with himself.

"And this adds up to *Diamond Sutro*?" Cantrowicz grunted.

"Exactly," Sugarman said.

Cantrowicz glared at Bahnson for a minute. Finally Burt

said, "Ah, I wonder, Mr. Sugarman, if we might have a little refreshment. Ah, liquid refreshment, that is, ah-ha." He grinned.

Sugarman buzzed for his secretary. He spoke a few words and she disappeared into a side office.

"I'll tell you, Stuart—it's okay if I call you that? You call me Arch, okay, not Archie?—I'll tell you," Cantrowicz resumed, "I don't want anybody fucking up a valuable property. You know? I don't know why some shows you do so good and some you just bitch up."

Sugarman inclined his silvery head toward Amos Elliott. "One of our brightest men. Fine credits. And it won't hurt any in getting minority market exposure, you know."

"That isn't what I mean. Look—" He stopped talking as Mrs. Shapiro reappeared with a tray.

"Here, let me help you," Sugarman said. He served drinks all around, then raised his glass. "Success!" he said.

Cantrowicz downed half his drink and deposited the glass on the edge of Sugarman's desk. "I don't watch TV myself," he said. "Too busy earning a buck. But my kids have a color set and they tell me what's going on. Now if you want *Diamond Sutro,* aside from making the bucks right—"

"We won't go less than first class, Mr. Cantrowicz." That from Melody Warwick.

"Okay, good, we'll see about getting into some solid figures in a little while. You know, adjectives are nice, but I like numbers better."

He clenched a fist and struck the top of Sugarman's desk with it. "But you aren't going to butcher *Diamond Sutro* the way you killed that *Shazam* show. It's written for two-year-olds! And no Saturday morning ghetto, either! Prime time, and adult scripts! And the syndicate has to retain a veto over casting and stories or it's no deal!"

Sugarman looked at Elliott, then at Melody Warwick.

They both shook their heads.

"We'll have to see about that. I mean, we definitely appreciate getting your inputs, Archie, but we won't try to tell you how to run a comics syndicate and you mustn't try to run our studio. They're completely separate areas of expertise, you see."

"Sure I do. I saw what you did to *Shazam,* too!"

"Actually, we didn't do it," Amos interjected. "It was another studio."

"And another network," Melody added.

"All right, all right. You know what I mean." Cantrowicz tossed down the rest of his drink, held the glass to Sugarman for a refill.

"I do understand your concern, sir," Amos Elliott put in. "And I assure you, this will be a prime-time production with a top budget."

Cantrowicz shook his head. "I don't understand one other thing, though. Look, you guys did *Batman*—"

"I wish we had!"

"I mean, you guys, you guys in Hollywood. You guys in TV." He plucked his cold cigar from the ashtray where he'd dropped it. Burt Bahnson leaned over to hold a match for him. Cantrowicz puffed the cigar back into life. "Can't beat a Garcia and Vega," he sighed.

Sugarman leaned back and pressed a button on the window air conditioner behind him.

"What I'm telling you guys," Cantrowicz resumed, "is that you did right by *Batman* and then you turned around and botched the *Green Hornet.* Same trip, same kind of production. But one of 'em had it and the other didn't. Now if you want *Diamond Sutro* you've got to do a show that has it. You see?"

He looked around at the others.

"Because it's a successful strip," Cantrowicz continued, "it's picking up papers, picking up subsidiary sales. It's turning a lot of bucks and I want it for the long pull, not for a flash in the pan and tomorrow it's dead on its feet, you see? Back to a handful of papers. I don't want that. I won't put up with it."

Sugarman said, "Okay. You want to dump Amos? We'll put somebody else on the show."

Amos Elliott choked.

"Nah, that's all right. But we keep our hand in or you can go buy somebody else's super hero."

"I know that. Frankly"—Sugarman leaned across his mahogany-topped desk—"we've taken options on a couple already. Eh?" He grinned, reached across the desk, closed his fingers around Cantrowicz's biceps for a moment. "But the quiz kids say *Diamond Sutro* has the best chance to make a real breakthrough."

He inclined his white head toward Amos and Melody.

"And," he continued, "it's my favorite strip!"

Cantrowicz got out of his chair and walked once around the room. He pulled back a curtain and looked out onto the New York of seventy-five years before. "Absolutely amazing."

He pointed down at a painted storefront. "See that candy store? I bought the *Forward* in that store. A few years later, I think, than the way you have it. But the same place. I drank egg creams there. They had a cat in the store, a big black and white tomcat.

"He had a white face with a little dark place like a mustache and a little goatee. We used to call him Trotsky."

He turned around and faced the others. "Okay, those are my conditions. I want to hear some numbers and if I like what I hear we can turn the legal beagles loose."

Sugarman beamed. "There is one little problem from our end, Archie. We can leave the other things for the lawyers and the accountants, eh—as long as we like each other we can work together. But there's one little thing that we have to get out of the way."

Cantrowicz grunted an interrogative.

"This, ah, this thing that happened in Virginia," Sugarman began.

Cantrowicz looked at him stony-faced.

"This whole mess with your cartoonist and that murder case."

Burt Bahnson said, "But Buddy was acquitted. The judge ruled that it was temporary insanity, he had experts in court. Besides, that fellow Schrieber—"

"Of course, of course." Sugarman nodded, looking sympathetic. "Who could blame him anyway? Scum like Schrieber, huh! But this involvement with that nazi group, that fellow Washburn. Very bad. Very, very bad."

Melody put in: "Negative exposure. Could push us right off the screen. Bad for other network shows, too."

"What we need to know, Archie," Sugarman said, "is whether you can get rid of this Satvan. Quietly. If you can, we're ready to go ahead with a two-part pilot and the network will commit themselves to prime time. If the pilot draws any kind of audience—which I'm sure it will—then Melody says they're prepared to take the series."

He steepled his fingers, peered over them through glittering gold-rimmed glasses. "Except for this fellow Satvan. We can't have a killer hanging around our necks like an albatross."

"But the court," Burt countered, "and the psychiatrists. They ruled that Buddy and this Washburn character were both victims of a mental disorder. They're both fragmentary segments of an, ah, of a dissociated personality. There was no conviction!"

"Doesn't matter," Melody Warwick purred. "Bad publicity. The old saw that all publicity is good may apply in some businesses but not in ours."

She smiled at Arch Cantrowicz. "Who owns *Diamond Sutro,* Mr. Cantrowicz? The syndicate? Or this little cartoonist?"

"Little cartoonist!" Bahnson exploded.

Cantrowicz silenced him with a hand on his arm. He put his cigar down and signaled to Burt for some papers from the briefcase. Cantrowicz shuffled folders, picked up his glass and sipped from it.

"I checked that out before we flew out here. We own *Diamond Sutro.* The syndicate does. We can dump Buddy Satvan in a minute. But he's our talent. We're in the same boat that you are—a million people with technical competence but just a handful with what you'd call real talent."

Stuart Sugarman beamed benignly. "Dump him, Archie. You have anything lined up for tonight? I'll ask Mrs. Shapiro to phone my house and have them set an extra place. Do you mind pot luck?"

Melody Warwick said, "I have to issue a caveat, Mr. Sugarman, Mr. Cantrowicz." She was fishing in her own folder, pulling out interoffice memoranda and typed reports.

"Eh? What's the matter?"

"Our legal department—at the network—checked out some recent court actions at my request. Not that I expected any problems." She smiled at Sugarman, then at Cantrowicz. "But just in case."

She slid a manila folder out of the leatherette cover. "You

see, there've been some challenges to the whole system of publishers buying characters. It goes all the way back, you know. The whole question of what a publisher is buying—limited rights, outright title to a specific work, and so on. But the precedents for buying a story and them claiming ownership of the characters are in jeopardy."

Cantrowicz turned toward Bahnson. "God damn it, Burt, get on the horn and get our lawyers off their ass! What the hell are we paying those bastards for?"

"Maybe you could buy him off," Sugarman suggested. "Could you do that? Or kick him upstairs, just get him out of the spotlight."

"We'll have to see about that."

"Well, it's getting late," Sugarman announced. "Shall we ask Mrs. Shapiro to type up a little memorandum of today's meeting? And then I suppose we can continue some low-budget exploratory work while we settle this other problem."

Bahnson turned and saw that Arch Cantrowicz was perspiring heavily. "I'm sure we can get it settled," Arch said, "I'm really very sure we can."

3. Sravasti

HE could see and hear what was happening, and gradually he found himself able to control his body. Could blink his eyes, wiggle his toes, flex his hands into fists and then relax them again.

It would have been almost pleasant to lie there savoring the returning control of his muscles, but there was a rush of information pouring into him. Pictures and sounds from some source seemed to well up in his brain. The sensation was like that of ancient, faded recollections rising spontaneously to consciousness.

He tried to sit up and was pleased that he could. What strange place was this? He had no idea. He had only limited ccess to Washburn's memory, and the dim, purply-gray nurk in which he found himself was vaguely familiar. Vashburn's recollections, to which he looked for some inkling f what was happening, were blurred and jumbled with the nformation still welling up so disquietingly within his mind.

He raised one hand, put it to his forehead in a characteristic esture, and found the metal band. The band was connected y a wire or lightweight cable to—he couldn't tell. The other nd of the thin conduit was lost in dimness. But he was sitting n some sort of table or raised pallet, and he could see, not far way, a similar platformlike device with another figure lying n it.

The figure was black, not as a black man was, but as if it had een coated in a dull, nonreflective substance like lampblack, hen shrouded in billows of soft, funereal gauze. The result vas a shape only vaguely human, visible as little more than a ilhouette more intensely dark than the darkness around it. But he could see that the figure lay motionless, a band of metal round its head and a cable stretching from it into the gloom vhere it was lost like his own.

"Phew!" he hissed. "Thanks for bringin' me back! I don't now what's goin' on here, but I thought we were maybe ettin' someplace before, startin' to get someplace anyhow, vhen I blacked out." He peered into the gloom, searching the oom, saw a couple of indistinct figures standing in apparent bservation of himself and the reclining shadow.

"It's me, Buddy. I'm back again."

The welling of memories ceased. One of the shadowy forms tanding and observing stepped to the platform where the ther lay. It bent to its dark companion, touched the metal irclet on its head, then remained bent over, moving slightly as f engaged in agitated conversation.

It rose finally and turned toward Buddy. "You are . . . atvan. You are . . . Washburn." The figure made a gesture. The movement was not quite human, yet it was clearly in-icative of puzzlement.

"I'm Buddy. Yeah, Washburn, too, I suppose. I've been, h"—he ran a hand nervously through his disordered hair— ah, sick. Yeh. There's this, you know, ah, it's called multiple ersonality, right? You understand? Like, ah, there was even

this movie about it one time, people say, well, you understan
your, ah, condition, can't you just get over it?

"And I say well look, I don't like it, you know? But I can'
control the dam, ah, suppose you had a broken leg and yo
didn't know it, but you knew *something* was fiddlin' the matte
and somebody looked at your leg and said, ah, *look*, man, yo
got a broken *leg*, for cripe's sake, and you said, oh yea, I see
that's right, that's what's the matter!

"But that wouldn't make the broken leg all better, would it
You see?"

The two black figures, one recumbent, one standing ove
the other, seemed to look at him. Buddy tried to make ou
facial features on them, but he could only detect vague blurs
blobs of blackness against blackness that might suggest eye
and mouths or that might only be his imagination acting up

"Do you see?" he asked again.

"You are"—sound like rushing water—"two men? one ma
. . . two men?"

Oh boy, what a mess! "Okay, look, I'm Buddy Satvan, right
I do this super hero strip for a living, right? I do the script an
some roughs, my detail man does the finishes, right? Bac
comes Diamond Sutro, defender of the universe. Eighteen
twenty million readers in thirty-seven newspapers."

Whispering, crackling. "Sutro . . . men?"

Wow, these characters just don't dig it. Buddy decided on
new tack. He put both hands on the metal band circling hi
forehead. "Look, what *is* this?" He pointed to the recumben
shadow, then to his own forehead, to the band, repeated th
question slowly, separating each word.

The standing shadow answered. "Ah . . . ahh . . . yes. T
give you"—swish, crackle—"tell you . . . pictures, Sutro
Pictures, Satvan?"

The figure placed an appendage—Buddy tried hard to se
it as a hand—on the head of the other figure, then lifted th
appendage again and crossed to where Buddy sat. With gentl
force the shadow pressed Buddy's hands away from th
headband.

"You must"—whir, sigh—"think"—sigh, pause—"see in
side."

The shadow pointed with a vague, looming arm. At the ark figure recumbent on the pallet. At Buddy. It pressed ack on his chest, pressed him down onto the pallet again.
Buddy let himself be pushed down so that he lay supine, his reath—at least the air of this strange place was breathable— hallow and fast. He had to stay in control. This weird situa- on was bad enough without letting his control lapse, without gain being overtaken by Roland Washburn.
Alien memories began to well within Buddy's mind. He ied to push his own consciousness through the headband, own the cable that he realized must be connected to that of he dark figure.
He saw—the universe! Some sort of gigantic, cosmic erspective that envisioned astronomical bodies—and dis- ances—far beyond his own grasp. He saw the frightening range-rimmed nullity, the blot that seemed to devour space self, its deformed edges writhing like glowing embers on a noldering log.
As the figure grew it blotted out glowing bodies. Buddy ould not even guess at its size or at what the bodies were. On he gigantic scale of the image in his mind it was impossible to istinguish individual objects. He tried to analyze the great lowing forms, determine whether they were stars, clusters, alaxies, clusters or metaformations of some scale beyond ven the reach of vocabulary.
"What are you showing me?" he shouted.
There was no response. He blinked his eyes, shut them tight nd tried again, driving the metal query down the cable, oping to reach the enigmatic dark mind that lay at the other nd of the connection.
"Hello! Hello there!" He gritted his teeth, smirked angrily t his own banality. And yet. . . .
"Yes! I am here. Can you understand me?"
The response rushed into his brain. Joy, relief, communica- on! Not the painful, half-coherent burblings of the standing hadow. This was a presence in his very brain, not a voice but he suggestion of a voice: eager, innocent, almost childish. Not question, not words but the suggestion of words. Some sort f pulsing, rushing sensation that Buddy could almost feel his

brain work to sort out, to decode, to unjumble—to set int conceptual form that his consciousness could handle, coul deal with and respond to.

"I can do it!" He laughed with pleasure. "Gotcha!"

He drew a breath, closed his eyes. "I'm Buddy Satvar creator of Diamond Sutro also known as Dr. Goodlaw. Wh are you? How did I get here? What is this place? What' happening to me?" The questions came as fast as he coul frame them, tumbling one after another through his mind

The enigmatic presence on the other end of the cabl seemed to catch his enthusiasm and to respond to it.

"O great joy! We have much to tell you, much to understan together. We beg you for the greatest of deeds. We offer t you the ultimate of challenge."

"Yeah, s-sure. But start with the simple stuff, okay? Like ah—" Buddy started to sit up again, to gesture in keeping wit his question. "Like, one thing at a time. Um. . . ."

He let his thoughts trail away, overwhelmed by th puzzlement that swept over him.

"Of a certainty," the alien voice asked inside Buddy's mind Then he felt his brain somehow reworking the unfamilia rushing message, turning it into the familiar argot of home "Sure. One thing at a time, Buddy Satvan. Please proceed t ask your question. One thing at a time."

Buddy blinked at the remote, murky ceiling above him. H cleared his throat a couple of times for false starts, then h asked, "Uh, okay, for firsts, where am I?"

"We call this place Sravasti, Buddy Satvan."

"Sravasti?"

"An arbitrary name."

"But that doesn't tell me anything. The last I knew I was in the, ah, hospital." Nothing to lose here, he decided. "I was in the, ah, the violent ward. You know?"

A moment of silence. Confused images swirling through his mind, uncertain memories jumbling and wavering. "Your mind is not yours alone, Buddy Satvan? Another, this Washburn . . . ?"

"Yeah. And more. I think."

"But then. . . ."

"But never mind that now, okay? Okay?" Vague affirmation. "The hospital, it was in Virginia, you know?" Vague negation, vague disappointment-with-self.

"In America, right? No, huh? Earth? Sol?"

Negative. Regret.

Good cripes, that was really far-out *bad*! "Look," Buddy persisted, "maybe you try and tell me, hey? This place where we are now, it's called, ah, you said Samasti?"

"Sravasti."

"Right, okay, Sav—uh, Sravasti. I mean, is this a new planet I never heard of or what?

"Is it what the Martians call Mars? Or—" He made a mental shrug, felt somehow that it got through to the other. That it had made it through the cables that connected their headbands. That he had communicated at least his question.

"A planet? Ah." The alien mulled over the concept, Buddy could *feel* that much through the metallic band.

"A planet. No. Yes. Ah!"

"Come on, pal. Try!"

"Yes, yes, I understand. How to . . . ? Yes, very well, Buddy Satvan. This . . . place . . . Sravasti. It is not a planet as I detect the concept within you. No. But close enough."

"Yeah?"

"Sravasti was, hmm . . . created, yes?" Buddy nodded, pushing an image-concept of understanding down the cable.

"We created Sravasti. We, Yakshis. We are not beings like yourself, Buddy Satvan. We are—" Buddy saw a mental image of the dark being, a group of dark beings, rushing together, assembling themselves from hordes of infinitesimal black dots, essences of being.

"You see, Buddy Satvan?"

"Then you—aren't living creatures at all?"

A kind of puzzled flow seemed to bubble into Buddy's mind. "We are . . . living? Not-living? I cannot grasp the concepts fully, Buddy Satvan. We are conscious beings."

"Good enough."

"Long ago we built this . . . Sravasti. It is a, ah, *Sravasti.* I cannot . . . Buddy Satvan, try to see, I will make a picture."

An image welled into Buddy's brain, a recollection he had no inkling that he owned. In the vacuum of space great machines worked to build a construct of immense size and complexity. Something as large as a minor planet, thousands of miles in diameter.

Something roughly globular in shape but with girders and stanchions of staggering dimension being towed into space by rocket-boosted gliders, shoved and jockeyed into position by tiny guidance flares while the whole thing drifted in orbit high above a world the likes of which he had never imagined.

The memory seemed to skip like a series of stop-action sequence photos. From a few giant girders to a rapidly growing network of spidery shafts and installations . . . to a final application of gargantuan panels, facets of polished stuff that gave the final construct the aspect of a giant polyhelical toy revolving slowly like an artificial moon, reflecting the glare of the local sun and the reradiated daylight of its primary planet from one surface after another.

Briefly, giant specks of light danced across the face of the world below illuminating ruddy, rich, red-brown land masses, lushly vegetated greenbelts, glimmering ice caps and huge, tranquil seas.

Then by some means that Satvan failed to fathom the polyhedron began to drift away from its planet, its orbit altering from a circle to a slowly broadening spiral until it broke away and seemed almost to carom farther—and faster—from the sun.

It crossed the orbits of other planets and groups of multiple planets. Flares of shuttle craft appeared and disappeared as the polyhedron made a grand tour of the worlds of its parent solar system. Then as the last of the mites dropped away and sped back to their home worlds the polyhedron accelerated completely out of the system.

With a final jolting increase of speed it . . . disappeared. In its place was nothingness.

Buddy blinked at the pseudomemory image, calling it back from the depths of his mind. It came. It came back to him as if the newly implanted recollection had been his own from the start.

The polyhedron, spiraling outward from the sun, crossing the orbit of the outermost planet of the system—a tiny, frostbound rock that itself caromed through a wildly irregular track—seeming to shift into higher gear for a brief period of increased acceleration—simply vanished.

Buddy asked, "What was that? Where did it go?"

The reply was a new picture in his mind. A different view of—space. For incalculable distances in every direction there was nothing, nothing but the hard vacuum of space. It was a vacuum that made the emptiness of solar space seem virtually a sea of dust and smaller free-drifting particles.

The concept came to him from the alien, Asoka, of degrees of hardness of vacuum. To the vacancy of solar space, the vacuum of interstellar regions was orders of magnitude harder, more nearly vacant of any matter. To the vacuum of interstellar regions, that of intergalactic space was further degrees more vacant. To that of intergalactic space, the regions between clusters of galaxies were still harder. And to those void regions between the great meta-formations was the hardest vacuum of all.

Nothingness.

Nothingness as close to absolute as existed anywhere within the bounds of space.

And here, into a region representing as nearly as the concept could be dealt with at all, the very center of the physical universe, the void between the metaformations of galactic clusters—the polyhedron reemerged.

Through the implanted memory he had received from Asoka, Buddy saw the planetary-sized construct spring instantaneously into being. From the viewpoint of his borrowed memory he could see the light of distant galactic clusters, light incredibly ancient, reflecting off the regular geometrical surfaces of the construct.

From his viewpoint it was impossible to tell whether the polyhedron revolved slowly or whether it remained stationary, anchored to the fabric of space itself, while the distant radiances wheeled deliberately about their central fulcrum, their reflected radiations making a dismal, dignified pavane for the eye.

"This was done long ago," the statement-concept impinged on Buddy's mind like a startling shout, interrupting his fascinated absorption. He realized that it was the alien shadow adding a commentary to the pictures he was showing to Buddy through their headbands.

"How long?" Buddy asked.

"I cannot tell you. The concept, the, ah, notion." The alien lapsed into puzzled silence for a few moments. Then he said, "The clusters of galaxies that surround Sravasti have completed their circuit twice. In your terms—give me your concept, Buddy Satvan, of time."

Buddy mulled that over. Minutes? Years? He summoned an image from an old drawing sequence he had once worked on. It represented the earth being formed hot and molten, then cooling, evolving, bringing forth primitive life . . . the growth of the reptiles, the ice ages, the emergence of the early mammals and the development of man. A quick sequence of human history and a final picture of himself lying as he now did with the cable running from his headband into the murk.

"Ah," the alien seemed to whisper. "Very well. Sravasti has been in this place for as long as your planet has existed, and for that long a time again, and again, for as many times as your planet has circled your sun."

"That's impossible. Dang, no!"

"Yes, Buddy Satvan. Why do you doubt me?"

Buddy felt himself cringing beneath the weight of Asoka's concept. "It's just—" He gave up, tried another tack. "Look, what *is* this place *Why* is it here? And what are you—*you*?"

"Sravasti is—the name is arbitrary," the alien responded. "It comes as much from your mind as from my own. So does the name you give me, Asoka. And the name of my—people—Yakshi.

"This place was once used for many things. A meeting hall for star-races. All were welcome who cared to come, all were heard and dealt with. It was a university, a great seat of study, both for great scholars and for ambitious students. Many came to learn what beings already knew and stayed to push outward the bounds of knowledge when they found that the object of their . . . curiosity . . . was unknown even to the teachers.

"It was a library. It was a laboratory. It was an observatory. For some it was a place of mystical retreat.

"The races rose and fell. The galaxies teemed with life. nly the smallest numbers of peoples were ever represented ere at Sravasti, but even they numbered in . . . your concept eems to be *trillions.* Does that have meaning for you, Buddy atvan?"

Buddy nodded, barely remembering to project the essence f his assent to the dark alien.

"Then in the great flow of cycles and epicycles, interest in ravasti grew less. Fewer races traveled between the galaxies. here was war, there was decay. Great peoples still rose, but or every civilization attaining to greatness there were many hat fell away from it.

"No one understood why this was happening. Here at ravasti a great congress of the most brilliant minds of all was onvened. Many believed that intelligence throughout the niverse was in a long downward spiral from which it would ventually rise once again. Others more pessimistic held that ivilization, perhaps life in its very essence, was a mere mporary anomaly in the fabric of existence. That it had had s day and was now disappearing spontaneously from the cene, never to return.

"The conference ended in disagreement on this basic issue. ut it was decided that Sravasti would be stocked as a torehouse of as much knowledge as intelligence had ever chieved. Great machines were built to preserve all learning hat could be stored in them. Scanning devices and systems for etrieval of that knowledge were built.

"And caretakers—the Yakshis—were placed in charge. ike Sravasti itself we are creations of living intelligence, but e are not children of nature. We were—made.

"The scholars, the researchers, the students—went home. aboratory animals that had any ability to survive on the urface of Sravasti were turned loose there. The machines ere adjusted to idle at their lowest rates of activity, powered y radiation from the very essence of space.

"And we have remained here ever since."

Buddy sat bolt upright, jumped from the pallet where he ad lain. "Then why did you bring me here? What do you ant? And why me?" He heard himself shouting, felt the ushing in his head, the dimming of his eyes.

"Can't you see I'm a madman? What can I do to help you
What do you want of me?"

He fell to the floor, flung his headband away.

He collapsed into darkness.

4. Virginia

THEY weren't completely insensitive to human feelings, eve
those of patients. They let him out of the camisole and gav
him clothes that looked almost like street garb. A pullove
shirt, a pair of formless, beltless slacks, a set of canvas slip-o
shoes. He dressed himself.

They let him shave, too. With an electric shaver, a cordles
model.

And they let him meet with his visitor in a room not to
different from an ordinary sitting room. You'd hardly notice
unless you were on the lookout, how carefully the furnitur
was selected. It offered no pointed corners, no sharp edges
no glass surfaces that might be broken off to make weapons
The lighting fixtures were all firmly recessed. The chairs an
couch and table were of massive design, too heavy to b
quickly or violently moved.

And they let him and his visitor sit together over the coffe
table with only one muscular orderly in the room, and th
orderly sat quietly, unobtrusively, by the far wall. You'd hard
ly notice his presence at all if you weren't on the lookout for a
orderly.

It was a pretty humane arrangement. The revenue fron
the comic feature took care of that. Buddy had a good lawye
and a loyal staff, and it was fortunate that he was able t
work—sporadically but still often enough, and effectivel
when he did—to pay the bills and keep himself in reasonabl
comfort.

His stretches in the violent ward . . . well, they were anothe
matter. But even there the staff used a minimum of force. Th

orderly now standing by in the visiting room, Simon Timmons, was a strong, gentle man who avoided abusing patients who were at his mercy.

If it hadn't been for *Diamond Sutro* and the money from the comics syndicate, Buddy would long since have been stuck in the state hospital for the criminally insane. He understood that thoroughly, and he shuddered at the thought.

He took Tara's two hands in his and heaved a deep sigh. "No pens or pencils, you know. Too dangerous." He laughed bitterly at his plight. "But they let me have crayons and this floppy newsprint to work with. I have some detailed notes here and a few rough sketches."

"I brought the cassette machine," Tara said. "We can work over the material and I'll take the sketches and the tapes to Willy to put in shape, is that right? As usual?"

Buddy looked into her large, dark eyes and the glossy black hair that set off Tara's olive skin. He sighed. "Right, as usual, Tara. Got a cigarette?"

She handed him a pack and book of matches. He lighted one and started to lay them down when the orderly moved toward them. Tara took back the matchbook and the pack of cigarettes and slipped them into her purse as Buddy drew on the one he had lit.

"Okay. How are we doing?"

"The last adventure—the plot to blow up Tibet—has about six weeks to run. They're really very happy about it at the syndicate. Burt says the front office thinks they may land a TV series sale on the strength of how well we're doing. But we have to follow up the Tibet sequence with at least as strong a yarn."

"Good. Okay." He was starting to feel more relaxed now, getting into his work, beginning to forget the hospital environment and creating the newest exploits of the man of mystic power.

"It's been a while since we did a rundown on the character and background, so I want to recap in the new story. We start with a couple of teaser scenes, then—"

Tara interrupted. "Is there a name for the new story?"

"I think, 'The Jackal Laughs.' What do you think, Tara?"

"Oh, yes, I like that."

"Or maybe 'The Jackal's Laugh.' "

"I like that, too. I think I like it better than the other."

"Good. So do I. All right, 'The Jackal's Laugh.' Now I haven't done a panel-by-panel breakdown on this. Haven't been able to. Too much, ah. . . ."

"I know, Buddy." Concern clouded Tara's face. She leaned across the table. "How can they keep you here? You're such a decent man, Buddy, how can they lock you up? How can they blame you for the things that awful Washburn did? How can they keep you here?"

Buddy smiled a dour smile. "Washburn is me. I'm Washburn. There's nothing I can do about that. I can't get separated from him legally. Or—physically, I guess." He gestured as if separating himself from something invisible.

"And the doctors, Buddy?"

He shrugged, hands held before him, spread helplessly. "They insist that we're one person, that we got split off somewhere along the way. Ettmann is trying to find the key to it so he can, ah, put us back together and rebuild our original personality. Our complete personality.

"I feel like, you know, a piece in a jigsaw puzzle waiting for somebody to come along and fit me into the next piece. I don't even *know* Washburn. Everything I can find out about him tells me that he's a slimy punk, some kind of despicable creep tyrant. It's probably for the best that he shot his deputy. He belongs in here!

"Or in a jail! Or in front of a firing squad, I don't know."

"But how can they blame *you,* Buddy?"

"They can't. They don't. But he can come any time he wants to, you see? That's why *he's* here." He jerked his head toward the orderly Simon Timmons sitting near the doorway. "Washburn takes over, he might try to attack you, Tara. Anything. I don't know." He heaved a sigh.

"I don't *want* to reintegrate my personality with that filth."

They sat quietly for a minute.

"Well, let's get on with *Diamond Sutro,"* Buddy said. He shuffled the sheets of soft grayish paper he'd brought into the room with him. "Here we go."

"First day of the new story we'll do a standard three-panel layout. Opening panel, I want an atmospheric medium-long shot of London. Usual thing—fog, Parliament buildings, Big Ben. Hands on Big Ben show ten o'clock. Lettering says 'BONG! BONG!'

"Narration panel says, 'London! In the very shadow of the cradle of democracy. . . .' "

"I thought Greece was the cradle of democracy."

"What's England?"

"Ah—I think the mother of parliaments, isn't it?"

"Well, make the line read 'symbol of democracy', nobody can shoot us down for that. Okay?"

Nod.

"Okay, second panel, cut to interior shot, laboratory scene. Distinguished looking English scientist at work. Give him a white lab coat, put a monocle in this eye. Willy can handle that. Has to say English all over him. 'Sir Percy Dillingham'—what would you think of Dillingham-Smythe? Too much, hey? Yes. "Sir Percy Dillingham, DSO, England's leading physicist, works late at night.' "

Tara shifted, held the little hand mike toward Buddy.

"Okay, the laboratory, tell Willy to put in a lot of electrical stuff. Maybe a computer. Not too many test tubes, chemistry's dated.

"Dillingham is thinking, 'If I can finish before the minister calls in the morning. . . .'

"Okay, final panel. Narration—'An assistant breaks in.' Shot of Dillingham from the rear, tell Willy to put him in silhouette. The assistant is a gorgeous blonde. Lab jacket, too, very formfitting. She says, 'A visitor. Very urgent.' Dillingham says, 'Good! I was expecting him!'

"Okay, that's the first day."

Buddy stood up and walked around his chair. The orderly stirred, watching, but stayed in his place near the doorway.

Tara said, "Are you okay, Buddy?"

"Sure. Danged cumbersome way to work, that's all. I should either have these panels roughed for Willy or at least type up a script for him."

"I'll transcribe the tape, Buddy. And Willy will understand. He knows *Diamond Sutro* inside out, he's the best assistant in the business. He'll be able to do it."

"I suppose."

"Maybe you could just summarize the story. I'm sure Willy could handle the actual panel breakdown."

Buddy paced back and forth. "I suppose he could just take over the whole thing!"

She didn't reply.

"Well, okay, Tara. Maybe I'll just do a straight running narrative and let Willy break it down. Okay."

He walked the length of the room, getting his thoughts in order. Then he came back and sat down opposite Tara. "All right. Tell Willy. . . . Here"—he took the cassette recorder Tara had been holding and put it back on the table between them. "Here, Willy, can you hear me? You crackin' well can, I know that. Listen, I have confidence in you, boy. I'm going to take Tara's suggestion and give you a straight rundown on *Diamond Sutro* and 'The Jackal's Laugh.'

"You see if you can do the panel breakdown yourself. If you run into problems, you come on out here and visit me and we can get it fixed up. Okay?"

He blew out stale air and took a deep breath, then resumed his dictation.

"The visitor is muffled against the chill. Slouch hat, collar up, you know the style. He and Dillingham step out the door. Dillingham's assistant asks if he's coming back and he says he doesn't know. Okay? That should take the second day's strip.

"The minister arrives in the morning. You know, chauffeur, Rolls-Royce, morning clothes, the whole trip. No Dillingham. Assistant is beside herself. Tells the minister that he just stepped out with a visitor and never came back.

"Okay, we do a 'Meanwhile' on that last panel. Right, Willy? Meanwhile in Milan. . . . Okay, Willy, same trip, you do the breakdown, we have Italy's leading physicist Luigi Serengetti disappear the same way.

"We do some more quick meanwhiles, from the end of each sequence into the next. Cut to Paris, show the Eiffel Tower, you know. Let's do a beautiful lady scientist, I know you like to draw beautiful ladies, Willy. We'll call her, uh, Marie, ah . . . Marie Charbonnet.

"Moscow—Boris Tuporov.

"Peking—Chiao-Tsu P'eng. Okay?"

Tara interrupted. "Doesn't sound quite right, Buddy."

"No? Well, ah, turn it around, then. How's about P'eng Chiao-Tsu? That better?"

"Fine."

"Good. Okay. Now, we do about five of those for teasers. Then I want to cut to San Francisco. The last few kidnappings were paced faster and faster, right? Circling the world from London to China, Now we're back in the US.

"Now I want to lay back for a little while. Going to give the old *Diamond Sutro* recap, man of mystic might and so on. Any new readers, this should really get them to know the character. The regulars always like it too, long as we do the art a little different each time."

"That's how I became your secretary, Buddy. I guess I was the only *Diamond Sutro* groupie in the world."

"Okay, good. 'While the greatest scientific minds on earth disappear one by one. . . . In San Francisco, fabulous Bagdad-by-the-Bay—" He looked up suddenly. "Did you say something, Tara?"

"Uh, I just wondered if that wasn't a little bit—"

"Hackneyed?"

"Well, since you mention it. . . ."

"This is a comic strip, you know, not a Pulitzer Prize novel."

"I know, yes."

"Thank you. Okay, Willy. Now we're into the who-is-this-man-of-mystery bit, right? I'll leave it up to you to lay it on right, right? Okay, some atmospheric panels, cable cars, Victorian houses. Soft-pedal the beatniks, all right?

"Okay, 'Behind the innocent facade of a gingerbread-encrusted mansion atop San Francisco's Nob Hill,' right, that kind of stuff. We bring in the man of mystic power, Diamond Sutro. Glamorous-looking shots, don't forget his confidante and faithful aide, the beautiful Astaroth Anderson.

"I want a montage to recap his most recent two or three cases, the Tibet thing, the mummy from Atlantis, the zombie-master yarn. Okay? Now we cut to an ancient civilization, all sorts of superscientific-looking gadgets, sleek machinery, futuristic buildings, art deco-looking people.

" 'Before Egypt, before ancient Cathay, before mighty

Atlantis and lost Lemuria,' that stuff, you know, Willy. 'The greatest master of the mystic arts, the man known as He Who Declares the Truth.'

"Lay on the stuff about foreseeing the coming shift in the earth's poles, the coming of the ice, placing himself in a trance. 'But there was one other, the archfoe of Dr. Goodlaw, the infamous master of evil, Professor Anubis.'

"The ice age comes, whole *shmear* gets wiped out, only our boy in his trance lies unharmed beneath the ice for uncounted centuries. When he revives he finds a world in need of his powers and so is born—Diamond Sutro!"

Buddy paused and finished his cigarette, then went on.

"He establishes several secret identities for himself including that of Arnaud Subhuti, millionaire San Francisco socialite. Tall, slim, dark-haired, elegant. His speech is cultured and touched with just a hint of some exotic accent—which accent, no one can identify.

"Course not, *heh-heh-heh.* Right, Willy?"

He cleared his throat and looked at Tara. "As Arnaud Subhuti, Diamond Sutro is the world's leading high-energy research physicist. Okay, now the recap is done. What does Dr. Goodlaw do?"

Tara answered, "I don't know, Buddy. What?"

"My dear, can't you guess?"

"He goes on TV and announces a breakthrough in interplanetary communication through his researches. Hmm?"

"Right! Hear that, Willy? Tara got it on the first try. That's exactly what he does. Calls in the network newsboys. And when somebody as rich and famous as Arnaud Subhuti says he has an important scientific announcement to make, they come.

"He tells 'em, 'I have developed a new ray which I call the Zircon-Iridium-Neutron-Gas-Astro-Radiation-Ray, or ZINGARR. With it we will be able to communicate instantaneously with any scientifically advanced race in the universe!' Think you can handle that, Willy?"

"I'm sure he can," said Tara.

"So am I. And then what happens, my clever amanuensis?"

"Subhuti gets kidnapped?"

"Right again. And who—now, Willy, you listen to Tara's

answer and see if she has it—who is it who kidnaps the great inventor Arnaud Subhuti?"

"Doctor Anubis?"

"Head of the class, my dear!"

"Buddy, isn't this all a little bit, ah. . . ."

"A little bit what?"

"Well, oh—*obvious*?"

"Obvious? But, my dear, if the reader can't psych out the comics, what's the point of it? George Herriman I'm not, you know."

"I know."

Buddy reached across to the cassette recorder and flipped it off. "You don't really think too much of *Diamond Sutro* any more, do you, Tara? I know you were a fan once but you've lost your sense of involvement."

She gazed at the machine for a while before she answered. "I think it's good fun," she said finally. "I guess it serves some function. Relaxation. Amusement."

Buddy said *hmm.* They laughed together. "You really think I ought to quit, don't you? Do something else?"

"I don't know. I mean, you make your living. You make a good living off the strip. But it isn't *serious.*"

Buddy laughed again, louder. "Isn't serious. You're right. You know"—he leaned forward, lowered his voice to a conspiratorial whisper"—I've had a secret ambition for years. I'd like to do a serious comic strip. Something mature. Something about real, believable people facing really important decisions.

"Something that would help the poor schmo in Oshkosh or Macon or wherever come to grips with his problems and try and work them out instead of something to help him avoid them."

He sat back in his seat again, raised his voice to its normal level. "Oh, with plenty of excitement, too. It would still be a comic strip for cripe's sake. But by golly something that the reader could relate to, that would relate to the reader's real needs. Not just a five-minute euphoric once a day and then back to the computer works."

He made an interrogatory gesture with his hands. "You know what I mean?"

"Yes," she nodded emphatically. "I'd love to see it! Have you ever tried to sound out Burt Bahnson with that idea?"

Buddy shook his head ruefully. "Sure I have. A million times."

"And?"

"And he says, 'Buddy, you know Arch Cantrowicz. Good old Arch. Feed the public the same old crap, just modernize the looks every ten-fifteen years so they won't recognize it.' Cantrowicz is from the old Mencken school. Nobody ever lost money by underestimating the intelligence of the American public. Or whatever the hell he said. Something like that."

"But what does *Burt* think?" Tara persisted. "He's the editor!"

"Burt's the editor, but Cantrowicz is the boss. Burt's scared out of his jeans of Arch. So that's where it ends. And Diamond Sutro is good fun and a nice living, so let's leave it at that, all right?"

Buddy held out his hand for another cigarette. Tara started to give one, but he changed his mind, gestured it away. Tara receded from him. "Get that to Willy, Tara. It should break down to four or five weeks of strip. I'll rough out some more while he works this up."

She was miles from him.

He rose and turned toward the orderly waiting near the door. "Out, Tara"—over his shoulder—"thanks." He lurched toward the orderly. The room seemed endless. His ears roared. "Simon, quick!"

The orderly crossed the space in slow-motion bounds, each stride taking eternities. The room grew darker. Buddy felt himself fading into nothingness, losing control of his being.

From some remote universe he heard two voices shouting.

A woman's—"Buddy! Buddy! Mr. Satvan! Are you. . . ."

A man's—he tried to see the orderly's face, to sync the sounds with moving lips—"Hold on! I'll get you to your room!"

Halfway down Buddy felt his body slip totally from his control. He caught one moment of sensation as a new stance, a new muscle tone overtook his system. Before he regained himself, regained his balance and stood upright again he was out of control.

The orderly reached the blond, pudgy patient before he nished falling to the floor. He got a quick grasp on his houlders but was amazed to find the patient rising under his wn power. The orderly said, "Mr. Satvan? Are you okay, r?"

"Satvan? That clown? You are addressing the leader."

The orderly looked at him dubiously, stood with his hands ill on the patient's shoulders.

"Well, stop pawing! Do you not recognize Roland L. K. Vashburn?"

"Oh, ah, sure, Mr. Washburn. We'd better get you, ah"—ver the pudgy man's shoulder, to the dark-haired woman olding the cassette recorder—"I'll get him back to his room, iss. I don't think you'll be able to talk any more today, with im."

The patient twisted his shoulder away from the orderly's rasp. "Now, Mr. Washburn, let's not have any struggle."

"Summon your chief at once! What's your name?"

"Timmons, sir. You want to talk to Dr. Ettmann?"

"At once!"

"All right, sir. You come along with me to your room and I'll et him for you."

Washburn turned and glared at Tara. "You!" he grated.

She looked as if she was about to burst into tears.

"Come on," the orderly said. "I'll get the doctor for you."

"Timmons, eh? You look like a strong man, good physique. Ve can use your kind. Ever serve in the army?"

Timmons had him by the elbow, carefully steering him back oward the room he'd come from to see Tara. "Yes, sir."

"Do you realize what's happening to this country, Simmons? For thirty years we've been slowly sinking beneath a ea of socialist mongrelizers. Ever since the traitor Roose-elt—or Rosenfeld, eh Simmons?"

"Timmons, sir."

"—tricked us into attacking the Reich and the forces of urity. Foreign interests, moral degenerates. . . ."

He turned to face Timmons, craning his wattled neck to eer up into the orderly's face. "Those who join now will be he leaders when we throw out the weaklings and traitors, eh, immons? You understand?"

"Yes, sir."

"Well then—"

"Well, you better talk with Dr. Ettmann first, sir."

"All right." He looked into Timmons' face again. "Ther are openings in the League for those who can see what' coming in this country. Bourgeois democracy is disintegrat ing. If something drastic isn't done—and soon!—this countr will fall prey to the mongrel weakling doctrines of radlil apologists. Look at Europe! Look at Asia!"

"Yes, sir."

They halted in the doorway of a smaller, quieter room Timmons said, "If you'll promise to behave I'll get Dr Ettmann to come up here. Otherwise it's back to the padde room. Will you promise me?"

Washburn nodded.

"Good." Timmons walked him through the doorway, the left him and pulled the door shut.

Washburn paced up and down the room. He went to th door and looked out through the small glass panel built into it center. He tried to open the door, but it wouldn't budge.

He paced some more.

Finally the door opened again and Ettmann came in clipboard and manila file-cover in hand. He was shorter tha Washburn, nearly bald, with thick, round-lensed tortoiseshel glasses.

Washburn said, "Good afternoon, Doctor."

Ettmann fixed him with a glance. "Good morning, ah, Ro land. It is Roland now—not Buddy Satvan?"

"That is correct, sir."

"Very well. Let's sit down, Roland. Will you chat with me fo a little? How do you feel about your situation?"

"My only concern is that it interferes with the vital work o the National Revitalization League of the United States Doctor. For myself, it hardly matters. A minor inconven ience."

His eyes blazed. "But the nation is in dire peril. The League is her only true sword and buckler. And with the League' führer incarcerated, the League is stymied."

"Hmm, well. Yes. The thing, is, Roland, I wonder how you feel about the times when you are, ah, not in control. You understand? We've discussed this before."

Washburn nodded.

"The times when you aren't Roland Washburn at all, but ıat other fellow, Buddy Satvan. You know who I mean?"

"Of course."

"Well, Roland, do you think you could express some ttitude toward Buddy Satvan?"

"Better for you to talk to him yourself, Dr. Ettmann."

5. Sravasti

UBURN Sutro blinked his eyes against the violet-lit mist of ravasti. He was lying on the floor of a room he'd never seen efore, a room whose depths were filled with equipment nfamiliar to him.

Shadowy forms glided through the murk. Two of them pproached him, loomed overhead. They bent and lifted him his feet.

Auburn blinked again, trying to focus on the shapes that ere helping him, but somehow he was unable to get his vision eroed in on them. Even their hands as they lifted him from ıe floor had seemed fuzzy-edged and vague for all their trength.

He allowed himself to be carried a few paces to a slab of ome sort. They laid him gently on it. The top was contoured ke a recliner, and seemed to adjust itself to his body as he hifted his weight.

He lifted one hand to his forehead—a characteristic gesture hat he made when puzzled or deep in thought—and found to is surprise that he was wearing a headband. A thin coaxial able ran from the band to. . . .

He turned and saw a compact control console. Beyond it a imilar cable ran to another slab that had a vague figure lying n it.

An almost tangible pressure seemed to rise in Auburn utro's brain. A pulsation—no, not quite a pulsation. More

like a steady flow, the advance of the tide on a beach. It ros
with each wave, fell back with each trough, but its leve
advanced nevertheless as the tide moved in. It seemed obviou
to Auburn that the phenomenon was associated with th
headband he wore.

He raised one hand to remove the band, then halted, hi
fingertips resting on the smooth surface. He was not re
strained. He seemed to be unharmed. The creatures who ha
helped him from the floor to the slab had made no effort t
harm him.

He would simply ride with the events, he decided, whateve
they might be. At least for a while.

His office could do without him. He didn't know where h
was or what had happened to him but he was going to find ou
He lay back and relaxed, opening his mind to whatever migh
try to enter.

And a presence seemed to seep into his awareness, risin
into his consciousness from some unknown depth. It wa
almost like a forgotten image returning unbidden and un
expected to confront him: a scene from his childhood, ho
many years before. . . .

He sat in an attic room, hardly more than an unfinishe
garret, the canted beams rising from the floor to the narrow
angled roof. He could sense himself, could relive the moment

He gazed through a small dormer window down into th
street, watching the town. It was an old town. The roadwa
was cobbled, and trucks and automobiles moved slowly alon
its rough surface.

Across the way rose old buildings like the one where h
crouched, structures half-timbered and peak-roofed in th
fashion of olden days. The ground floor contained shops
The upper stories were divided into apartments where th
shopkeepers and their families lived along with occasiona
apprentices or boarders.

There was Mijnheer van der Roest's cheese shop. Ther
was Mijnheer van Loen's bakery. The boy remembered bein
taken there by Mamma and Paps, remembered the deliciou
odors of Mijnheer van Loen's fresh bread and Misiz va

Loen's cookies. The boy Pieter had loved the visits and the delicious pastries.

Beside the bakery was Mijnheer Rosenthal's little tailor shop, so narrow that one person could fill the space between Mijnheer Rosenthal's work bench and the shop wall. And then there was his own Mamma and Paps' bookshop, Wachtel's bookshop. They had gone away now, leaving him with Mijnheer van der Roest and Misiz van der Roest. They were his Tannie and his Oom now. They made him stay in his garret room beneath the rafters all the time.

Pieter had very little to do. He had one tattered magazine to look at. He could read Dutch, but the magazine was from another country and he could not read it. He looked at the pictures. The magazine was full of pictures.

He looked out the window now. Both Mijnheer Rosenthal's little tailor shop and Mamma and Paps' bookshop were closed, boarded up. They were all gone away. Mijnheer Rosenthal must have gone away with Mamma and Paps, Pieter thought. Perhaps he would ask Tannie or Oom when they brought him his dinner.

The cheese shop was still open. Both Tannie and Oom worked there each day, leaving Pieter alone in the house, but they always locked the door of his garret when they left the house. Even when they came home at night they would visit him, but they did not let him come downstairs. Not ever. When they were out he would turn the pages of his magazine or look out the window.

He could see the cheese shop now: Tannie van der Roest was wrapping a package for a customer, Oom was talking with another. The bakery was open as well. Pieter could see people coming and going: townspeople in their somber coats and woolen caps, and the others in their gray uniforms and their black uniforms.

On the other side of the closed bookshop Mijnheer van der Maaten's wineshop was still open, too, although Mijnheer seemed to have gone away, leaving Misiz to run the shop. At the end of the street, at the great avenue, Mijnheer Mechanicus' coffee house was filled each day with people.

Pieter felt lonely. He wished that his Mamma and Paps were

with him. He wished they had never gone away. Tannie and Oom van der Roest were kind to Pieter, but he did not like living in the little garret room, and he missed his Mamma and Paps.

He looked down into the street, and from the great avenue saw a gray car turn and move slowly over the cobblestones. It drew up before Mamma and Paps' boarded-up bookshop. Three men climbed out of the car.

They wore gray uniforms.

One went to the bookshop and peered between the boards. Another entered Mijnheer van der Maaten's wineshop. The last entered Mijnheer Mechanicus' coffeehouse. For a little time nothing happened. The man who had peered between the boards of the closed bookshop moved on a few paces and peered into Mijnheer Rosenthal's boarded-up tailor shop. Pieter could see him shake his head and then walk away toward the wineshop and the coffeehouse.

Soon the two other men came out of those shops. The three conversed for a moment, then they began to walk back toward the bakery and the cheese shop. One man entered each shop. The third remained in the street. He looked toward the building where Pieter crouched and watched. Tannie and Oom had warned Pieter to stay away from the window, but it was so lonely in the little room, Pieter had so little to do, he had memorized the pictures in his magazine and the stories he had built around them.

He peered down into the street. Tannie and Oom were closing the cheese shop. Oom doused the light. They came out of the shop along with the man in the gray uniform. Oom turned back and locked the front door of the shop.

Now Tannie and Oom stood with a man in gray at either side. They looked frightened. They looked very upset. Tannie seemed to be sneaking little looks up at Pieter's garret.

Pieter did not like the men in the gray uniforms. Clearly they had done or said something that had upset Tannie and Oom. Pieter looked up into the gray, late-afternoon sky over Amsterdam. Maybe the big man with the scarlet cape would come and hit the men in the gray uniforms. Then he would pick up Tannie and Oom, one in each strong hand, and fly with them to Pieter's garret window. That would make Pieter happy.

The man with the scarlet cape was Pieter's favorite from his foreign magazine. The man wore tight golden clothing. On his chest was blazoned the image of an all-seeing eye. His hair was black and curly, and he had scarlet boots and a scarlet cape that flowed behind him when he flew and that hung from his shoulders in graceful folds when he stood. Sometimes he wore ordinary clothing and lived like other men, but when a mighty whirlwind appeared in the magazine he was changed to the man with the scarlet cape and then he flew.

Down in the street Tannie and Oom and the men in the gray uniforms were coming toward the house where Pieter waited. He could hear the key in the door downstairs. He could hear the door open and the men come in with Tannie and Oom.

Suddenly Pieter was very frightened.

He could hear voices downstairs. He heard Tannie van der Roest and Oom van der Roest, and he heard the other voices, nasty voices that he could hardly understand because they made the Dutch words so strangely.

Pieter began to cry. He ran to the window again and looked into the sky, hoping desperately that the man with the cape would appear. He would be flying. Did he ever come to Amsterdam? Pieter could hear footsteps on the staircase, Tannie's and Oom's and other, heavy, booted footsteps. He stuffed his magazine inside the waistband of his trousers. If only the flying man would come! If only the whirlwind would come!

The whirlwind could come and give Pieter a scarlet cape and golden tights and an all-seeing eye! Pieter clung to the window, his sight fixed on the gray sky, waiting for the whirlwind to come and change him.

The door behind him opened. Pieter could hear it. He did not turn back. He heard a harsh voice bark, "Pieter Wachtel, *jude, kommen sieh!*"

Auburn rubbed his forehead above and below the thin band. The push of a mental presence into his mind was continuing, gently ebbing and flowing, but it was never gone. He dropped his hands to his sides and tried to open his mind to whatever was pushing. He sensed that it was something benign. He was not afraid of it.

He closed his eyes.

The other presence entered his mind. It seemed not so much to speak to him as to well up from the depths of his mind. It was as if the message were placed in his memory and left there for him to examine.

"You are Washburn?" the presence asked.

Sutro *thought* his response. *No, not Washburn.*

"Then you are Old Buddy?"

No, he replied mentally. *I am Auburn Sutro. I am a mining engineer. I live in San Francisco. What—what happened? Where am I now?*

The message was a repetition of the explanation given to Buddy Satvan and Roland L. K. Washburn. Auburn Sutro lay quietly, absorbing the data. The brilliant, orderly mind that had created the electron beam earth reamer and revolutionized deep-core mining was sorting information, storing it away, readying it to be set into a pattern.

Sutro zeroed in on the headband, the cables and the console that connected him to the Yakshi on the second pallet. He demanded a schematic of the console, found it streaming into his mind. It was a simple enough device, he decided. A kind of sophisticated bidirectional encephalographic decoder/encoder. The console contained a compact memory array that built up messages from incoming EEG impulses and retransmitted them through the cables.

A little more earnest questioning—all of it mental—showed that the console was linked to a larger device, a machine with huge storage and processing capacities. Sutro explored the larger machine using the little console as an input/output device. What the—Yakshi—lying on the other pallet thought of this Sutro didn't know.

In any case the creature didn't object, none of the other shadowy forms in the room interfered, so Sutro assumed that his inquiries were acceptable to them.

Finally he called for some tools. He had a hard time getting the messages into and out of the machine—he was using commonplace engineering specs, but the computer—for that was surely what it was although its capacity was incredible orders of magnitude beyond anything ever dreamed of by earthly designers—the computer had to be taught Sutro's terminology, his metric scales, the principles and assumptions of Sutro's methods.

Finally a Yakshi approached. He carried a case of some smooth material. He placed it on the floor beside Sutro's pallet. Auburn sat up, removed his headband, wondering if any of the Yakshis would interfere but none did.

He squatted beside the case of the floor. The Yakshi ran a—finger?—along one edge and the top slid aside. Sutro saw a set of fine tools, as beautifully crafted as precious gems. All of the tools and all of the materials he'd wanted.

He laid the headband on the top of the case, modified it with the tools he'd been brought, disconnected the cable from it and from the console and rolled the cable into the tool kit. He slipped the headband on and tried it. It worked perfectly.

The Yakshi lying on the other pallet, Asoka, rose and held his own headband toward Sutro. Auburn modified it as he had his own and Asoka donned it again.

Through the headbands Sutro asked once again how he had been brought to Sravasti. Asoka answered, "The machines brought you, Auburn Sutro. The machines that were built by the greatest of the old star peoples, and left in the care of the Yakshis."

"The machines?" Auburn repeated. "You mean this console, the big computer? That's just a data-processor, powerful as it is. How could it bring me here from earth?"

"The machine that you call the computer is only one, Auburn Sutro. The star people left us three great machines. All were needed to bring you here. The computer was one of them. The others you will learn of as needed. From us—or from the machines themselves. The circuits of the computer have access to the library of the star peoples. All that they knew is yours to use, Auburn Sutro. Merely ask us—or the machine."

Sutro raised his hand to his brow.

He'd been at work in his office on Folsom Street in downtown San Francisco. An assistant had worked out some modifications to the Sutro Earth Reamer, and Auburn had asked for details on the proposed changes.

Engineering specs, anticipated performance, financial projections on the new product from data-processing time needed to labor and materials for a breadboard model to testing to marketing and production costs. Would it pay out? Would it help the company or was it an expensive frill?

And then he'd felt himself slipping into blackout.

Nobody knew about his blackouts. Apparently when they came over him he left his office—his staff said that he sometimes walked away in the middle of meetings and remained incommunicado for weeks on end. He disappeared from all his familiar circles. His friends had to accept it as an eccentricity that went along with genius.

But how much time had passed since that last blackout in the Folsom Street office? Where was he now? The explanation that the machines had brought him here was no explanation at all.

"Okay," Sutro murmured aloud. Then he stopped and repeated a message, pushing the concepts through the headband. "The only way to go about this is by being orderly. Can I communicate directly with this computer?"

The reply came from the Yakshi Asoka wearing the twin headband to Sutro's own. "You can communicate with the computer in pseudoverbal dialog. That might be best. Or if you wish you may attempt to drive your own consciousness down through its receptors into the circuitry itself. By so doing you might experience directly the dimensions of the machine, Auburn Sutro."

Auburn's thoughts flashed back to his student days, writing programs at Stanford. Then the development of the office terminals and conversational mode compilers. To enter the computer itself with his naked mind and experience what the machine knew and felt—if such terms could even be applied—was a fascinating prospect. But some native caution made him hold back from it.

"I'll try dialog," he told the Yakshi. "I'll just stay here and see what I can learn for a while."

He lay back on the pallet again, adjusted the headband for comfort and gazed around the room once more. The Yakshis hovered in the misty atmosphere, the purplish glowing light. Auburn couldn't distinguish them from one another—Asoka must still be lying on the other pallet, prepared to monitor Auburn's communication with the machine. Not a bad idea, that. The others—Kalinga, Nanda, still more—seemed rather to flow in and out of the room than to walk.

He laid his head down and closed his eyes. Somehow, during his blackout, he had traveled from Folsom Street to the remote and puzzling place called Sravasti. He'd always recovered from earlier blank periods in familiar San Francisco surroundings—this time was unsettlingly different.

Learning something about the aliens' machinery wouldn't, of itself, solve the puzzle for him. But it would certainly be a start!

Hands at his sides, eyes closed, he shoved a mental inquiry at the computer. Where to start? What to ask? "What is your storage capacity?" he finally queried. "And what is its structure?"

In the pause that followed Auburn could almost feel the machine searching for the information. He must have imagined that it cleared its throat before it answered him.

"My memory is hierarchic," the response came after a pause. "Prime storage access time is point-oh-oh-one picosecond. Prime capacity thirteen trillion trits—"

"Hold it!" Auburn interrupted. *"Trits*? What are trits?"

"Triskidecimal storage units, each subject to values ranging from zero through twelve."

Auburn actually laughed. Thirteen-base numbering! What kind of strange creatures had designed *that* system! But if it worked, it worked.

The machine went on. "Secondary storage, picosecond access time, 2,197 trillion trits. Supplemental storage in various media, access time dependent upon medium selected, capacity unspecified and available through slaved handlers and channels for stacking into secondary or primary storage."

Auburn queried the machine about its processing capabilities—arithmetic functions, logical operations, instruction repertoire, input and output formats. The answers were stunning. It was the ultimate computer. It was not a manlike mind, not an aware, creative intelligence—but the ultimate tool for amplifying the power of a true mind. A machine that could calculate, store, retrieve, sort, respond. A superb tool.

But inferior, still, to the meanest living intellect.

Auburn shot a thought at Asoka. "Have you been monitoring?"

"I have."

"Then stand by and be ready to haul me out if I get into trouble. I'm going to try and explore this thing directly." He opened his eyes and got a look—if he should miscalculate what he was about to attempt, it might be his last look—at the world outside. At the physical, tangible world, strange as it was here in Sravasti, still it was seen through his living, biological eyes.

Then he dropped his lids again and willed himself into the machine. Not merely a message this time, not merely a question. He willed his very self, his ultimate ego, into a tiny speck. He hurled himself through the headband, through the console, through the alien circuitry built uncounted eons ago by unknown hands or tendrils or projections of pure force—and into that great, ultimate computer.

And he felt himself, suddenly, a new being. His mind seemed to expand, screaming outward like a vast explosive mass, growing to a size it had never before known. He tried a few simple calculations. Multiplied his social security number by the ninety-third root of *pi,* transformed the product into eights-complement Polish notation, raised it to the power of the number of electrons in the Crab Nebula and subtracted his age in picoseconds.

Almost before he had formulated the problem he had the answer to ten thousand decimal places.

He started to ask the machine who had built it, then revised his mental technique and instead strained to *remember,* instead, the experience of being built.

As the machine, he recalled its first "experience," the first opening of its input channels, the first "knowledge" that it had ever had of its own existence and of the outer world. Through the machine's memory—his own memory, now—he felt the tools and the forces that had built him.

Did the machine have a visual input capability? It did, and he saw its builders—creatures of many races, some a travesty of the human form, others vaguely suggestive of other species, of insects, of angels, of incredible monsters, of intelligent plants.

He nodded, or would have nodded if his consciousness had been located in his body instead of the circuits of the machine.

All right! Now, at least to some extent, he understood the machine. What it was, what it could do, how it had been created.

But what was it for?

Again he plumbed his memory, and this time the answer that came was more baffling than helpful. The machine was—"he" was—created for the service of intelligent life. Any time, anywhere in the universe, once *mind* arose it was the experience of the ancient star races that that mind sought out other consciousness. Basic to the philosophy of the ancient peoples had been the belief that whatever self-awareness might exist, regardless of the nature of its body or its location, it would wish to reach out to others, to share with them its strengths, its insights, its creations, its attainments. And to learn of theirs.

Any intelligence that preferred to avoid other minds, or worse yet to subdue or destroy them—was to precisely the degree that it did this, sick and defective and in need of assistance.

And it was to the service of any intelligence which ever again might rise in the universe, that the machines had been left by their benevolent creators.

Enough.

Enough, Auburn thought. He could take only so much of the immense, and overwhelming, experience of inhabiting the machine, of having its mentality for his own. He felt himself half involuntarily slipping away, away from the mighty brainlike machine. He found himself no longer possessed of the huge storage capacities, the incredible numerical and analytic powers of the machine.

He was back in his human body, back on the pallet lying near the Yakshi Asoka. He sat up, started to raise a hand to his brow. In a final flash of communion with the machine he hurled a parting question.

"What have you done?" he asked. "You were built to serve intelligence, but what have you *done*?"

The reply came, a direct factual statement. Auburn had felt that the machine, for all its incredible capacities, had no true awareness of itself, no real personality. It was not a living thing. In this sense, for all its intricacies and powers, it counted for less on the cosmic scale than an amoeba.

Yet its answer seemed to carry the suggestion of a sardonic chuckle. Auburn Sutro rejected that idea. He must have interpreted that into the reply, imagining the inflection atop the information that the machine offered.

What had it done?

"I brought you to Sravasti," the reply came in a bolt of pure mental force. "I brought you here, Auburn Sutro."

6. Sravasti

THE experience of entering, feeling, *being* the titanic computer had been overwhelming. I won't do that again, Sutro decided. At least for a while. The machine's capacities were staggering. While he was in it, while his personality had been melded into the circuitry of the computer, he had possessed all the abilities, all of the memories of the complex system.

But they had not all been present in his mind at once. Not any more than a full lifetime of experience is present in a man's mind at one moment. It was all there, yes, every bit—or *trit*—of data recorded in the machine's vast memory banks, just as every experience in a human life is recorded somewhere in the brain.

But precisely as the human consciousness holds only a very limited amount of recollection and awareness at any moment, so Auburn Sutro while sharing the circuitry of the machine could grasp only chosen blocks of its memory or processing arrays at a given moment. And now that he had left the machine, the access which he had held to its storage and logic quickly slipped away.

Yet, at the same time he felt the return of certain human characteristics—human, or at least *living*—that the machine, for all its immense capacity, simply lacked. Curiosity came back. Purposiveness returned—not as a filled storage register but as a *felt* force. And ego, the pure sense of self, reappeared in his mind.

The "thinking" of the machine was immensely powerful, dazzlingly rapid, minutely precise. But still it was mechanical. The thinking of a man, for all its vagaries and imprecisions, was clearly of a superior sort.

Auburn requested and obtained additional headbands for the other Yakshis, Kalinga and Nanda. He quickly modified them to function without the restrictive cables. Then they made their way together from the room of the pallets and the console and found a place that might almost have passed for the comfortable sitting room of a plush, old-style club like the San Francisco Miners' Association so familiar to Sutro.

The chairs weren't quite chairs, the tables were of unfamiliar shape. The soft stuff underfoot wasn't exactly a carpet and the walls weren't quite lined with richly leather-bound rows of books. But it was all close enough. Sutro could nearly fool himself into thinking it was the venerable Miners' Association on Sutter Street.

"All right." He projected the thought at the Yakshis. "I really like solving problems, that's my profession. But I need more data than I've got. A lot more. And that computer gives me *too much.* I don't know where to look! You've got to help me to define the problem and to find the tools I'll need to solve it."

The Yakshis seemed to receive the message as clearly as if they were all using normal speech.

"You understand Sravasti?" the message returned. "You have learned where you are, what this place is?"

"I learned that from the computer. I don't understand how I came here. I was in San Francisco. I think I blacked out. The computer says *it* brought me here, but I don't understand that."

"Ah, ah!" The Yakshis seemed to exchange a knowing, sympathetic glance. "You only know the one machine."

"What are the others? The computer spoke of *machines.*"

"The star peoples left behind three great devices. One is

that which you call a computer. The others—do you wish to consult the computer about them?"

Auburn shook his head. "Maybe later for specs. But I'd rather *see* the others first. Are they here?"

"All are in Sravasti." The Yakshis nodded agreeably, identical blurry shapes, like the same object viewed front-left-right-in a tailor's mirror.

Like old Mijnheer Rosenthal's mirror, Auburn thought. And then, where did that come from? Had he ever *known* anybody called. . . . Well, never mind. The matter at hand. . . .

"Are they near by?" he asked the Yakshis. "Can we get to them now?"

A nod, a gesture repeated by three identical vaguenesses there in the murky violet-lit hall. The Yakshis rose in perfect unison and led Sutro through an archway into another hall. The building they were in seemed to be huge, but he had no idea of its real size or arrangement, The computer would have that data, Sutro thought, but I don't want to go back to that. Not now.

"This is the star peoples' second machine," one of the Yakshis (or perhaps all of them) communicated to Auburn. "You would call it a—" He projected a concept at the engineer.

"Oh yes," Auburn nodded. "A scanner. Very well." He stood gazing at the machine. Either the lighting was improving or his eyes were adjusting to the weird effect. Best optical system in the world, he thought. Dim the light, more comes in. Brighten it, the iris closes down. Throw a color filter over it, half a minute later you've adjusted, corrected, everything looks normal again.

He went to the machine.

It must have been built for a human or at least a very humanlike operator. There was a seat, there was a simple control panel, and there was something that had to be a headset. Not really too different from a diving helmet, only from its looks lighter and more compact.

"Appears to be simple enough." He sent the message at the Yakshis. "May I try it out?"

"Don the headset. Manipulate the controls. You cannot

ımage it or yourself. The only peril is an input overload. An ıtomatic monitor will cut in should that occur."

Sutro climbed into the seat and reached for the controls of e scanner while two Yakshis lowered the headset over him. e still wore the communication band around his forehead. Vill this work inside the headset?" he asked.

Affirmation.

The vague, chill touch of a Yakshi hand guiding his own ld Auburn where the master switch of the scanner was. He cked it on.

Instantly it was as if the headset had been removed.

He could see the control panel with his hand still on it. He rned and saw the Yakshis patiently waiting while he used e machine. He slid a lever upward and felt as if he were sing. Looking down, he could see himself where he sat.

It was uncanny. Like floating out of his own body and oking down at the top of his head. He could see the scanner eadset resting lightly on his shoulders.

He slid the lever down again, merged with his body, conıued the downward movement, felt as if he had dropped rough his own feet, moved through the girders and conıits of the underpinning beneath the building. He dropped rough miles of machinery, emerged on the far side of avasti and looked around. To his surprise the artificial nstruct seemed to possess soil, weather, even life.

The dominant color was still the purple-violet of the ıilding's lights. The ground—it might have been placed ere by some ancient hand to add to the aesthetics of the tificial world, or it might be the natural accumulation of llions of years of vacuum particles—was thinly coated with ıow. A few plants stuck up through the blanket, and small eatures moved among them.

For a moment Sutro felt strangely touched. The persistence life, however remote from his own, however alien from imself, plucked some chord within his being.

Then he rose farther, hovered above the thin atmosphere Sravasti. He spun his perspective—back in the hall of the achine he could still detect his body, could still will his ngers to manipulate the controls of the scanner—and looked ıt into space.

Except for one narrow sector the sky was filled with an arra
of breathtaking splendor. Giant galaxies hung in etern
suspension, their spiral arms curling as they spun out the
billion-year-long choreography. Dust clouds, supernova
scintillating bundles of matter that might once have been sta
and that might now be climbing back up the hard rungs
another cycle of flame.

He felt a message from one of his guides on Sravasti, move
his hand from the lever where it rested and placed it on
ratchetted dial. He swung the scale of his perceptions up an
down through the wave lengths of natural radiance. By in
frared, objects that had glowed visually faded to a mino
brightness and other, dimmer sources flared. He moved th
ratchet to tune on radio frequencies, to ultra-violet, to X-ray

He was the first man to see singularities hovering in spac
sucking in matter and radiation toward the ultimate a
cumulation of new primal atoms.

And in one narrow sector of the sky he saw—somethin
else.

Fire worms writhed and twisted. Uncounted lines of glow
ing color grew gnarled and warped and shivered and dance
in the void. He couldn't tell whether there were millions o
tiny segments making a complete circuit or whether a singl
glowing entity struggled to maintain itself. In either case, th
ring was complete.

Outside its expanse the sky was full of the objects and th
radiations that populated the sidereal universe, the wonder
that man's endless curiosity had revealed to him object b
object, class by class, from the days of Sumerian astrologer
priests to the building of space-platform-mounted electro
telescopy.

Inside the expanse—nothing.

Not mere blackness. Not mere vacuum. The annihilation o
space itself.

Sutro's hand shoved a lever forward, forward, as far as
would move on the scanner panel. He felt himself, again as if
disembodied consciousness, driven at mad speed toward th
nothingness that dwarfed the concept of the black hole to tha
of soft vacuum.

He saw the fire worms, things of flame that devoured the very fabric of existence, looking like gargantuan embers on a winter's log. And then he experienced—the nothingness.

No sight.

No sound.

Total sensory deprivation.

It was worse than any blackout that Auburn Sutro had experienced. It was not as if he had ceased to detect the presence of the universe, but rather as if the universe itself had ceased to exist. The sensorium of Auburn Sutro remained. It was offered no input of any sort.

For a moment he thought that it was the experience of death, but even that was less than the annihilation he had experienced. In death the individual ceased to perceive the cosmos, but the cosmos still existed. In this state it was as if the cosmos itself had been wiped away to the uttermost speck.

Then Auburn Sutro found himself seated again at the control panel of the star peoples' scanner. Two Yakshis had removed the headset from his shoulders and were carefully restoring it to its place. The third shadowy form had gently lifted Sutro's hand from the lever where he had clamped it. As Auburn watched, the Yakshi restored the controls of the scanner to their original neutral position and cut power from the device.

"What was that?" Auburn asked. "What was that phenomenon?"

The nearest Yakshi seemed to be nodding, its body swaying back and forth in an earnest effort to share with him. "We do not know. That's what you were summoned to undo. To stop it before the universe is destroyed. To set it back if you can."

Violet-black against violet-black, the Yakshi swayed and whispered, its thoughts carried to Sutro by the headbands they both wore.

"The volume of space already annihilated—" The Yakshi expressed a figure so huge that Sutro made him repeat it over twice before he accepted it.

"Whole metagalaxies are gone, Auburn Sutro," the shadow whispered, "more races of beings have been destroyed than there exist individual members of your species."

Sutro put his hand to his brow. "What—blackness beyond blackness. That—complete nothingness. You have no data beyond that?"

"Nothing."

"How long has this been spreading?"

The Yakshi told him—a surprisingly brief period. Then it was advancing with terrifying speed! As vast as was space, it would *all* be devoured, at this rate, in a horribly short time.

"Your own world will be destroyed," the Yakshi concluded, "in about one million years."

Sutro rocked back at that. A million years! Did it matter, then? Would there even be humans on earth in a million years? "What happens in the meantime?" he asked.

"Death," the Yakshi hissed. "Hundreds of worlds are consumed each day. Billions, trillions of intelligences."

Auburn's mind flashed back to a statement he'd once heard—or overheard—in a Maiden Lane bar in San Francisco. He'd stopped in for a drink after work, and found himself beside an off-duty newspaperman who'd done the same. The newsman was lecturing to anyone who would listen. His subject was news values, and his words had made a vivid impression on Auburn Sutro's memory.

"A dog fight on Main Street," the newsman had said, "is more interesting than the earth opening up and swallowing twenty million Chinese!"

Did the fate of trillions of intelligences matter to Auburn Sutro? Even if none of them were on earth—and even if earth was safe for another million years?

Auburn decided that it did matter. He said nothing, but the sense of his conclusion must have been transmitted subliminally through the headbands.

The Yakshi nodded.

Sutro asked if there were a way to project a physical entity rather than a remote scan into the burned-out area.

"Oh yes." The three Yakshis nodded. "That can be done. The third of the star peoples' machines can do that. We have done it. But—whatever, whoever is projected into the nothingness does not return. We have tried. We get back—nothingness."

Even so, Sutro wanted to see that third machine.

It had another console installed in the room where Auburn had first found himself when he arrived in Sravasti. That, and huge volumes of circuitry and power plant buried beneath the floor penetrating deep into the guts of the artificial planet.

"With this we can send anything, grasp anything we need. The star peoples told us to use the grasper sparingly. In fact, to use all of their machines sparingly. We were not placed in Sravasti to pursue ends of our own, but to serve as caretakers for the races to come."

"And you sent for me."

The three Yakshis nodded.

"Look here," Sutro said, shaking his head, "this whole thing is really too much to take at one shot. You know, we were still debating on earth whether there was other life anywhere in the universe, no less intelligence. People brought arguments, but they were all statistical in nature, you see?"

The shadows nodded patiently, their attitude attentive.

"What I'm saying is, we calculated that there were so many galaxies in the universe. Or that there were in the universe that we could perceive, anyway.

"And so many stars in each galaxy—at least on an average. That made for a total number of stars so huge, maybe as great as ten-to-the-twenty-second—a hundred billion hundred billion—that, well, it didn't matter *how* scarce intelligent life must be. If it existed in any statistically significant portion of cases—if we ourselves weren't a unique fluke of nature—then there must be vast numbers of intelligent races scattered throughout the universe."

He stopped, all but panting with the magnitude of his own statement. In unison the three Yakshis seemed to gather and rise to give their response.

"Entirely correct, Auburn Sutro. Why, then, do you find this all so hard to accept?" They gestured, the motion indicating all of Sravasti.

"Because—" He stopped, pounded a fist on the arm of a chair. "Because it was only a statistical surmise. This is *reality.* It's like living all your life talking about heaven and believing in it or telling yourself you believe in it anyway. And then you die and you wake up again with the angels singing all around you and clouds of glory and you're absolutely amazed because for all that you said you believe, it never really sank in. Never really. And then it turns out that it was all true all along and you can't believe *that*."

A Yakshi drifted toward him, hung quivering in the air. "The references are—very difficult to follow."

Sutro laughed. "I should think so. All right, never mind that. Here I am." He looked down at himself, seemed for the first time to notice the outfit he wore. "You—want me to save the universe from that spaceburn phenomenon out there. How in hell—never mind *that*—just how did you pick *me*? And I *still* want to know how you got me here! And how am I supposed to *fix* that?"

The three shadows gathered, merged, separated. One of them drifted close to Auburn Sutro. "We delivered the problem to the star people's machines. We told the one which you call their computer of the disaster taking place. Somehow it resolved the needs of the problem into a description of such a mind as might—only might—prove the salvation of all being.

"The computer guides the operations of the other machines when they are not controlled directly as you controlled the scanner. Under the guidance of the computer, the scanner searched all of space, all of being, and found one creature alone that might prove able to accomplish the task.

"You, Auburn Sutro-Old Buddy Satvan-Roland L. K. Washburn. You were that one.

"And the third machine, the grasper, brought you to Sravasti. To us, having found you on your own planet. So. . . ."

The creature mimicked the Asian gesture of pressing its hands together before it and bowing toward Auburn Sutro.

"So—you will save the universe. Or it shall be consumed."

7. San Francisco

FIRST WEEK: As a glaring orange sun disappears into the black Pacific dusk, an icy gray fog slithers through the fabled

Golden Gate and creeps sinisterly up the famous hills of San Francisco. High atop world-renowned Nob Hill stands a fabulous mansion. Its Victorian towers pierce the icy, windswept sky. The grounds are dark, patrolled by a legion of fierce, wraithlike Afghan hounds, their sharp eyes and alert brains ever ready to pick out any intruder who dares enter this dark sanctuary, their mighty fangs sharpened and tipped with surgical steel in a clandestine veterinary.

No light pierces the stygian murk that surrounds this house, no sound challenges the mournful hoot of foghorns rising from the chilled Bay except the restless pad-pad-pad of the majestic warrior dogs.

The grounds of the mansion, lushly planted but now overgrown with the product of studied neglect, contain a strange mixture of botanical life drawn from the four corners of the world. Tall palm trees sway in strange companionship to mighty redwoods while mutated orchids suck sustenance from the sap of unfamiliar hosts. The *lazo de necios,* a giant remote cousin of the Venus's-flytrap found deep in the Amazon rain forest, opens and shuts is fibrous claws restlessly. There is the occasional scuttle of an armadillo, the almost ultrasonic screech of a rare, intelligent pygmy bat found only in certain shunned Saharan oases—and within these shadowy grounds!

What keeps the prying eyes and restless feet of passers-by away from these exotic—but deadly dangerous—confines?

A tall, spike-mounted fence. And within this, shadowed by the cast-iron barbs, a heavy brick wall, ivy covered and decorative—unless you've ever tried to climb it, and found what lies on its broad top! And within the brick wall—other barriers best left undescribed.

Yet outside these concentric barriers, these rings of danger, there lurks a dark figure. Shards of fog drift and swirl, seeming almost to wrap themselves around him like vile and fawning beasts at the feet of their evil master.

Half visible in chiaroscuro silhouette, the intruder lurks, crouching low beside the cast-iron fence. Is there something strange, something foreboding about this shadowy being of the fog and of the night? Is there something odd in the shape of his demoniac features?

Perhaps the ears are longer than they ought to be. Perhap
the nose is drawn to a sharper tip than an honest nose ought t
be, and perhaps that tip twitches and snuffles like the snout o
something not quite human. Perhaps the eyes gleam with
light not decently come by, and the teeth, when thin, cruel lip
are drawn back in an inscrutable expression somewhere between a smirk and a snarl, show a length and sharpness n
proper man's teeth ought to show.

Yes. This is—Professor Anubis. Holder of degrees from th
great citadels of the ancient world, doctor of science, doctor o
philosophy, doctor of medicine, doctor of war. Possesssor of
cold, brilliant, piercing mind. As sinister and as dazzling as
teardrop-cut emerald, this is one of the two truly towerin
intellects in the world.

The figure crouches. He explores the inside of his emerald
lined midnight-black satin cloak. Long, taloned finger
emerge bearing a vial of some noxious, bubbling fluid. A
Professor Anubis grasps the vial in emerald-gloved hands it
contents spring to a frantic boil as if they were alive an
responding to their evil master's will.

The sinister doctor pulls the cork from the mouth of th
tiny vessel. Its bubbling sea-green content foams upward
sublimates into a thin, ugly gas. Before it can escape to merg
with the still-swirling sheets and fragments of fog Docto
Anubis raises the vial to his long, thin nostrils. He inhale
convulsively. His already brilliant eyes blaze forth as i
illumined from within by the fires of hell itself!

A passing San Francisco foot patrolman, swinging hi
nightstick gaily as he congratulates himself for the hundredt
time upon drawing the posh Nob Hill beat after eight years i
the seamy Tenderloin district, halts. He leans, stares, reache
to rub his eyes.

Wasn't there a man there just a moment ago? Some oddl
made, deformed figure, possibly a derelict wandering acci
dentally away from the quarters that San Francisco re
serves for its down-and-outers, blearily stumbling onto th
rich confines of exclusive Nob Hill?

But no. The patrolman stares. There is no one here. Fo
just a moment he thought that there was. Then the figur
seemed to grow transparent, to fade into the darkness, and a

it did so to walk right through the wrought-iron fence and disappear! Impossible, of course. A trick of the fog and the uneven illumination. The wealthy denizens of Nob Hill do not like to have their privacy disturbed by too many bright streetlamps.

The patrolman continues to walk his beat. There is nothing even to report—no incident that the sergeant would believe, anyway, and he certainly wouldn't want to be accused of drinking on the beat!

SECOND WEEK: Deep in the bowels of the rich, dark earth beneath Nob Hill, Arnaud Subhuti labored long into the San Franciscan night, alone in his ultramodern laboratory. This was the same secret redoubt from which a series of inventions had emerged to stun the scientific establishment of the world and to win the undying gratitude of its struggling millions.

From these secret and heavily armored precincts had poured a flood of brilliant achievements. The superentonometer that had revolutionized the science of radium reduction. The ultra-dynamic electrohydrolicizor. The atomic nuclear phosphor-radonomograph.

And now Arnaud Subhuti stood, crystal octite held to raving laser radiation, completing the last preliminary experiment before the public demonstration of his newest invention, the crowning achievement of an already incomparably brilliant career. The ZINGARR—the Zircon-Iridium-Neutron-Gas-Astro-Radiation Ray!

His white laboratory outfit reflected the lurid glow of the laser beam as it flooded the room with mysterious coherent light. His serious, blue-gray eyes gazed intently at the crystal octite, protected from accidentally glancing laser beams by thick, smoked-glass goggles. His strongly muscled legs reached to solid, crepe-soled lab shoes custom designed to provide uninterrupted traction in the dangerous environment of the scientist's laboratory.

In one corner of the room a computer hummed and blinked softly to itself. Occasionally it broke into the steady, throbbing hum that filled the room and chattered angrily to itself as a row of complex equations appeared on its high-velocity video readout screen.

But the computer's chatter did not interrupt the concentration of Arnaud Subhuti. When the wizard stood engrossed in the researches that marked his amazing rise in the world of science, interruption was nigh impossible. The keen mind of the world's greatest scientist could be brought to bear upon any given problem until that problem was cracked—that was part of the secret of Arnaud Subhuti's brilliant string of inventions.

But tonight, that very power of concentration that had served him so well would lead Arnaud Subhuti to something near disaster!

In the laboratory behind the great scientist a shadowy form seemed to seep through the very walls themselves. The entrance to the secret laboratory led through the gracious, antique-filled halls of the lovely old Victorian mansion that sat atop San Francisco's Nob Hill. Few were the confidantes of the wizard who were privy to the secret of this building—to the rest of the world it was the palatial residence of a millionaire recluse who had appeared mysteriously some years ago, holding a fortune of undisclosed origin and speaking English with a faint but strangely unplaceable accent.

There was a second passageway that led into and out of the secret laboratory. This passage was known to Arnaud Subhuti alone. No one else had even a whisper of its existence. *No one.*

How, then, had the newcomer entered Subhuti's *sanctum sanctorum?*

The noxious fumes of the foaming sea-green liquid were already wearing off. Doctor Anubis, whatever he may have been, was not a physical coward. He had risked all to use the contents of the vial.

He had risked all—and he had won!

A chilling laugh echoed from the chrome-vanadium walls of the laboratory. There was a single loud report and the laser beam shining on Arnaud Subhuti's experimental crystal octite winked out. The room's illumination level fell back to that provided by its ordinary fluorescent tubes.

Arnaud Subhuti spun in his tracks, his custom-designed crepe-soled lab shoes tracking unerringly on the laboratory floor.

"Doctor Anubis!" he exclaimed.

"At your service, Mister So-Called Wizard of Science."

"I did not choose the title," Subhuti rejoined good-naturedly.

"No," Anubis sneered. "Well, my friend, you shall have a new one soon enough. You shall be one of my faithful servants, laboring at my hidden headquarters high in the Andes Mountains."

"Collecting scientists, are you, Anubis?" The wizard seemed surprisingly relaxed and nonchalant for one whose sanctum had been invaded and whose life was at stake. Perhaps he had reason to breathe easily. Or perhaps his nonchalance was all a front.

The fiend hissed his arrogant reply. "You guessed, then, did you? Well, there's no need to deny it! Yes, I have them all!"

"Sir Percy Dillingham . . . Luigi Serengetti . . . Marie Charbonnet."

"A most charming lady, Madame Charbonnet."

"Boris Tuporov . . . P'eng Chiao-tsu. I congratulate you on getting Dr. P'eng out of the People's Republic. No mean feat, that, Doctor."

"Thank you, Arnaud Subhuti. But I cannot afford to waste more time in banter. We are both awaited in the Andes. You will come with me or—" He gestured with a strangely shaped weapon.

Subhuti's eyes narrowed behind the smoked-glass goggles he still wore over those steely blue-gray orbs. "I see you come here with no ordinary armaments," the wizard said.

"I would not so insult my most formidable opponent!"

The gun—if such a term may be applied to the weapon—hissed softly. The wizard of science slowly crumpled to the floor of his laboratory and lay unmoving.

THIRD WEEK: The haunting, mysterious notes of an Incan flute drifted eerily across the snow-crowned peak of Mt. Huascaran some 22,205 feet above the chill gray waters of the Pacific Ocean where it raved and crashed against the rocky coastline of the Republica del Peru. Cosmopolitan citizens of bustling Lima, busy Callao, sybaritic Arequipa went about their daily business, blissfully unaware of the activities being perpetrated high on the slopes of the tallest peak in the Peruvian republic.

Perhaps some of the natives in the darker quarters of Puno,

the glittering resort city on the shores of Lake Titicaca, might have had an inkling of what was taking place. Surely some of the strange, taciturn residents of ancient Cuzco, onetime capital of the great empire of the Inca Atahualpa, had received word of the dark activities taking place among the peaks of the Andes.

But if any did, none spoke of what he knew. Long trained in the wisdom of holding their own counsel, these descendants of the ancient Incans gave no hint to outsiders of what knowledge they concealed.

But within the walls of the ancient redoubt built into the living rock of Mt. Huascarán ages ago, and secretly restored by sinister forces in recent years, there was a buzz and hum of activity. Furnaces roared, crucibles of rare metals glowed with white heat. Great electrical generators gave off earsplitting whines as they spun to power the giant machines buried deep within the mountain.

Most portentous of all, huge and awesome flashes of lightning seemed to burst from the very peak of the mountain, turning hundreds of square miles of almost uninhabited Andean slopes into a sinister, glaring wasteland for fractions of a second at a time.

But now the hum and bustle of the peculiar establishment was interrupted by the remote *chop-chop-chop* of a high-speed rotor blade. The mountain fastness, inaccessible through all of the annals of time save for a tortuous, winding footpath that led up the steep, deadly slopes of the Andes, had at last yielded to that ubiquitous modern tool, the helicopter.

The silvery, dragonflylike craft soared high in the thin mountain air, hovering in bright morning sunlight over the peak of Mt. Huarascan. A secret radio signal was transmitted over a predetermined wavelength that changed every hour. A section of sheer granite seemed to roll away, revealing a small but ultramodern landing pad carved from the flank of the living mountain.

The helicopter, sunlight glinting from its whirling rotors, descended gracefully and settled onto the pad.

The mountain closed.

Inside the aircraft sat two men, a living contrast in human types. One, the pilot, seemed hardly human at all. His ears were long and pointed, his nose preternaturally sharp. There was a look of feral shrewdness in his eyes. There seemed, somehow, almost more of the jackal in this man than there was of humanity.

The other man, weighted down with a mass of heavy chains and strapped into place as an involuntary passenger, still manifested a courage and nobility that branded him far the moral superior of his captor. There was a look of farsighted dedication in his clear, blue-gray eyes. Captive though he was, this was clearly a man with whom to deal!

Mute slaves in ancient Incan costumes ran to the doors of the helicopter, tugging them open even before the ship's rotors had ceased turning. They looked to the jackal-headed man and received instructions from him in a secret hand language unknown elsewhere in the civilized world. Wordlessly they dragged the form of the passenger, chained and unresisting, from the cockpit of the helicopter and set him roughly on his feet.

"Well," the jackal-headed man sneered, "what do you think now of my little establishment, Subhuti?"

The chained man glared contemptuously about him and said nothing.

His captor, suddenly livid, ran to the chained man's side and struck a vicious, furious blow to the face. "Answer when I speak to you! No man defies Doctor Anubis, the Lord of All Living Things."

The chained man stared stonily ahead.

"Very well," Anubis almost shrieked, "we will see if you remain silent when you have sampled a taste of my hospitality! I can be generous to those who cooperate with me, but those who make themselves my enemies regret it!"

He turned to the silent natives and delivered a complex series of gestures. The natives took Arnaud Subhuti by the elbows and directed him from the landing pad.

Inside the building they quickly reached Doctor Anubis' main research quarter. Subhuti, still chained but as upright as a young athlete, looked about himself. His keen eyes took in with appreciation the wealth of modern scientific equipment that filled the cavernous room.

But those eyes widened in horror when he saw the dull,

zombielike figures whose silent, dispirited movements seemed somehow to sway in time with the sound of a distant Incan flute.

Sir Percy Dillingham.

Luigi Serengetti.

Madame Marie Charbonnet.

Boris Tuporov.

P'eng Chiao-Tsu.

An involuntary exclamation escaped the lips of the great scientific wizard. "You fiend, Anubis," he whispered, "you inhuman fiend! What have you done to them?"

The jackal-faced figure threw back his head and laughed, a bloodcurdling sound utterly without trace of mirth. "Exactly what I will do to you, Subhuti—if I must! But I would prefer to obtain your voluntary cooperation. The scientists you see before you are most useful assistants to me, but they do, I will admit, seem to have lost something of their—creative spark."

"Never!" Subhuti ground out. "I would rather die!"

"But my dear Arnaud," Anubis purred in response, "you have no choice in the matter. There will be none of this for you, do not worry. I shall yet realize my dream to become in fact the Lord of All Living Things. And you, the wizard of science, shall become my willing deputy. I have far grander plans for you than mere laboratory work!" The self-styled Lord gestured once more, addressing his native servitors in the secret sign language. One of them advanced and held a velvet-lined case toward his master. The other two grasped Arnaud Subhuti by his still-manacled arms and held him immobile.

FOURTH WEEK: With the wizard of science held helpless in his heavy bonds, the haunting music of the Incan flute and the mad whine of giant electric generators providing an insane duet of accompaniment, Doctor Anubis plunged the ugly hypodermic needle into his archfoe's arm.

A red-hot agony flowed through the wizard's veins. It was as if every nerve in his body had been connected directly to a source of throbbing electrical current. The sight before his eyes was flooded with red as his keen brain took note that the quintet of world-famous researchers working in Anubis's ırall continued their labors, apparently unmindful of the orror transpiring before them.

A mad buzzing filled his ears and suddenly Arnaud Subhuti elt every muscle in his body turn to ice water!

As he slumped heavily to the floor, borne down by his ıassive chains, his last thought was a prayer to whatever ower there might be: *Whatever happens, let me not become an gent of the monster who gloats over me!*

FIFTH WEEK: Subhuti regained consciousness in another oom. Luxurious drapes hung from a crenellated ceiling to a ıick, sound-deadening carpet. Cressets hanging from tanchions provided a flickering, lurid illumination. A sweetly loying incense hung heavily in the musty air.

The wizard looked at his hands and feet. His chains were one. No straps or clamps held him in place. He could rise and ıove about as he wished, but somehow, while his mind eemed to be entirely clear, he discovered that he had no will hatsoever. He had been reduced to the role of a passive bserver, a virtual passenger inside his own skull!

"Subhuti! Subhuti! Look at me, Arnaud!"

He turned his head. There stood a gaunt figure, so tall that lthough stooped it still towered over him. It had the outline f a man but the head—the head seemed to be that of some east with pointed ears and a feral snout. A jackal. The figure ore a black satin cloak lined with brilliant emerald green that lashed as he moved.

"Good, Arnaud Subhuti. My serum worked on you, as I new it must. But as I told you, it is not my wish to hold you in nwilling thralldom. I would rather have your willing ssistance. Your value to me is limited while your intellect is ulled with drugs. So—I will enroll you in my service by a orce so great as to hold you long after the drug has worn off.

"Rise, Subhuti!"

The wizard of science willingly complied. He stood, now, waiting whatever might come next, his mind void of any hought of action or resistance.

The jackal-headed man turned toward a place where two anging draperies met. Ignoring the wizard of science—for e clearly had no fear of the helplessly drugged man—he poke:

"Come, my darling daughter. Come, my beloved Aphrité."

The curtains stirred, were parted by some unseen agency human or mechanical, that lurked behind them. Beyond in a chamber glowing with lurid light, stood a figure tall and slim nearly as tall as the jackal-headed man himself.

The figure advanced through the drawn draperies and stood silently, lips parted, gazing at Arnaud Subhuti. The helpless wizard of science, robbed of all will and volition, gazed back, his passive mind registering the vision of the woman who stood before him.

Her face was a pale, milky white, her complexion so smooth that it must never have known any but the kindest of ministrations. High, jet-black eyebrows arched above long, curling lashes. Her cheeks were smooth, pale, high-boned. Her lips were full and deep crimson. Her aspect was strangely suggestive of some exotic race.

But her most fascinating feature was her eyes. The whites were as pale as high Andean snow. And the irises were—not the honest brown or blue, green or hazel or gray of ordinary mortals, but—a deep, ruby red.

Long tresses of rich, dark hair hung over her shoulders and curved gracefully over high, generous breasts.

She wore a cloak of flame-colored, flame-patterned satin. It hung from her sensual shoulders to her pale, naked feet.

"Aphrité, my dear," Professor Anubis said, "this is the man of whom I spoke to you, Arnaud Subhuti. Will you not greet him?"

The most beautiful woman in the world advanced slowly, gracefully. When she stood before the wizard of science her eyes drew his irresistibly to hers, hardly lower than his own. She raised long, graceful arms and slid them around his broad shoulders.

He could see that beneath the flame-satin robe she was nude—magnificent—breathtaking!

She pulled his face down to hers, raised her lips to his.

Her kiss was as if he had been cast into a pit of excruciating pleasure: her mouth on his was searing in its passion, her incomparable body pressed against his was a pliant conflagration.

When at last Aphrité drew away from the helpless wizard of

:ience a strange expression was imprinted on her lovely
:atures. But behind her the laughter of a jackal seemed to fill
1e room, rising to its high rafters and echoing sinisterly.
"Now I can apply the antidote," Doctor Anubis screamed in
iumph. "Now he will be mine—willingly—forever!"

* * *

"What do you think of it, Willy? I transcribed the tape and
dited a little for the *umms* and *ahhs* but that's pretty close to
erbatim." Tara put down her notebook and rose, walked to
1e hot plate for a cup of coffee. "Want a refill while I'm at it?"
Willy shook his head, no. "Thanks, Tara, but I have enough
ouble sleeping." He ran a hand through thinning, tangled
air. "The man is amazing. Absolutely amazing. What kind of
1ape is he in? Did Dr. Ettmann say anything? Is he getting
etter?"
Tara turned, steaming cup in her hand. She picked up a
ained spoon and stirred in a pinch of powered cream. "It's
eartbreaking, Willy. I can understand why you say you can't
o there. Buddy seems absolutely normal. Well, he's a little
epressed, but who wouldn't be! But he keeps track of
usiness, he's very excited about the TV deal. His mind is as
lear as ever. Look at the work he's already done on 'The
ackal's Laugh.' But then—"
She shrugged helplessly. Willy put a hand toward her and
1e took it, shaking. She had to put down her cup so she
ouldn't spill the coffee on the studio floor.
"Then he changes. It's terrifying. He becomes that—other
1an. That nazi. Washburn. He seems actually to change, his
hole bearing, his facial expression, the way he talks. It's like
ossession. It's—god damn it, Willy, where's the brandy? Let
1e put a slug of it in the java before I start to cry."
Willy reached into a low drawer and pulled out a quarter-
ıll bottle of amber fluid. "Don't blame you," he grunted.
"But how do *you* feel, Willy? I mean, about this story. Can
ou do the panel breakdown yourself? Buddy wanted to draw
1e roughs, but he gets so discouraged working with crayon
nd newsprint and they won't let him have anything else
ecause of—of—of—"

"Siddown, Tara, for godsake try and relax. The story's fin
No problem doing the breakdown. I think it'll fly."

She looked at him through tear-brimming eyes. "You'r
sure?"

Willy scratched a huge, freckled ear. "Well, the fourth wee
is a little skimpy. No dialog, just that hypo sequence. But w
can fill that up with reaction shots from the other zombies, yo
know, Percy Dillingham and them."

"Yeh. Gimme a Kleenex, damn it."

"And that babe whatsername, Aphrité—"

"Yes."

"That's some hot stuff. Hey, do you think Buddy's, al
getting any there in the booby-hatch?"

Tara wiped her eyes.

"Well," Willy rambled on, "we'll have to tone the babe dow
just a hair. Not show that open cloak, anyhow. But th
syndicate's getting pretty loose these days. We don't want t
lose any good papers, but if you get clipped now and then it
good promo. Remember what happened to *Doonesbury*."

Tara nodded.

"Come on, sweety, it'll fly. Don't worry about it." He looke
down at his watch. "Hey, it's getting pretty late, why don't yo
toss that stuff down the sink and we'll go find a bar and I'll bu
you a glass of real booze."

Tara put down her cup and managed a tremulous hal
smile. "Okay, Willy," she said.

8. Sravasti

"WHAT this amounts to is nothing less than the annihilatio
of the universe."

"Yes, Auburn Sutro. That is why your mission is so urgent."

The engineer sat down and faced the shadowy Yakshi. H
stifled a low, bitter laugh and shook his head. "This ought t
be a glorious adventure, you know that, Asoka? No, I suppos

ou wouldn't. But it's the kind of wildly melodramatic stunt
iat every kid I ever knew dreams about. A chance to save the
orld!

"Only I have to get *myself* straightened out first. I've still got
assimilate this whole thing, and I have to avoid more
lackouts. I don't know what happens when they come. You
iid that I was several other men? That I changed from
erson to person right here on Sravasti?"

The Yakshi nodded—or transmitted whatever impulse that
utro's mind interpreted as a nod of agreement. The engi-
eer gave a low whistle, rubbed his head.

"I guess—" Sutro stood up, began to speak, interrupted
imself and started over. "Can I leave this building? I mean, is
iere an atmosphere outside that I can breathe? Is the
mperature outside safe for humans?"

"The surface of Sravasti bears life, Auburn Sutro. The star
eoples created an outer shell to preserve the atmosphere.
here is a unique ecology on the surface of Sravasti. Full
etails can come from the computer of the star peoples, but I
an say—you will be safe from surface conditions."

Sutro nodded. "Good. Uh—this may sound odd to you, but
'd really like to go for a walk outside. This building is—
omehow it isn't exactly comfortable for me. Psychologically.
'd rather—I'd like you to come along, too, Asoka. I want to
nderstand more about these other peoples who lived on
ravasti."

The Yakshi assented.

"And maybe I can learn more about Sravasti from in-
pecting it anyway. I can plunge back into that computer if I
eed to, but I want to get the feel of the place through my own
enses."

The shadow moved close to Sutro, guided him through the
uilding. "I can go with you only a short distance," Asoka said.
The star peoples wanted the Yakshis to remain close to this
lace, not to wander across the face of the planet. We are—
ou must accept this concept—not beings of stable matter like
ourself.

"Our patterns—you understand?—the structure of energy
hich gives each Yakshi his being—is maintained by the

machines of the star peoples. If we go too far, the structur disintegrates."

He made an odd, touchingly human gesture with hi shadowy hands. "It would be—very roughly, you understanc Auburn Sutro—it would be as if the Yakshi had died. Nc precisely. We are not precisely alive. But—roughly so.

"Then the machines would create a new Yakshi within th building to take the place of that which had—faded away.'

Sutro turned to face the being. "But you Yakshis seem t share your memories, to have a common mind. Don't yo continue to exist then? And what about the ones—didn't yo project some Yakshis into the burned-out area? What becam of them?"

"Gone." Asoka seemed to shrug.

They both turned, walked through a final, irising archway and stood looking out of the structure, across the surface o the artificial planet.

Sutro lifted one foot, placed it on the ground outside. H took a breath. The air was breathable indeed, and not merel that. After the dead, ozone-tinged atmosphere inside th Yakshis' building, the atmosphere of Sravasti held a sweet organic flavor that Sutro savored in his mouth and nostril and lungs.

He looked at the ground. It was covered with vegetation Low, knobby growths that seemed to lie somewhere betweer moss and true grass in structure. The stuff stretched across a flat landscape. At the horizon—a very close horizon—the surface of the planet seemed almost to be chopped off. Bu clearly it wasn't: things rose from beyond the edge, things tha could almost pass for trees.

The sky was black.

A few pale clouds seemed to drift across it, but where cloud didn't obscure the sky it was sprinkled with a vast array o stars. If Sravasti was truly located at the center of the siderea universe, there would be an even distribution of stars in al directions. Sutro stood awestruck, gazing upward.

The brilliance of the stars dotting the blackness was close tc that provided by sunlight on earth. The density of the star was overwhelming. Their number was beyond guessing.

But—Asoka had touched him on the shoulder; the feeling

f the Yakshi's not-quite-material hand sent a shiver through utro. Wordlessly the Yakshi raised an arm and pointed to a egion of the sky near the horizon, off to the left of where they tood.

To Auburn Sutro's naked eye the vision was tiny, incredibly inier than it had appeared through the ancient star peoples' canner. But it was far more terrifying, for all that, when it was een directly.

The fireworms writhed and spun. Beyond the perimeter of heir movements the heavens were sprayed with multicolor oints of brilliance. But within the region of the fireworms vas—nothingness. A dead, utter blackness.

Sutro stared in fascination, then tore his eyes away from the errifying vision. He felt weak. He dropped to sit on the soft egetation, his back to the sight. He looked up at the Yakshi. Before I even address that, I need to understand myself etter. I need to control my faculties. You see, Asoka?"

A nod.

"Tell me about the other men."

"Ah"—the shadow-form gestured—"when the star people's nachines summoned the man here, he seemed different from ou. Shorter, round and soft. He said he was Old Buddy atvan. A—soft—person. But soon he changed. He drew imself up, taller, stiff. He commanded. There is no need to ommand Yakshis, man. But this man *needed* to command.

"And then—he called himself Roland Washburn—he ecame—you.

"Auburn Sutro. Another man. You see? All in one body. ut three men. You see?" The Yakshi seemed almost lesperate to make himself understood. He leaned toward utro, said again, "You see?"

Auburn leaned his head against his knees, rubbed his temles with the tips of all his fingers. *Did* he see? He racked his rain trying to grasp what Asoka had said. He saw—and tried o avoid what he saw.

Images flashed through his mind. Sensational psychiatric ases. Exploitation films based on clinical books. He saw all too vell!

Old Buddy Satvan.

Roland Washburn.

And himself, Auburn Sutro.

He'd never heard of Satvan or Washburn, was totally unaware of their existence. But—wasn't that sometimes true of cases like this? What were they called? Multiple personalities. *Grand hysterie.* There might be two, three, fifteen—any number of personalities trapped in a single body, split away at some early age from the original identity and living independently of one another, sharing the use of the body through some mysterious algorithm of the psyche.

Sometimes they were aware of each other—sometimes not. Some of them could sit like passengers in an airliner, watching the other personalities in action, eavesdropping on their thoughts and memories. Others totally lacked the power, lived what passed for normal lives while they were in control, in phase. Only they suffered from periodic blackouts when other persona took over.

Periodic blackouts!

And for how long? How long had it been since Sutro last left his office on Folsom Street, his club on Sutter, his comfortable home in suburban Mill Valley? How many hours—or how many *years*—had Satvan and Washburn alternated in control of *his* body while he slumbered away in psychic limbo, a black region as vacant as the burned-out sector of the fireworms.

Auburn raised his hands and stared at them, blocking out two palms' worth of the heavens. Did they look old, those hands? Were they liver-spotted and trembling? Had he been in limbo for *decades*?

He dropped his hands again, rose slowly to his feet and faced the Yakshi Asoka who had stood patiently while he had gone through his chain of thoughts.

"Please," Auburn Sutro said through his headband, "let's just—let's just walk for a while." He linked arms with the shadow-being, taking comfort from the contact despite the odd feeling of the creature of not-quite-matter.

They walked in silence.

The horizon seemed to draw nearer with each pace rather than receding to keep a uniform distance as Sutro expected. The puzzle was actually a relief for him—a temporary escape from the despair his own condition provoked. The universe was in danger!

Images of heroic cinema spacemen battling galactic menaces rose and faded. But Sutro faced a far more personal, and imminent, problem. Unless he could get himself back together, how could he hope to save the universe?

He shook his head, as if shaking off the problem like a dousing of water from a swimmer.

The trees—or treelike growths—beyond the planet's close horizon grew taller and more beautiful as they approached. At last he stood with Asoka at the edge of the world. Sutro looked down at the ground beneath his feet, and this time he laughed aloud, a laugh of relief at solving *any* problem.

Of course!

Sravasti was an artificial construct, not a natural world. Its core was a webwork of girders and cables, not a ball of molten rock and metal. And its surface was made of—flat plates laid out in neat geometrical parquet.

He stood at the edge of such a plate now, looking back toward the building of the Yakshis, then ahead, again, into a richly blooming garden, or something that might easily have passed for one. Not that there was any of the geometrical precision of an old-fashioned formal garden like the few that persisted around the surviving Nob Hill mansions.

But graceful plants lifted colorful leaves and blossoms to catch the rays of a trillion distant suns. Auburn raised his eyes to the wispy clouds above, as he continued his slow advance across the surface of Sravasti. Possibly it rained or snowed on Sravasti. Where the soil came from, where the spores of the ancestors of these plants had originated—never mind that, he would ask the computer if he needed to know that.

Later on, later on.

He turned and saw Asoka, still near-by but hanging back. Sutro asked the reason. The Yakshi's response seemed weak and discontinuous. He was clearly at the limit of his power. Much farther and Asoka would simply fade away.

The temperature near the building had been comfortably warm; as Sutro and Asoka moved away it had grown more and more chill. The engineer blew out his breath. It misted up in the cold air.

"Auburn Sutro," the Yakshi said, "I cannot——" His later words were distorted, faint, lost.

"Go on back," Sutro began, "I want to—" He stood, transfixed, his eyes riveted on the sky. The wispy clouds had gathered, deepened. A thin, dry snow was beginning to fall. And in the now dimming light of the sky, he thought he could see—

Shapes.

Humanlike shapes, swirling and drifting with the cold flakes, slowly swaying downward through the gray-purple twilight.

They were—angels.

Angels? *Angels*? Sutro asked himself. Great, winged beings as pale as snowflakes, drifting down. Many of them. Uncounted angels. With great white wings like those of giant seabirds.

Blond, flowing hair.

Pale, blazing eyes.

One drifted toward Sutro. It held a great sword, hilt downward, bathed in flaring, sparkling flames. As the angel neared the violet-tinctured ground Auburn ran forward to meet it. Behind him a voice cried "No, do not—"

The voice ceased.

Sutro stopped and looked back. He saw a vague outline thinning and fading in the snow-flecked twilight. The outline disappeared utterly. A glimmering hooplike object that had circled its head tumbled onto the vegetation, struck silently, crumpled and lay still.

Sutro turned away. He stood face-to-face with the angel. The being was huge—well above the tall engineer in height, broad-shouldered, massive. It stood with feet spread, firmly, holding the flaming sword like a firebrand.

Auburn Sutro opened his mouth, closed it again, managed to stammer something. The angel did not answer. Sutro spoke again. "You—how can it be? Is God—?"

He stopped, stood paralyzed before the mighty form.

Snow fell on Sutro's head, crusted his hair, melted and ran on his face. His cheeks and hands were cold. His breath clouded with each exhalation.

The flaming sword seemed to create a barrier of heat or of pure force around the angel. The snowflakes fell larger and more thickly now but as they reached a point above the angel's head they curved away, falling in a circle around his naked feet.

The angel took a single pace forward. He raised his sword to shoulder level, the flaring blade held directly before him, its long surface parallel to the ground, its tip a hands's length above Sutro's shoulder.

Slowly the angel lowered the blade. Sutro could hear the snap and rush of the flame. He could feel its heat on the entire side of his head. The brightness of the fire dazzled his eye while the other, shadowed by the bones of his face, peered through the swirling flakes into the pale, blazing eyes of the angel.

The blade touched him.

The soliders permitted Tannie and Oom and Pieter to take some belongings with them. Each was allowed one suitcase or bag. Tannie and Oom took changes of clothing, shoes, soap, bread, cheese and sausage. Oom packed his razor. Tannie, silent, filled a bag for Pieter. It had to be light enough for him to carry by himself.

He stood wide-eyed, watching Tannie pack for him. She asked him if he had anything he wanted her to put in and he shook his head, no. He clutched his blouse tightly around his belly, feeling the foreign magazine with the picture stories. He would take the great man with the scarlet cape, the golden suit, the all-seeing eye, along with him. His bag might become lost. The magazine was safer inside Pieter's blouse.

One of the men in gray who were taking them away spoke to a companion. He called him by name. His name was Untersturmführer. The other man—Pieter did not learn his name—did whatever Untersturmführer told him to do. Untersturmführer also told Tannie and Oom to do things, and they obeyed.

Oom told Pieter that he too must obey the men in gray. Pieter looked down at the floor and clutched his blouse when Oom told him this.

When Tannie had finished packing Pieter's bag she pulled a white kerchief from her pocket and wiped her eyes and nose with it. Then she took Pieter's hand. With his other he made certain that his magazine was securely wedged into the waistband of his trousers, hidden beneath his blouse, then picked up his little bag that Tannie van der Roest had packed for him.

Tannie and Oom picked up their suitcases. Oom put his hand on Tannie's shoulder for a moment. Oom was a very big man with a round, bald head and great dark mustaches that moved up and down when he spoke. Suddenly Oom put down his suitcase again, went and picked his big meerschaum from off the mantelpiece and slipped it into his pocket. He took a fat pouch of tobacco and matches also. Then he lifted his suitcase once more and said something to Untersturmführer.

They all walked downstairs.

Outside the house Oom van der Roest turned and locked the front door, dropped the key into the mailbox of their neighbors, the Mejuffrou van der Maaten and her old father, who owned the wine store between the closed bookshop and the coffeehouse.

Untersturmführer and the other man pushed them toward a truck that was waiting in the street. The men did not seem especially unkind. Merely bored.

There were many people in the back of the truck. Some of them reached down and Oom van der Roest picked Pieter up and handed him to a strong young man wearing a gray cap and a dark blue overcoat. The young man smiled at Pieter and lifted him into the truck.

Tannie van der Roest handed Pieter's bag up after him. Then people helped her and Oom into the truck.

Untersturmführer gave a signal to the other man in gray and he closed the tailgate of the truck. Then they both went to the front of the truck and got in.

The engine started and the truck began to move.

Pieter did not understand what was happening. He heard many of the people in the truck talking in low voices. He heard the words *Juden* and *Deutscher* many times, and once somebody pointed to Oom and Tannie van der Roest and said *Weissjuden, Weissjuden,* and then in Dutch also, white Jews. Pieter did not know what white Jews meant.

They rode in the truck for a long time. Finally they came to a place with a fence around it and the truck stopped. Pieter tugged at Tannie van der Roest's hand and asked where they were. She said Westerbork. He didn't know where that was, but he was glad to be told the name of the place anyway.

Westerbork.

Pieter stood up as tall as he could. He felt the magazine underneath his blouse and smiled to himself. He looked around. For the first time he saw that a man was sitting up high, at the front of the truck. He wore a gray uniform like Untersturmführer's, and he had a rifle in his hands. He looked bored.

Pieter wished that the great man with the cape would fly down from the sky and hit the man with the rifle and take Pieter and Oom and Tannie back to their house, but he didn't come.

Soon the fence opened and the trucked rolled inside. After a few minutes the truck stopped yet again. There was a long wait, then Untersturmführer came and opened the back of the truck and everyone climbed out. The young man in the cap and overcoat handed Pieter down to Oom.

Everyone stood around, apparently not knowing what to do. Pieter kept a tight hold on Tannie's hand.

After a little while a man came over and somebody whispered that he was Obersturmführer. Pieter wondered if that meant he was Untersturmführer's brother. Obersturmführer pointed to Tannie and Oom and said something Pieter couldn't understand, but Tannie and Oom started to walk away from the group of people from the truck, holding Pieter tightly between them by both his hands. Oom had taken Pieter's bag.

Obersturmführer began to shout at them. Oom shouted back. Obersturmführer ran up and hit Oom. It was the first time that Pieter had ever seen anyone raise a hand to Oom, but Oom just stood there. Tannie began to weep loudly. Obersturmführer continued shouting at Tannie and Oom, and Tannie kept hugging Pieter and crying. Obersturmführer came and stood very close to Tannie and shouted some more.

Pieter was terrified.

Finally the young man with the blue overcoat came and put his hands on Pieter's shoulders and talked very softly to Tannie. He talked and talked. Obersturmführer backed away a step. Slowly the young man with the overcoat lifted Pieter out of Tannie's arms. Another man in a gray uniform came and Tannie and Oom went away with him, holding onto each other and looking back at Pieter.

Then Obersturmführer shouted something and everybody began to walk the other way. Pieter had his bag in one hand, and with the other he held onto the young man with the blue overcoat.

9. Sravasti

HE was floating somewhere. Nowhere. In the dark. In the nothing. He would have shaken his head in bewilderment but he seemed to have no corporeality at all.

It was—

It was—

He couldn't carry the thought any farther. There was no place to go with it.

Always before when he'd been under, the soft fool, the buffoon Buddy Satvan had been out. Washburn had always been able to observe Satvan's actions, to monitor his activities. In fact, it had been a very useful relationship for Washburn. He could conduct his own affairs as needed, could act and speak as he saw fit. And when he had any need for Satvan, he could summon the weak, flabby personality from its dormant state and pass control over to him.

Then Satvan had to cope.

It was really very handy. That way Satvan was able to carry on his puerile career as a comic-strip writer and sketcher, earning the money it took to keep them both—Satvan and Roland L. K. Washburn—in comfort. One thing about leading a noble struggle for an unpopular cause was the continuing need for financial support.

Without *Diamond Sutro*—with all its bourgeois vapidity—Washburn would have been forced into a series of cold-water lofts and basement offices, threadbare uniforms and crudely mimeographed manifestoes. That, or find a wealthy mentor. But he had no wish to make himself beholden to any master other than himself, and his ideals of purity, discipline, struggle, the will.

And Satvan was handy when Washburn faced a situation, as he occasionally did, which he did not choose to handle personally. Then he could simply pass control to Satvan, as he had the time when—he stopped. He still didn't like to think about that. With Satvan he was committed to a private institution. Without him it would have meant a state hospital, or worse. Or worse.

But now—now Satvan was not in control. Not as far as Roland Washburn could determine. *Nor was he* . . . as far as he could tell he had been unconscious. Not exactly sleeping, but something much like it. And he had recovered awareness to find himself in this limbo. Like a ghost, a disembodied consciousness. It wasn't really unpleasant. Merely—odd.

He tried to relax and achieve union with this new state of being. His mind seemed to drift back to the boyhood he had labored so hard to recover, to reconstruct, to recreate. Back to his only really happy days, back to the days of the *Hitlerjugend,* to the happy sense of community, of obedience, of communal superiority to ordinary folk.

Wearing the gray uniform, the visored cap, the swastika armband. Marching to the steady *rat-a-tat* of snare drums. The *Jugend* had struck fear into the hearts of every enemy, every subman. Their own parents had quailed before them!

Tramp down cobbled streets, thick-soled shoes sounding a march-step, eyes flashing with stern pride. Halt! Music! Drama!

Massed uniforms: SA, SS, *Wehrmacht, Hitlerjugend.* The leaders, the great leaders, the leaders.

The Führer himself, the embodiment of the Will.

All gone now. The ignominious end of the war. Bombers and slovenly enemy soldiers in baggy uniforms, their beards unshaven, careening through the city with bottles and women.

And for him a new country, a new name.

New ideas. Soft, slovenly ideas. Better had he gone to the

East, for all the faults of the Slavic submen. The Party's teachings had been that the submen of the East were low and bestial races, but they had somehow pulled themselves together into a disciplined, orderly society.

The West, where he had found himself—the West was worst of all. Soft and sloppy, sinking daily in a sea of self-indulgent luxuries. All of it was manipulated and commanded by the very lowest of the submen, the worst of them all.

But Washburn would lead the people.

He would bring about a renaissance of right thinking, a return to traditional ideals. He would put an end to mongrelization, to self-indulgence, to the disgusting licentiousness of the so-called Free World. Beneath his banners the great spirit of the Struggle would revive. The subhuman cancer would be cut out of the body politic and cast away.

Then would come the true triumph of the Will! Then would come the vindication of the Struggle! Then would come the final rehabilitation of the fallen Heroes, the Martyrs of Europe!

He could feel himself swelling, throbbing, thrusting forth to the mighty hour of victory and glorification! The cheers would resound, the torches would flare in the night of his apotheosis! It was—

It was—

With a mighty surge he felt himself coming, coming out, coming into control. No soft, whining Buddy Satvan to thrust aside with a psychic snarl.

Now Washburn burst from the darkness, felt himself in control of his body, his fingers clutching as if they held a blade, a sharp knife, a javelin, a mighty weapon, a club, a heavy club with knots and spikes on it, a round-barreled, long-barreled round heavy throbbing peni—*no,* a submachine gun, yes, a bucking chattering submachine gun to kill the bucking chattering submen, yes. . . .

Panting, spent, he opened his eyes.

He was lying on the earth, his face pressed to a soft, primitive blanket of vegetation, his mouth open, slack, some of the pale violet-tinted vegetation clinging to his wet tongue. Roland moaned, rose stiffly to his feet.

He was outside the building where he had previously ıcountered the shadowy Yakshis. He was standing on a plain some sort, vegetation underfoot, trees nearby.

It was snowing.

He had been in his room in the private psychiatric hospital Prince Morton County, Virginia. Then he had been in the range room with the weird purple shadow-men. Then—en the blackness, and now he was outside somewhere.

It was almost dark out, with the soft, diffused light of a late idwinter afternoon when the sun is almost gone and what ght it provides is softened and spread by thick snow-clouds.

It was very silent. He could hear his own breathing, ragged ıd loud, slowly adjusting itself toward normal. He felt some-ing on his forehead and reached with one hand to see what was. It was the communication headband that he had worn side the building. But it was disconnected from its cable.

He shook with a tremor as a gust of wind brought heavier ıowflakes pelting onto his face. They were wet now, and ruck and ran down Washburn's face like absurd tears. He ırned in a circle and discovered that one of the Yakshis still aited nearby. In another direction a tall, slender, very pale gure stood, all but lost against the falling snow. And beyond , the suggestion of other, many other such beings.

Washburn faced the Yakshi and opened his mouth, shut it gain, decided to try the headband, asked "What are those—ıings?"

The answer came garbled and unclear.

Washburn turned his back on the Yakshi, began to walk ward the white, ghostly being. In his head he heard a weak y. The shadow-man was pleading with him to stop, to turn. Washburn laughed and strode ahead. Again the plea. e turned back and looked toward the shadow-man. The akshi was struggling feebly after him, reaching out to grasp im. Washburn moved faster. The Yakshi grew fainter and isappeared into the snow.

Roland Washburn halted. He peered back at the shadow-ıan, or tried to. Was he simply obscured by the falling snow nd the darkness? Washburn ran back a few paces. No sign of ıe Yakshi. Washburn looked carefully at the ground. No ody. But—a headband like his own.

He pulled his from his forehead, shoved both into the wai
of his trousers, pulled the bottom of his tunic over the band
For a moment he felt an odd sensation as he did this, then
passed off and he ran after the tall, white shape nearest him.

Without apparent motion it maintained its distance. Rolan
shouted at it. The being halted. As Washburn moved, no
more slowly, the distance between them closed.

"I have come," Roland announced, "to enlist your people i
the great struggle."

The white creature toward above him, regarded him wit
strange eyes. It was vaguely humanlike, but no more a tru
man than was a Yakshi a true man. The angel did not respon
to Washburn's words.

Roland made another attempt. "Yours is a great people
You are the master-race of this world. You must—"

The creature threw back its head. It arched it shoulders. I
spread its great pale limbs—Washburn couldn't tell whether i
had raised immensely long, slim arms and, wearing its loos
robe, had raised long folds of pale cloth with them—or wheth
er it actually was a winged creature, a gigantic bird of som
sort whose form in the snowstorm had misled Washburn. H
thought of the great condor of the Andes.

With a great slapping sound the creature swung around,
thumped its feet on the snow-covered vegetation, rose into the
air. The sound of dozens of like beings made a brief, deafen-
ing dissonance, like the flapping of wings of a great flight of
birds. The white creature grew smaller as it rose into the sky.
Within seconds it and its fellows were lost to sight.

Washburn stood, his own head back, eyes raised squinting
against the cold. Millions of specks of white drifted and spun.
Which were snowflakes, which flying creatures? He could not
tell. He did not even know now whether the things had flown
with wings of their own bodies or whether they had used some
device hidden beneath their flowing gowns to carry them
away.

He stood, shaking his fist angrily and cursing them, until his
eyes and throat began to smart. Then he stopped to rub his
eyes, to swallow a few times and relieve his throat.

Where to go?

He retraced his steps toward the place where the Yakshi

ıd disappeared, where he had found the abandoned :adband. He still had his own and tried to send a call for help rough it. He had no way of knowing whether it had been ceived. He heard no reply.

The place was now completely silent except for the steady w-pitched *slush-slush-slush* of heavily falling snow. Washburn gan to worry. The Yakshi garments had kept him markably comfortable, but he did not want to stay here definitely. The snow continued to fall. He had no food. ventually he would weaken from hunger or fatigue. If he :pt in the snow he might freeze. Even if he didn't freeze—he dn't want to stay here!

He tried to align himself very carefully in the direction of e Yakshi's movements. He began to walk. The ground was easantly springy, the snow still not deep although it was cumulating each minute. The darkness had thickened with e increased heaviness of the snowfall.

Washburn realized how chilly he was. He began to jog. very dozen yards or so he would stop and look back to see if : was leaving a straight trail in the snow, if he was running raight or if he was falling into a curved course and losing ack of his goal.

In a surprisingly short time he came to the place where the ound seemed creased. The plain on which he'd been running came to a sort of seam in the earth, and another plain or ate began at a slightly different angle. He stepped carefully :ross the angle and saw—what must be the building he had me from.

How he had got from the building to the field with the white ing-creatures he had no idea, but he knew that safety lay ithin the walls of that structure.

Panting and sobbing, Roland L. K. Washburn ran.

Willy checked the office number in the building directory as : did every time he came to the syndicate's headquarters. He und that it was 1526, the same as it always was. He waited for ı empty elevator, hefted his artist's portfolio and made his ay to the back of the car.

Upstairs the receptionist gave him a dazzling smile, arched er eyebrows in an expression that might mean anything from *good morning* to *the sky's the limit,* and waved him straig through to Burt Bahnson's office. Willy nodded diffidently the bright young art school grads who as usual clustered in t reception area, each nervously juggling his thick folder samples, and maneuvered his lanky frame through the inn doorway.

Bahnson was waiting at the entrance of his own cluttere cubicle. He crushed Willy's skinny hand in his beefy one, to the proffered portfolio and shoved an ancient blond-woc chair at Willy. Then he spread the portfolio on his drawi board and bent over the *Diamond Sutro* material.

Willy watched Bahnson for a few minutes, then got u cleared his throat a couple of times and wandered off to t crusted hot plate for a cup of coffee and a stale half donut th someone had rejected earlier that morning. He looked at t old notices on the bulletin board, nodded vaguely to a coup of homesteaders in the bullpen and ambled back to Bu Bahnson's cubicle.

He perched nervously on the edge of the blond-wood chai "Well?" He blinked faded eyes behind tortoiseshell ey glasses.

Bahnson smiled, his square-cut face creasing to the ear "It's fine, of course." He shrugged. "Always is. You ought stop worrying and get a little confidence in yourself, Will Did you really think—what, that I'd say this stuff was lou and you had to do it over? You're one of the top men in th field today, you know that."

Willy shrugged. "You're very kind to say that, Burt."

"Huh!" Bahnson consulted an oversized calendar th covered most of one wall of the tiny office. "Let's see, th carries us through—umm—" He ran a grease pencil light across the calendar page. "—end of the quarter. Fine. Loo Willy, it's a good thing you brought this in yourself instead sending it by messenger."

"I never—"

"I know, I know, it isn't that, don't worry. It's because Arc Cantrowicz asked me to bring you around when you came in. was going to phone you and ask you not to use a messenge but it slipped my mind but everything worked out anyhow.

Willy's eyes widened. "Arch *Cantrowicz*? The head of the syndicate?"

Burt nodded.

"What does Cantrowicz want with me?"

"I don't know, Willy, but it has to be something good. You know he always passes bad news through hatchet men. I've pulled that duty myself a couple of times, and, *phew*!

"So if he wants to see you himself it has to be good. Maybe a bonus or something. You know *Diamond Sutro*'s picked up six papers this quarter. And the TV people have been around a couple more times since Arch's little West Coast excursion. I think it's getting close!"

"Then what do you think—?" Willy adjusted his hand-painted brown necktie so a little more of it showed between the long points of his white-on-white shirt collar. He tucked the end of the tie inside his gray suit pants.

"I don't know," Burt shrugged. "But here, this'll help you get ready." He poured a glass of bourbon for Willy. Willy tipped it up and rose to his feet. He started for the doorway of Burt's cubicle.

"You coming with—?"

Burt shook his head. "All the best, Willy. He said send you in, not bring you in. But *illegitimus non carborundum* and all of that, you know? Stop by on your way out and tell me what he says."

Willy made his way to Archibald Cantrowicz's office. It was the largest in the syndicate suite. Cantrowicz had a private secretary. She was middle-aged and wore a 1955 suit. She smiled through rimless octagonal eyeglasses at Willy and ushered him into the inner office. For the first time Willy laid eyes on the president of the syndicate.

"M-Mr. Cantrowicz?"

The man was around his desk and shaking Willy's hand. He was in shirtsleeves. He had a hearty manner that made Willy feel relaxed but at the same time worried.

"I want to talk to you about your strip, Willy. About *Diamond Sutro*. You know where we've had pickups?"

Willy looked blank.

Cantrowicz sat Willy down in a leather swivel chair, trotted back to the other side of his glass-topped desk and picked up a sheet of paper. "Omaha—Macon—Muncie—Bakersfield—Vancouver BC—Cuernavaca. Cuernavaca in Spanish, of course."

He dropped the paper and grinned delightedly at Willy. "What do you think of that, fella? Make you proud of yourself?"

Willy felt his face flush. "That's very nice of you to say, Mr. Cantrowicz—"

"Arch, please."

"—Arch. B-but you know *Diamond Sutro* is Buddy's strip. He still plots it. Tara brings tapes of the, from the, ah, from the hospital. Even roughs sometimes. I just do the breakdown and pencils. I even hired an inker. With Buddy's approval. Ivy Lawton. She's very good." The red had climbed from Willy's collar to his ears.

"Yeah. Look, Willy, that's what I've wanted to talk to you about. You know, Buddy Satvan is a brilliant creative person. And a prince. I love that man, Willy."

Arch's eyes grew misty. "But we have to face facts. There hasn't been a really big adventure strip in years. In decades. There's nothing like the great days of *Tarzan, Prince Valiant, Flash Gordon,* you know. Our strips, the competition, it's all the same. *Mandrake, The Phantom,* even the early days of *Superman,* Ah, Willy, Willy, *Brick Bradford,* Willy, *Dick Tracy.*

"Those were the days, those were the days."

He dug into a maple console behind his desk and pulled out a bottle and two glasses, poured himself a stiff hooker of Scotch and extended one for Willy Albertson. "Bottoms up, fella."

Willy dipped his tongue into the Scotch.

"Even the funny strips," Arch rambled on, "remember the Lena the Hyena contest that Capp ran? National craze, national craze. Made the cover of *Life* magazine, remember that?"

Willy nodded vigorously.

"Well, nowadays the public just wants to laugh, that's all. *Peanuts* and *Emmy Lou* and that damn politician *Doonesbury.* But we have a winner here, fella!" Suddenly he was serious, powerful. He hunched forward across the desk, elbows spread, forefinger pointed at Willy. "*Diamond Sutro* is the wave of the future, Albertson. We're going to ride this thing to the top. We're picking up papers, we're getting into reprint books, we'll probably have a paperback novel soon, it's super.

"But TV—"

He leaned back, looked dreamily at the ceiling.

"TV, that's where the big money is, and the network is on the verge of signing for the Diamond Sutro rights. Except for one little thing, one little thing." He paused, clearly waiting for Willy to ask what the one thing was. Willy failed to rise to the cue so Arch answered the question anyway.

"They're scared of the publicity about Buddy. So all we have to do is. . . . You're really running the strip now anyway, Willy. Loyalty is a beautiful thing but let's face the facts. We have to ease Buddy out. I'm not going to fire him, don't worry about that. I love that man. Even though I could fire him, you know. That moral turpitude clause would do it in a second but I wouldn't do that to Buddy. We'll just pension him off and put your name on the strip where it belongs anyway, and everybody will be satisfied.

"Hey? How do you feel about that?" Arch gazed eagerly across the glass ocean of his desk top, waiting for Willy's agreement.

"That wouldn't be fair." Willy shook his head. "Besides, Buddy didn't do anything. That's exactly what the judge ruled. That's what Buddy's, uh, that Dr. Ettmann says. It was that other guy, Washburn, who did it."

"And Washburn turns up in *Diamond Sutro,* too," Cantrowicz said. "Willy, Willy, there's millions riding on this, don't shoot craps with it!

"Now you listen here! I don't want to discuss it any longer. If you won't take over the strip I can get somebody else to do it. You know how many artists there are would give their eye teeth to get a crack at a daily strip? Especially a winner like *Diamond Sutro*? There must be fifteen kids a day come through this place, and all of them are damned good, damned good.

"I'll just tell Bahnson to hire somebody tomorrow. If you won't play ball you'll be out on your ass along with your precious Buddy Satvan!"

Willy shook his head. "I can't do that to Buddy. At least I have to check it with him. I mean, what becomes of Buddy?"

"Oh, shit." Cantrowicz shook his head. "I told you we'll take care of the guy. I can get him a job helping Jensen or something. Or let him be a silent partner, I don't care if *he* gets of Sutro, I just want his *name* off it!"

Willy spread his hands. "Let me talk to Tara and see if I can find out how Buddy feels. Just give me a few days, Arch."

10. Virginia

THE elder Ettmanns—both long in their graves, so there was in truth no point in attempting to call them to account—had surely had their reasons for selecting the names they bestowed upon their youngest child and only son. Actually, either the first or the second of the names they gave him would have been quite acceptable. But, taken together, they were just too much of a good thing, like a rich syrupy beverage taken with sugar added.

Noble St. Vincent Ettmann.

If the family name had been something a little more elegant they might have settled for more modest given names—at least *one* more modest given name. But there it was. There *he* was. Noble St. Vincent Ettmann. And if he'd had an easier time with that name, if he'd taken less abuse and felt less need to defend himself all the way from kindergarten to high school, Noble St. Vincent Ettmann might have settled for Noble S. Or maybe even something simple like Vince.

But somewhere around the time of his third bloody nose or his fifth or sixth shiner, the boy had decided that he was either going to have to stand up to his enemies and not yield an inch, or else he was going to cave in all the way.

He stood.

And today he was Noble St. Vincent Ettmann, MD, DSc, and he had the whole thing spelled out in gilt, serif letters on the grainy maple-laminated sign that rested on his desk.

He sat behind the desk, neatly garbed in conservative tweed business suit, his fingers interwoven behind his neck, fluffing the modishly long hair there. He smiled warmly at the patient who sat opposite him. Both of them were using comfortable, genuine leather armchairs.

Dr. Ettmann's chair had a swivel base, however, while the patient's or visitor's chair rested on four fixed legs.

To Ettmann's pleasure, the patient initiated the conversation. "I am favorably impressed to see your pride in your name and attainments, Doctor. The name is German, is it not? Well. Your academic credentials are enviable. At one time I considered pursuing an academic career myself, several leading schools had asked me to enroll, you know."

The patient sighed as if reliving an ancient, difficult decision, one that had been made properly but that still caused him mild pain to recall. "When one is involved in a vital movement—a virtual crusade, one might almost say—there isn't time for campus frolics or for ivory-tower intellectualizing. One must *act.*"

He gestured to emphasize his point—a vigorous, chopping motion closely resembling a karate blow.

"Not that theorization has no point, you understand." This, added in a manner designed to placate the listener.

Ettmann smiled, a more confidential, personal smile than the one he had used to welcome the patient. "I'm glad that we can have this relationship, Mr. Washburn. It *is* Mr. Washburn today, isn't it?"

The other man shook his head in puzzlement. "Of course, Did you mistake me for someone else, Doctor?"

Dr. Ettmann smiled and shook his head. "Is there any reason why I should?"

"Of course not!"

Ettman smiled and nodded. "Mr. Washburn, we've had a number of these chats, but I somehow feel as if we've never really come to grips with, ah, with the real problem." He steepled his fingers and gazed across them at Roland.

"The only real problem is my release from this place, Doctor. I appreciate the comfortable accommodations, but I really ought to be getting on with my work. I cannot do that here."

Noble St. Vincent Ettmann smiled still again. It was something of a generalized, noncommittal response to patients' statements: encouraging, nonthreatening, vaguely approving and supportive, yet it did not specifically associate him with the patient's statements. A delicate balance, a thin line to walk, and Ettmann had worked long to learn to do it.

"You must assign a date for my release," Washburn went on. "I think I have been as reasonable, as cooperative, as could be asked. Well, there have been one or two little incidents, to be sure. But I was highly upset. You can understand that, anyone could understand that. A man engaged in vital work, taken away from it in the prime of his career and forced into this, ah, involuntary retirement.

"But I'm completely ready to return to my work, and every day that you delay me only adds to the huge task which I face."

"Mr. Washburn." Ettmann poured himself a glass of water from the carafe that stood on his desk, offered one to Washburn, accepted Washburn's negative gesture and continued speaking. "Do you—this is really quite important—do you understand where you are? What this place is?"

"Of course!"

"And what *kind* of place is this, would you say?" Ettmann's eyes remained fixed on Washburn's, friendly, encouraging.

"It's—it's—well. . . ." Washburn shook his head.

Ettmann waited. His expression remained friendly, patient. He was very well paid, had a limited patient load, could afford to extend to his patients his patience. He grinned inwardly at the play on words.

"It is a kind of rest camp. A resort," Washburn blurted. He looked distressed at the statement.

"Yes." Ettmann nodded enthusiastically, offering support. "It *is* a kind of resort. But why do people come here? It isn't, oh, just a place for vacation, is it? Or is it, would you say?"

Washburn's complexion grew slightly flushed. Beads of perspiration appeared on his forehead.

"Would you like a sip of water, Mr. Washburn?"

Roland shook away the question. "I really have been here long enough, Doctor. I really need to return to my work. I am needed. It is unfair to keep me here any longer. I must pack my clothing and return to Washington. I am needed. My movement needs me.

"I am the leader of the movement, you know. You have been very kind to me here, very patient, but I must go. I must leave now." He started to rise from his chair.

"Please." Dr. Ettmann shook his head. "Just a little longer. Surely you can stay and chat with me for a few minutes." He glanced at his watch. "Soon it will be dinner time anyway. You wouldn't want to miss dinner. Shall we just stay here and chat until then? Eh?" The smile, the head cocked just a bit from the vertical.

Washburn subsided.

"Have a look at this, Mr. Washburn." Noble St. Vincent Ettmann pulled open a desk drawer, extracted a sheet of expensive letterhead bond, passed it across the desk-top.

Washburn accepted the paper with one hand, ran the other through his neatly trimmed short hair.

"Can you read me the heading, Mr. Washburn?"

Roland blinked his eyes, rubbed them, stared at the paper. "It's, ah—the glare in here. . . ."

"Make yourself comfortable, Mr. Washburn. Take your time. It's just a sheet of writing paper. I'm a little vain, it's my personal letterhead. You see, over there in the corner, where it says 'Noble St. Vincent Ettmann, MD, DSc.' But what is the actual heading on the stationery?"

Washburn squinted. "It says Morton Prince Memorial Institute. Uh, Prince Morton County, Virginia."

"Yes, thank you." Ettmann reached for the paper, returned it to the desk drawer. "A remarkable coincidence, don't you think? The Morton Prince Institute being in Prince Morton County, I mean? I've always found that very amusing."

Washburn stared at him dourly.

"Do you know who Morton Prince was, Mr. Washburn? No?" The smile again. The patient was not a rival to be bested in debate nor even less an enemy to be defeated in battle. Rapport must be maintained if we are to help the patient help himself.

"Morton Prince was the first man to describe the *grand hysterie* of multiple personality. Prior to his work, what we know as multiple personality was regarded as a complex schizophrenia—or even as demonic possession. Ghostcraft. Witchlore. Does this sound familiar to you, Mr. Washburn? Does it mean anything, what I'm saying?"

Roland shook his head. "Intellectual calisthenics, Dr. Ettmann. That name is German, isn't it? Or is it Austrian? It isn't Jewish by any chance, is it? Ettmann? Ettmann?"

And don't get led down side-trails away from the subject. If the patient is leading the topic away from something it means that he realizes—on some level—that he is being reached. On some level.

"Mr. Washburn, the Institute is a hospital. A mental hospital specializing in cases of *grand hysterie.*"

He leaned back in his soft leather chair. "Mr. Washburn, do you understand why you are here? Why you are a patient here?"

"I do, Doctor. Jewish medical forces are keeping me here to prevent the completion of my mission. But they will fail. My mission is sacred and it cannot for long be stayed!"

Involuntarily, Ettmann sighed. "Mr. Washburn, does the name Oskar Schrieber mean anything to you?"

Roland wrinkled his brow in concentration. "Schrieber. Of course. My deputy! A martyr! They murdered him, Doctor, but they will pay dearly. A Jewish life will perish for every drop of Oskar Schrieber's blood. He is—the Horst Wessel of our time!" Roland smiled at the bon mot. He would use it again.

"Mr. Washburn, do you know who—to use your own phrase—who it was who martyred Oskar Schrieber? Who shot him?"

"I do. I do, Doctor. I know who it was. I attended his trial in this very county and witnessed the miscarriage of justice."

"Mr. Washburn, who was it? Who murdered Oskar Schrieber?"

"It was that moronic cartoonist. The one who draws the comic strip. Satvan. It was Buddy Satvan."

"And what did the court decide, Mr. Washburn?"

"I can hear the judge as if I were there in his courtroom this afternoon. 'Not guilty by reason of insanity.' A miscarriage of the most severe degree."

Dr. Noble St. Vincent Ettmann leaned forward, elbows on his desk, fingers steepled beneath his chin. "Now Mr. Washburn, I want you to look at two photographs and to tell me what you think of them."

He rose and went to a file cabinet. He removed a dossier from one drawer, extracted two glossies and passed them to Roland.

Washburn examined one, then the other. He held them one in each hand. "What is there to think, Doctor? This is I. This other is the murderer, the cartoonist Satvan." He tossed the two photos onto the desk.

"You notice no, ah—resemblance?"

Roland leaned over the photos and studied them further. He shrugged noncommitally. Ettmann waited. Roland said, "Well, if you *want* to see a similarity, you can see one. But look: look at the weak face, the devious eyes, the soft expression, the almost Jewish debasement of this buffoon. Look at the nose. It's almost Semitic, wouldn't you say?

"My photograph is nothing like that. The whole face is different. The hair, The expression is different. No real resemblance. No. I see none. I don't see how you can compare these two pictures."

Ettmann nodded. "We have relatively little experience with cases of this sort. The whole literature hardly amounts to more than a handful of papers and a couple of popularizations. So there is no such thing as a standardized approach.

"Well," he mused, "that may be for the best. But it does appear that we need the cooperation of the several personalities. They have to *want* to get back together, and that's difficult to obtain because they have to surrender their separateness, their independence. Still, they usually do so if we stay with it long enough."

He paced back and forth behind his desk, then plunged once more into his swivel chair and reached for a drink of water. "The division of the original personality seems to come about as the result of childhood trauma. At least that much is orthodox." He laughed, mostly an inwardly-turned laugh, before turning a serious face to Roland. "We haven't even embarked on that search yet, although with your history. . . ."

He abandoned the train of thought.

"I wonder why you feel as you do about Buddy Satvan, Roland. Do you think it might be all right to talk about him for a bit?"

Roland snorted. "A clown. A buffoon. I don't know where he ever got the nerve to kill Schrieber. A weakling."

Dr. Ettmann only said *mmm.*

"Well, what more is there?" Roland demanded sharply.

Ettmann walked to a low table and shuffled a stack of magazines, paperback books and newspapers. He came up with a daily tabloid and brought it back to the desk, rapidly turning pages. At last he came to the comics section and folded the paper over, laying it before Roland Washburn.

"This is the *Diamond Sutro* strip for today. I wonder if you'd care to comment on it."

Roland shook his head in annoyance but when Ettmann made no further comment he snorted, "Very well. Let me look at it. These things are all trash, you know, Doctor. They merely distract the mind of the public from the weakness and corruption that is overtaking our society. It's part of the pattern, don't you see? An intelligent man like yourself, if they can fool you, lull you. . . ."

Roland looked at Ettmann, saw the doctor's eyes directed to the newspaper. The strip comprised three panels. The first showed the interior of a scientist's laboratory. A tall, handsome man stood gazing blankly ahead of himself. He was being embraced by a voluptuous woman in a flowing garment. A weird, jackal-headed being looked on in obvious approval.

The second panel showed the jackal-man in close-up.

The third was an exterior view of some sort, apparently of a mountain range.

"What do you think?" Ettmann broke in upon Roland Washburn's reverie.

"Eh? Oh!" Washburn's head jerked upward. He dropped the still-folded newspaper onto the desk. "The man draws well. Not that I have any artistic training myself, but his composition is pleasing and his line work is better than that in most of the other strips."

"Hmm, yes. That's your entire feeling?"

Washburn was fencing now, he understood himself well

enough to know that. But so was Ettmann. If only the man would ask directly the questions he wanted answered. But Roland was familiar with Ettmann's technique: the patient must be led to make his own statements, allowed to achieve his own insights. All right, he would play Ettmann's game a little longer. Maybe he could provoke the doctor into asserting his own interpretation for a change.

"You mean the story itself? You want my opinion of that?"

Ettmann smiled noncommitally.

"Typical lurid escapism. Some interesting uses of archetypes but basically an infantile fantasy. Ability to change into a supernatural being, overcome all of one's foes."

"Ah. How do you feel about the characters?"

Washburn laid his hand flat on the comic page, covering the *Diamond Sutro* strip. "As I told you, interesting archetypal imagery but essentially a puerile fantasy of power and wish fulfillment. On a plane with those cheap barbarian paperbacks one sees nowadays. You know—muscle-bound idiots in fur athletic supporters, that kind of thing."

Ettmann chuckled aloud at the image. "Yes, I quite agree about those cheap novels. Ah, but regarding the characters in Buddy Satvan's comic strip, I was particularly interested in your feelings about the hero's third identity."

Washburn's expression grew grim. "You mean when he is neither the physicist Arnaud Subhuti nor the superhero? A third identity?"

Ettmann nodded, nodded that eternal encouragement of his.

"It must be getting very late, Dr. Ettmann. I wouldn't want to keep you from your dinner."

Only the smile.

"Perhaps we could resume another time. I—if I am not to leave the Institute tonight as I had planned, why, ah, perhaps in the morning. Or another day."

Nothing.

"Look here," Roland exclaimed. He uncovered the *Diamond Sutro* strip again. "There is no third identity. He is either the hero or he is—as he is here—this scientist, Subhuti. Ridiculous names."

"In today's episode," Ettmann agreed, "but in others. . . ."

He walked to the file and drew a series of clipped comic strips from the dossier that had contained the glossy photos. He brought them back and spread them on the desk, standing over Washburn's shoulder, trying to encourage Washburn to open up.

"You see?" He pointed at a figure in the clippings. A slim, almost compulsively neat man with short-cropped hair and a military bearing. "Does this fellow look familiar to you, Mr. Washburn?"

Roland shook his head vigorously.

"I wonder if you'd mind reading me this caption block. The print is small, I know."

Roland bent over the clipping. He was sweating heavily. "Isn't it time for dinner?" He was suddenly ravenous.

Nothing.

"Oh, all right, all right! If you're so obsessed with a stupid cartoon I don't see why you don't just read it yourself. It says, 'At the headquarters of the Fraternal Order of the Fylfot, Kommandant Renaldo Warbuckle issues commands.'

"Are you satisfied? Are you satisfied, Doctor Ettmann, Doctor Jew Ettmann? Are you satisfied?"

Ettmann removed the clippings and returned them to the file drawer. "I suppose that's enough for today," he said softly. "If you want to go ahead and get your dinner, Mr. Washburn."

Suddenly Roland found that the perspiration from his forehead had rolled into his eyes and they were smarting and tearing. He looked over Ettmann's desk, spotted a box of soft tissues. "May I?"

The doctor nodded. "Of course."

Roland wiped his eyes, blew his nose, sat slouching in his chair, the damp, crumpled tissue clutched in his hand. "Perspiration in my eyes, nothing more," he asserted. He forced himself back to a more commanding posture.

Ettmann nodded, looking sympathetic. "Would you like to stay and chat a bit longer?" He looked at his watch again. "We can have the kitchen prepare something if we miss the regular sitting."

"All right. I suppose I can spare you a few more minutes." But Roland could think of nothing he wanted to say. He ɔpened his mouth a few times but was unable to get past an narticulate *uhh.* Finally he subsided. He made a gesture to Ettmann, a hand sign that meant *help me, help me.*

The doctor leaned forward. "I think this—no, I *know* this nust be very painful, very difficult for you, Roland. But it is he only way back to wholeness for you. And I want you to know that I'm on your side. I want nothing but to help you, to ielp you to achieve what you need to achieve."

Washburn nodded. "Well," He shook his head, an effort to lraw himself together. He pulled his shoulders back and drew n a deep breath. "All right, Buddy Satvan has a character in iis comic strip with a name vaguely resembling mine. He even nakes this Warbuckle look a little bit like me.

"So?"

Ettmann leaned forward. "The Fraternal Order of the Fylfot, Roland, isn't that a comment—don't you think that's a omment of some sort, on your own political movement? Do ou know what a fylfot is, Roland?"

Washburn shook his head, no.

Ettmann opened a dictionary and read. " 'A symbol or ɔrnament in the form of a Greek cross with the ends of the ırms bent at right angles. A swastika, gammadion, hakenkreuz.' " He shut the heavy book with a snap, looked up ıt Roland Washburn.

"I don't know why Satvan put me in his stupid cartoon—if his Renaldo Warbuckle is supposed to be me, which I do not oncede, by the way. And I'm not really that concerned, Mister Doctor Jew. I suggest that you ask Satvan."

Washburn stood up, threw his crumpled tissue contemptuously on the doctor's desk and stamped to the door. "If I have nissed my dinner I will simply wait until morning, thank ou!"

He slammed the door behind him. noticed the guard Timmons standing quietly outside. He headed for the dining oom and a cold, solitary meal.

11. Peru

SIXTH WEEK: The brilliant scientist, world-famed genius and inventor of the fantastic ZINGARR, Arnaud Subhuti, had known fabulous women the world around. A millionaire in his own right, as widely famed for his dashing good looks and sparkling wit as for his scientific exploits, Subhuti had been pursued by the beauties of five continents.

[Six? Seven? Tara, check this out before Willy gets it—BS]

But never—never—had he met the likes of Aphrité Anubis, crimson-tressed and ruby-irised daughter of the jackal-headed fiend incarnate, archfoe of Diamond Sutro, Professor Anubis. Not even Crystal Knight, faithful companion and assistant of Diamond Sutro, had ever ever pressed herself to him with the uninhibited passion of the fiery, demanding, lush-figured Aphrité. Not even Astoroth Anderson, his colleague in some of his greatest struggles against the minions of evil, had matched the sheer voluptuousness of this new eidolon of sheer sensuality.

Now, standing hopelessly drugged in the mysterious Andean retreat of Dr. Anubis, his naked libido violently assaulted by the satin-clad beauty, Arnaud Subhuti felt himself rapidly sliding, sliding into the oldest and most subtle of slaveries, the slavery of a mighty man to the wiles of a gorgeous and nubile woman.

Suddenly Aphrité dropped her arms from around Arnaud's neck. She pulled her warm, passionate lips from his. She drew her shimmering flame-patterned cloak tightly about her shoulders and strode from his side to the opposite end of the solid granite room carved into the living peak of Mt. Huascarán, 22,205 feet above the chill gray waters of the Pacific Ocean and part of the well-hidden, secret laboratory of Dr. Anubis.

The sinister, jackal-headed fiend placed an arm possessivey around the shoulders of his voluptuous daughter. A new ight seemed to gleam malevolently from his beady eyes and a gleeful cackle fell from his thin, cruel lips.

"So, Arnaud Subhuti, you have now sampled the pleasures of my daughter Aphrité. What my drugs could wring only nvoluntarily from Sir Percy Dillingham and the other great scientists of the world, a beautiful woman's lips can draw willingly from the greatest of them all, the high and mighty Arnaud Subhuti!"

Once more the blood-freezing cackle echoed from the rocky ceiling of the monster's retreat.

"Now that you are completely my prisoner, you will leave this little establishment. Here, high in the Andes of Peru, my silent Incan slaves and my drugged scientific zombies will continue their labors. But for you I have a higher mission! You will leave this place. You will travel with my daughter Aphrité to my secret master headquarters and laboratory that lie—nowhere on earth!"

With a swirl of his cloak, the evil mastermind turned. He made a curious gesture with one hand and marched from the room. His daughter, the fabulous Aphrité, smiled across the rock-floored chamber at Arnaud Subhuti. A cruel, sensuous expression crossed her incomparable face. "Come, my darling Arnaud," she hissed, and followed her father from the laboratory.

Subhuti started after the flame-caped woman. Slowly, with the vacant eyes and slow, wooden tread of the hopeless zombie, the world-famed scientist followed Aphrité and her father from the room. The exit they took led through a doorway Subhuti had not used before.

A silent Incan servant in breechclout and headdress stood holding back the heavy, decorated draperies. The jackal-headed Anubis stepped through the opening, followed by the dazzling, exotic form of his daughter and the zombielike wizard of science.

They stood in Dr. Anubis' private spaceport!

SEVENTH WEEK: The spaceport had been carved, like Anubis' secret laboratory, from the living granite of the mighty Andes themselves. A weird study in contrasts here

nearly four miles above the crashing Pacific currents, th
port's walls were monolithic mountain granite decorated wit
monstrous, leering portraits of mighty Incan deities.

[Tara: Have Willy check this out. Probably Larouss
will have enough for swipes, else he'll have to try the librar
—BS]

Powerful arc lights stood ready to flood the gantry wit
their lurid glare but the present illumination was provided b
flickering torches whose effluent of oily black smoke an
weirdly weaving shadows lent the ultramodern equipment
strange air of almost preternatural antiquity.

The roof of the room was a single rolling panel cunningl
designed with all the malign ingenuity of the world'
wickedest genius to fool any stray aviator passing overhead
There would be no reports of secret spaceports in the hig
Andes. There would be no investigations by government com-
missions, army expeditions or international scientific bodie
of the mysterious activities at the towering peak of M
Huascaran, more than four miles above the chill waters of th
easternmost Pacific.

[Tara: Check that four miles figure. Is it just *over* four mile
above sea level or just *under*? I can never keep that dang thin
straight. Should have been a mathematician instead of
storytellin' fool—BS]

The ship itself stood long and cool and graceful on it
launching ramp. Here four miles above sea level and near th
equator with its rotational speed of a thousand miles per hou
the craft would be launched from a sloping ramp that woul
carry it in a slanting, upward trajectory into earth orbit, an
ultimately to its mysterious destination in dark, terrifyin
space.

It was a small ship, a mere thirty feet in length. A gracefu
stingerlike point for its nose, a geometrically perfect curv
marked the form of its fuselage. Flaring tail fins would guid
it as it rose through the thin atmosphere above the Andes. It
propulsion was no crude explosion of chemicals, but a secre
ether-ray system developed in Dr. Anubis' Andes laborator
by the mightiest intellects of the scientific world laboring i
secret thralldom.

The shell of the ship was of a secret lucite composition, a

but invisible to the naked eye but wholly impervious to the deadly radiation that abounds in outer space.

Dr. Anubis gestured dramatically toward the ship.

"Aphrité, my precious child," he hissed sinisterly, "you will pilot the ether-ray ship to my main base and top-secret headquarters. You know its location, of course, my dear—in a place whose name is never to be mentioned lest our foes learn of it and pursue us there."

A knowing smile flickered upon the sensuous lips of the exotic Aphrité. "Fear nothing, my father. Your dutiful daughter will never fail you or your cause!" she hissed.

She took the unresisting hand of the wizard Arnaud Subhuti and led him to the almost invisible hatch of the ether-ray ship. With a confiding look back at her wicked father, Aphrité pulled the hatch shut.

Almost at once the rolling panel of the secret spaceport's concealing roof swung back, exposing the launching ramp to the outside elements. The Andean air more than four miles above sea level was sparse and chill with the whispered suggestion of dry, paralyzing snow. An icy wind, rising from the frigid, gray waters 22,000 feet below, whipped into the secret spaceport.

Dr. Anubis drew his rich, glossy cloak more tightly across his shoulders. He chuckled once, malevolently, and threw the heavy, filigreed switch that sent the ether-ray ship screaming up its ramp.

EIGHTH WEEK: The strange ship rose from its ramp. To the eyes of the few hardy natives, taciturn descendents of the mysterious Incan race of misty antiquity, the sight would have resembled only that of two figures, a man and a woman, moving through thin air almost faster than the eye could follow, surrounded by a ravening, gleaming nimbus of brilliant vermilion rays.

The glamorous Aphrité sat at the controls of the ether-ray ship, carefully monitoring the performance of the mighty but delicately attuned spacecraft. Her strange, ruby-irised eyes narrowed in concentration. Her rich, sensuous lips were pursed with effort. And beside her, strangely passive, was the form of Arnaud Subhuti, most brilliant scientist of the planet earth.

And what of Arnaud Subhuti?

The secret drug given him by the malevolent Dr. Anubis had worked its evil way on his will—or had it? Had it, indeed?

Had the brilliant mind of Arnaud Subhuti not anticipated the visit of Dr. Anubis to his Nob Hill mansion, the intrusion of the world's wickedest genius into the innermost *sanctum sanctorum* of the world's greatest scientist? Had not the mysterious disappearances, in rapid succession, of Arnaud Subhuti's colleagues Sir Percy Dillingham, Luigi Serengetti Marie Charbonnet, Boris Tuporov and P'eng Chiao-tsu served as warning to the wizard of Nob Hill?

Perhaps Arnaud Subhuti had prepared an antidote to the will-destroying drug of Dr. Anubis and injected it into his own veins, all in expectation of the mysterious visit which had occurred—exactly as expected!

Was this Subhuti's way of discovering that one great fac which had eluded not only the world's governments and the agencies of law and order, but even the mighty Diamond Sutro himself—the location of Dr. Anubis' secret ex traterrestrial headquarters??!!

The ether-ray ship rose above the last wisps of earthly atmosphere, climbed into the endless black night of the inter planetary void. The ship's skillful pilot, Aphrité Anubis leaned back on her invisible acceleration couch and stretched She did so with the graceful, sensuous movement of a muscu lar, deadly pantheress. She set the ship's controls on automatic and undid the straps that held her to her couch.

She turned toward the noble, muscular scientist who lay on the acceleration couch beside her own. "Ah, my darling," she lipped softly, "if only my father knew of the passions you arouse in my bosom! He would be furious! But I am glad And now you should be emerging from the effects of hi drug!"

Those were the very words Arnaud Subhuti had awaited His eyelids flickered, his body shook. "Wh—where am I?" he stammered. "I—I was in my laboratory. And now—" He looked out through the transparent, nearly invisible body o the ether-ray ship.

[Tara: For Subhuti's expression, tell Willy to look up a stil of Lugosi in *Frankenstein Meets the Wolfman*—the strapped-to the-table scene. I don't want the evil, of course, but Lugosi has just the flash that I need for this sequence—BS]

The earth and the moon could be seen suspended like a great blue-white Christmas ball and a smaller pale yellow one, standing against the backdrop of interplanetary space far behind the ship. The ether-ray vehicle coursed onward like a bullet of glass through the cosmic night. Soon it passed the shrouded mystery of cloud-blanketed Venus. Then the barren, meteor-pocked face of Mercury with its towering mountains and its rivers of molten, flowing lead.

On and on the ether-ray ship sped. Closer and closer to the searing, blinding flames of—the sun itself! Could the tiny craft survive the terrible heat and radiation of that solar furnace? Could even the greatest inventions of Professor Anubis and his corps of zombie-scientists protect the voluptuous Aphrité and her companion the noble Arnaud Subhuti?

Utterly bathed in those inconceivable atomic flames, the ship plunged toward the very heart of the sun itself!

[Tara: Do you think the ether-ray ship needs a name? Kind of adds a little fillip for the readers to hang onto? Ask Willy to try Larousse again. Stick with Egyptian motif. Maybe Uraeus would be a good idea. No, come to think of it, that doesn't sound so good. Horus? Styx? Charon? You two work it out between you and let me know what you come up with. Thanks—BS]

NINTH WEEK: Arnaud Subhuti, scientist/alter-ego of the great hero Diamond Sutro, and Aphrité Anubis, breathtakingly beautiful ruby-irised daughter of the world's wickedest man, have plunged into the searing heart of the sun itself, protected only by the virtually invisible hull of Professor Anubis' either-ray spaceship *Isis.*

[Tara: Tell Willy not to bother with Larousse, let's call the ship *Isis.* Has a nice ring to it, don't you agree?—BS]

For an instant the two space travelers stand, their lives in peril of instant annihilation. They embrace—the beautiful woman in her ironically flame-patterned satin cloak, the man in ordinary laboratory garb. The ship is bathed in the sun's nuclear fire. The hull of the *Isis* dampens to near opacity as its own vermilion ray-shield fades to invisibility against the dazzle of the sun.

"Have no fear, my darling," the lush Aphrité whispers to Arnaud Subhuti. "We are safe within *Isis* !"

"Have you flown through the sun before?" Subhuti questioned her grimly.

"Never," the ruby-eyed beauty responded. "Never has my mission been so urgent. But I have all faith in my father and in his works!"

"Yes." A serious expression filled the scientist's eyes. "Still, I notice that Professor Anubis entrusts this dangerous journey to you—while he remains safely in Peru!"

For an instant the interior of the ship was completely blacked out. Then the travelers saw what had happened to them: They had been swallowed whole, ship and all, by an indescribable monster that lives inside the core of the sun!

"Oh, save me!" In an instant the cool, confident Aphrité was reduced to the level of a mere woman, frightened and seeking the protection of a man. And Arnaud Subhuti did not fail to respond.

"A ship that could withstand the sun's own inferno can surely survive a trip through the gullet of a giant salamander!" He led the beautiful woman to her couch, lifted her for a moment in strong yet tender arms, then lowered her like a child onto the contoured surface.

The scientist strode to the controls of the *Isis.*

If we were in any real peril, he thought, *I could use my powers as Diamond Sutro to save Aphrité. Still—it is for the best that she not know that Arnaud Subhuti, famed scientist, and Diamond Sutro, Doctor Goodlaw, are one and the same man!*

Arnaud Subhuti's keen eyes scanned the indicators on the pilot's panel. The Universal Standard Vector Displacement Meter indicated that the ship was still moving at a breathtaking rate of speed—exactly as Subhuti had anticipated. So titanic was the force of the ether ray that *Isis* was carrying the solar salamander with her!

And—as *Isis* burst through the solar photosphere once again, as temperatures dropped from a billion degrees or more to a matter of puny thousands—the salamander grew sluggish . . . rigid . . . was at last frozen solid, at a temperature, of 6,000° Fahrenheit!

The vermilion ray envelope of *Isis* became visible once

again, seething and flaring about the little Lucite-hulled craft.

[Tara: You check on Lucite, will you? Is it a trade name or a generic? If the former, have Willy change *all* references to it to lucine, okay?—BS]

Subhuti turned from the control panel and smiled tenderly down at the slowly stirring form of Aphrité. Despite the villainy of her father she was a woman, and her womanly instincts had led her to place her trust in a decent man. There was hope for her moral rehabilitation!

"Are we—are we safe?" She trembled.

Subhuti sat tenderly on the edge of the couch. He took her long, tapering hand in his own strong, competent ones. "We are safe," he said. "Your father built well. But—"

He dropped her hand, rose and strode to the transparent hull of the ether-ray ship. He stood tall and straight, hands clasped behind his back, gazing thoughtfully into the depths of interplanetary space. Loudly, so his beautiful companion could not miss a word, he asked, "But where do we head for now?"

TENTH WEEK: Having safely traversed the searing depths of the sun itself and escaped the attack of the terrifying solar salamander, the ether-ray ship *Isis* is speeding away from the sun on the opposite side from the planet earth. Arnaud Subhuti, who in secret is Diamond Sutro, He Who Proclaims the Truth, has asked the gorgeous daughter of his archfoe Professor Anubis, "Where do we head for now?"

The gorgeous ruby-irised woman rose gracefully from her acceleration couch and floated to the side of the scientist. She took his arm, rested her flame-tressed head on his muscular shoulder, and pointed one long, satin-covered limb toward the transparent hull of the *Isis.*

"Do you see?" she asked. "Do you see that planet?"

Arnaud Subhuti's steely gray eyes widened in surprise. He was known as one of the world's three great astronomers, a mere sideline for him, and he knew that there was no planet where the breathtaking woman pointed! "How can—how can that be? We are already past the orbits of Mercury and Venus, and they and earth are on the other side of the sun now anyway! Is it—?" He looked wonderingly down into the ruby-irised eyes of Aphrité.

"It is—the planet Hathor," she whispered to him. "It shares the same orbit as earth, and has long been fabled under such names as Twin-earth, Counter-earth, or Vulcan. But it is none of these. It is—Hathor! It is—the secret headquarters and ultimate redoubt of my father, and of all of his agents.

"It was my duty to bring you thence, Arnaud Subhuti, as my willing slave, there to serve the bidding of my evil father! But instead your courage and your love have made you—my Lord and Master!" Impetuously she seized his muscular hand and pressed it to the red, fervent lips that had enslaved battalions of men before her fatal encounter with the alter ego of Diamond Sutro!

They stood then, for a long moment, side by side, gazing ahead of the *Isis* at Hathor, the world hidden forever from earthly eyes by the glare of the sun itself. Hathor grew larger and larger in the all-encompassing window of the ether-ray ship. Soon it was the same as earth's, its covering of ocean blue and cloudy white much like that of its transsolar counterpart. But—

But where earth had been despoiled by the greed and ignorance of modern man, Hathor's seas ran emerald-green and diamond-clear, teeming with fish of every description.

And where earth's solitary companion Luna brightened the night sky of half a world, Hathor was blessed with a family of variously tinted moonlets and with a set of whirling rings to put those of Neptune to shame.

[Tara: Don't leave this one for Willy, he's busy enough. Check out that Neptune reference—maybe it's Uranus that has those rings. Jupiter? Damn! Listen, dear, while you're at it, as long as I'm going to be cooped up here for a while, see if you can get me a good set of standard reference works, would you? A one-volume encyclopedia, I think the Columbia one is good. A current almanac, world atlas, you know the stuff. Thanks a lot—BS]

ELEVENTH WEEK: [I'm sorry, Tara, Willy. I wanted to do more on this tape, but I'm just wiped out. Bushed, you know. Had a bad episode with the Washburn personality, went after nice black Timmons the attendant and wound up in sedation again. Soon as he realized what he'd got himself into, Washburn left me to face the music. As usual.

[Anyway, I'm back out of the violent ward now, but I am absolutely exhausted. Between Washburn's tantrum, you know, and the sedative hangover.

[You guys are real heroes. I just want to tell you how much I appreciate what you're doing for the strip. Give my regards to Burt Bahnson and Arch Cantrowicz down at the syndicate, would you, Willy? Everybody's being just beautiful over this.

[As soon as I get out of here I'm going to throw a big bash and invite every one of you guys to celebrate with me—BS]

12. Sravasti

WASHBURN was out of the snow, the chill air of Sravasti's artificial atmosphere clean and cold and strangely, lightly perfumed in his lungs as he sprinted across the flat landscape. The building in which he had arrived from earth, the building of the Yakshis and the ancient star races' great machines loomed ahead.

It must be that building! He had never seen its exterior—he had left neither as himself nor as his despicable but nonetheless useful alternate Buddy Satvan. He'd have known if that had been the case. But—what else could this structure be?

It was a low building, a single tall story in height. Nor did it cover a very large area of ground. With the entire planet an artificial construct, it subsurface volume containing neither rock nor molten core but an intricate honeycomb of girders and rooms, there was no need to build high into the air. The total internal volume of the planet was available for use. The existence of the building that projected above surface at all was the anomaly, the quirk of the long-absent builders of the place.

Roland reached the building, searched and found a sealed portal and stood hammering breathlessly at it until it opened. He cast a last look back at the strange, artificial out-of-doors

and tumbled into the violet-lighted interior of the building.
Two of the dim shadowy man-figures hovered and wove before him. They wore headbands. Washburn did not. "Did you . . . are you. . . ." The figures hissed and rumbled. Washburn slipped his headband back on, found himself once again in communication with the Yakshis.

"You are unharmed?" The question poured into his mind, rose from some submerged well of the unconscious.

"I'm okay, yes. You'd better get me—" He thought of a hot, steaming mug of bitter black coffee. One of the Yakshis disappeared to whatever place they went. Washburn ignored the remaining shadow-figure and wandered through the violet-lit room, letting his eyes roam the alien decorations and furnishings. Finally he settled into a peculiar chair.

The Yakshi reappeared and extended a vague, wavering arm to Roland. He reached and took the mug, stared at it in amazement. He sniffed it, tasted its contents. It was coffee all right, to the last scent and flavor. The cup was of a familiar heavy design bearing the emblem of a quick-food restaurant in Falls Church were Roland had had a few snacks.

"Look, ah—oh, thanks. I thought there were three of you creatures. What happened to the other?"

When confused, do not admit puzzlement: demand clarification!

"We are Nanda, Kalinga," the two ghost-voices whispered in Washburn's brain. "The other, Asoka, was—lost." The Yakshis did not use the word, of course—or any word. But that was as close as Roland Washburn could come to verbalizing the message he received.

"Dead?" he demanded. "Or lost—strayed?"

"Dead?" The two wavering figures seemed themselves to be immersed in contemplation. "Ah, as nearly as a Yakshi can be dead. We are not precisely alive, Roland Washburn. We are—electronic constructs, you must understand. We are not organisms."

"All right," Washburn snapped back. "But that's the end of Asoka, isn't it?"

"No—no—n-o-o-o. . . ." The two shadowy beings stood a few paces apart. Between them the air seemed to shimmer and dance. A dim silhouette, vague and shaded at its edges, began to appear. It ballooned, shrank, danced, solidified—as much as a Yakshi ever did.

The two others closed upon it. Washburn watched them engage in what must be an embrace of some sort. "Brother," he thought he detected at the bottom edge of his awareness.

"Brother."

"Brother."

They separated again. The center Yakshi gazed at him with its deep, black-against-black eyes. One of the others disappeared briefly, returned with a headband and slipped it over the brow of the new Yakshi.

"I am Asoka," the being told Washburn.

"But—you were lost. They said—you were lost. Dead. Are you the *same* Asoka? Or a new one?"

The creature did not smile or shrug, yet to Washburn there was a distinct impression of such a response. His mind turned the Yakshi's answer into a semblance of words. "I possess all of the memories of Asoka. I am physically identical. To me there is complete continuity of being. But to him—is the old Asoka's consciousness continued in me, or is my possession of his memories a gift?

"An obscure philosophical question, Roland Washburn. We have more urgent matters at hand. More urgent matters. The—spaceburn.

"The spaceburn spreads. Metagalaxies have disappeared. All of existence, it appears, will be swallowed up unless you can resolve the threat. You. This the machines have determined."

Roland set down his coffee mug with a thump. The dramatic gesture, even in this alien place. The psychological advantage of position. He stood so that he need not look up to the Yakshis—another lesson of his painfully developed leadership skills.

"You Yakshis. The machines in this place. The whole power of Sravasti. But there is a menace on earth as well. Do your machines tell you how long it will take the spaceburn to obliterate my solar system? The earth?"

The Yakshis conferred. "You may enter the machines as you did before—as your other self did before. But if you wish not to. . . ." They stood in identical postures of concentration, somehow communing with their machinery.

Then: "By your measurement it will require some—million years, plus or minus a thirteenth."

Washburn laughed out loud. A million years! And these weird beings were concerned with that! Well, maybe on their scale the concern of a million years had meaning, but on his, a thousand-year reich would be splendid, a ten-thousand year reign of the Will would be more than satisfying. He laughed again.

"All right," he told them at last, "I'll help you out. I'll solve your little problem. But first I need to return to earth. There are things that I need to accomplish there. We have our own problems. They're mongrelizing the schools, they're poisoning the water with fluoride, they're communizing the economy! The great race of high men is being destroyed by the mongrels and the weaklings, and it must be saved. *Then* I can return here and help you."

The three Yakshis looked at one another, then back to Roland. "No, no," they whispered into his mind. "The universe is at stake. Everything is threatened. Your little problems, on a single planet. . . ."

He shook his head. Now was the time for firmness. "Those are my terms! I must return to earth. Later I can help you."

"But, Roland Washburn, beings in great numbers—worlds and civilizations die daily!"

"Those are my terms!"

The Yakshis conferred briefly. At last one of them—it might have been Asoka, Washburn could detect no visible difference among them but Asoka seemed most often to act as spokesman—loomed toward him. "If you must, Roland L. K. Washburn, then return to earth. If there is no other way."

"No other! Absolutely no other!"

The Yakshi faded, wavered back and forth, returned to its fellows. Then, "So shall it be." An air of regret permeated the shadow-beings. They stood in silent communication.

Elsewhere in the warrens and deeps of Sravasti circuits were activated, particles and waves of energy far below the level of neutrinos spun and flowed. Washburn stood with arms

folded, his face stern, his attitude dominant and demanding.
And. . . .

Buddy Satvan found himself standing in a grassy field. The sun cast a midafternoon radiance around him. The sky was dotted with white, puffy clouds and a pleasantly warm breeze was blowing. With an audible whoosh a jumbo airliner passed high overhead, its great altitude making it seem to crawl across the sky leaving a spotless white condensation track behind it, the sound of its huge engines following along the contrail far in its wake.

Buddy blinked, shook his head, clapped his hands to his own portly torso as if astonished to find himself there. He looked down at his clothes and saw that he was wearing an outfit of featureless gray cloth, a tunic and trousers and a pair of comfortable yet unfamiliar brogans.

He put a hand to his brow in puzzlement and felt something there—he slipped it off and saw that it was a soft metallic headband. He twisted it into a figure eight and slipped it over his wrist, up his arm until it tightened at his biceps.

He looked around again.

Behind him stood a wall of trees. Ahead of him, across the grassy field, he could see a highway, a few roadside businesses and billboards. He could hear the whine of tires, the roar of heavy truck engines from the road.

He ran both hands through his hair, took a deep breath and began to trudge across the field, headed for the nearest of the business establishments that rose ahead of him.

By the time he reached the building he was half-winded and drenched with sweat. He wiped his forehead with a sleeve of the gray, featureless tunic and looked up at the illuminated plastic sign. It was a quick-service hamburger joint. Buddy consulted his appetite and discovered that he wasn't hungry. Then he consulted his pockets—or the places where his pockets should have been—and found that he had none.

He walked into the hamburger joint and smiled uncertainly at the counterman, a teenager in white paper cap and blouse. On second look Buddy realized that she was a counterwoman, or rather a girl. She returned his smile with equal uncertainty, lifting one hand to cover, for a moment, the angry acne marks of her adolescence.

"How about a Jolly Jock-O?" the girl asked.

"Um—n-no thanks," Buddy stammered. Then, "Is there a phone here?"

The girl nodded toward a corner of the restaurant. Buddy walked over and picked up the telephone directory, scanning the cover. Prince Morton County. The current year. All right, then, whatever his strange experience had meant, he was at least somewhere near the right place and he had't suffered a very long lapse of time.

He lifted the handset of the telephone, groped instinctively for a coin where there wasn't even a pocket. He hung up the telephone and returned to the counter. The bored girl was watching him suspiciously.

"Something the matter, mister?"

"Uh. Um, this is very embarrassing. But, ah, could you, that is, do you th-think you could lend me the price of a phone call?"

Suddenly stony faced she shook her head, no.

"It's very important. Really."

"You want me to call the highway patrol?" she said.

Buddy wondered whom he *would* call. Suddenly he knew. "Look, miss, ah—I need to place a long-distance call. A long-distance call, person-to-person, collect. See? You see?" He made a palms-up gesture with both hands as if to demonstrate that he was harmless, not hostile.

"So?" she said noncommittally. "Listen, the afternoon rush starts soon, after-school and early commuters. I got to get a batch of Jolly Jock-O's and Jolly Jock-Ettes and Jock Juniors ready. I can't play games with you. I got no handout for you."

Buddy swallowed a sob of frustration. "Miss, I want to call New York. My office. *Collect*—see, they'll pay for the call, I just need to get the operator. So"—sudden jolt of cold panic—" what day of the week is it? Please!"

"Cripes, mister, are you all right? It's Thursday."

Of course. There wouldn't be school and commuters on a weekend. He'd better stay cool. "S-sure. Look, I really have to contact my office in New York. It's very urgent. I just don't happen to have any change with me. If you'll drop a coin in the phone I'll call the operator. You don't even have to hand me the coin, you can do it yourself. I'll just stand here."

There was cold sweat on his brow.

Slowly the girl edged around the counter and made her way to the telephone. Keeping as far from Buddy as she could she reached into her apron pocket and pulled out a quarter. She took the telephone handset, dropped the quarter in a slot and dialed for the operator. There was a brief exchange and she had her quarter back and handed the phone to Buddy.

He put through a call to Willy Albertson, collect, at the studio in New York. And breathed a sigh of relief when he heard Willy's odd, croaking voice accept the call.

"Willy, listen, this is Buddy Satvan!"

"Buddy, are you out? Are you okay? What happened?"

Buddy said that something odd had happened. No point in trying to talk about Yakshis and artificial planets and the fireworms eating the universe. Less than no sense: It would be disastrous.

"What do you want me to do, Buddy? Can you get here?"

"I don't know. I'm still in Virginia. Willy, where's Tara?"

Willy named a motel in Prince Morton County.

Another wave of relief shuddered through Buddy. "Look, Willy, right after I hang up I want you to phone Tara, will you? I'll give you the number where I am. It's hard for me to phone from here, but I'll stay put by the phone and Tara can call me back. Will you do that?"

"Sure. Of course."

Buddy read him the area code and number. Willy checked them back, asked Buddy again if he was all right. Buddy said, "Please, let's don't discuss it now, just get hold of Tara and have her contact me or if there's any screwup you call me back instead," and Willy said he would, and Buddy hung up the phone and found a counter stool and sat down.

The girl asked if he wanted to buy anything.

Buddy said he'd left his money behind.

She gave him a cup of coffee on the house and he sat nursing it till the phone rang.

Tara.

Buddy read her the location of the restaurant from the

front of an orange laminated menu and she said she'd be there in half an hour.

The counter girl smiled. Behind the acne she had pleasant features. In a couple of years the pimples would be gone and she'd be very pretty, maybe even beautiful. Buddy smiled back and said thanks for everything.

An hour later he slumped heavily on the edge of the bed in Tara's air-conditioned motel room. She came and half squatted, half knelt beside him. She put her hand warmly on Buddy's. He recoiled in surprise, then reached and took Tara's hand gratefully. It was a small hand, but Buddy held it with both of his, squeezing strength from it.

"Can't you tell me now, Buddy?" Tara asked. "You wouldn't in the car, I could understand that. But—what's going on? How did you get, I mean, well, how did you—?"

He looked up from the biege motel rug into Tara Sakti's large, dark eyes. She was a small woman with a dark complexion, remnants of a heavy crop of freckles, thick dark hair. Buddy shook his head and started to shrug. "How did I escape, you mean?"

"Not exactly. Well, yes. I mean—"

"That's understandable. I could—Tara, you understand my, ah, condition. Don't you?"

"Well, at the court hearing. And I've talked to your doctor, to Dr. Ettmann."

"Then you know I'm not always Buddy Satvan. That there's somebody else, another person. Inside me somehow." He took his hands from hers, put his fingertips on his chest and looked down at himself as if he were posing for a piece of cheap religious art.

Jesus about to expose the Sacred Heart to the faithful.

"Well, then."

Buddy stood up and paced around the room. Tara got off the floor and sat on the edge of the bed. She said, "I don't understand."

"Tara, it was one of those times when the other man had control. Usually when that happens I don't know anything that's going on, but sometimes a little bit filters down to me. Down to—wherever I am. This time—he was pretty violent.

ıttacked a man named Timmons, an attendant. They carted im—me—off to a padded cell.

"All of a sudden—*zip!*—he was out of there. *We* were. He 'as—someplace else, someplace foreign, alien—like another lanet. There were no people there, just machines and some trange, shadowy things. And after a while *I* came out. That's ıe term, you know. Like a debutante. We come out. I came ut. I met the . . . they call themselves Yakshis. And then I lacked out again. I guess the other, you know, Washburn, ame back.

"And then—then all of a sudden I was back in Virgin-ı! That's when I called you. Called Willy and had him call ou."

He stopped pacing, stood over her, his hands extended leadingly. She looked up at him. "Do you want to phone Dr. ttmann?"

He shook his head. "I don't know. I guess so. They must be ›oking for me."

She started to reach for the telephone beside the bed, then ›oked into Buddy's face and stopped.

"N-not yet, though. Please," he said.

She took one of her hands with hers. They stood facing each ther. With her other hand she reached for the top button of er blouse and began to open it. Buddy put his hands around er shoulders, one knee on the bed, and they drew their odies together.

Afterward Tara said, "Maybe we could just go back to New 'ork. Or away someplace. Let Willy handle the strip for a hile. Or just let him have it. I've saved some money, I—"

They were sitting in bed, still touching closely, warmly.

Buddy looked at Tara. "They'll look for me. And anyway, hen—when he comes out. . . . He—I—could be dangerous. 'iolent. You know how all this started, with Schrieber and the hole thing about that National Revitalization League. . . ."

"A crew of nazis!"

"But don't you see? When Washburn comes out, he's the iggest nazi of them all. He's their führer! And it can happen nytime! I'm surprised he didn't come when we were—

when—but I suppose it's his puritanism. A streak of that go
along with the other a lot of the time.

"Anyway"—he put his head in his hands—"I think you'
better. . . ." He waved toward the phone.

But when Tara called the Morton Prince Memorial In
stitute and spoke for a few minutes she turned to Buddy an
made an odd gesture. "Please, can you wait just a moment,
she said into the phone. "Just hold. I'll be right with you."

She held her hand over the mouthpiece of the phon
"Buddy, they said you're there! That is, that Roland L. K
Washburn is there!"

Thunderstruck, Buddy thought for a few seconds. Then
"Who says so?"

"Uh—I guess the office. The operator there."

"Could be covering up. They don't like to lose patient
especially dangerous ones. Or—or I don't know. Ask for, al
ask for Dr. Ettmann. He'll know."

She spoke into the phone again. "Yes. Please switch th
call." Several more minutes of conversation. Buddy watche
Tara's face grow alternately pale, flushed, puzzled, angry.

"No, this is not a joke!" she snapped at last. She jounced th
handset back onto its base.

"He refuses to believe me. I spoke to Dr. Ettmann himse
and he said, 'All right, if you have Buddy with you and he
willing to come along, just bring him back here. Do you wan
to do that? Do you want to go back there?' "

Buddy's throat tightened. He could just go away, go awa
with Tara at that. And—and turn at any time into Roland I
K. Washburn! Why hadn't Washburn come out by now
Buddy was puzzled, but he knew that the führer could emerg
at any time. That was one of the maddening things abou
his/their condition.

For some reason he, Buddy, could come out only when h
was summoned. He didn't control the mechanism, he wa
simply there, in control, part of the time. But Washburn, h
suspected, could control the mechanism of change. Unless h
Washburn, was simply too fatigued now by the Sravas
experience to exercise that choice—he was *leaving* Buddy out

But why was Washburn lying low?

And how long would he continue?

"We—we'd better go," Buddy murmured.

They drove out to the Institute in Tara's rented Dodge Dart. She pulled the car into the visitors' parking lot and they walked, holding hands, to the main entrance of the big brick building. The front door was not locked although they had to pass a politely manned guard stationed at the outer fence.

At the front reception desk they introduced themselves and stood waiting for someone to come out and meet them.

In a few minutes the main corridor doors swung open and three men advanced, ranging themselves side by side to face Buddy and Tara.

One of them, his hair black and his stolid face mahogany in contrast to his snowy starched attendant's uniform, Buddy recognized as Timmons.

Another, casually garbed in broadcloth shirt, woolen slacks and soft herringbone jacket, gasped in amazement. "You! But how—?" Dr. Noble St. Vincent Ettmann stammered to silence, staring at Buddy Satvan.

The center man of the three, able somehow to make even his plain, somewhat baggy ward clothes look like a military uniform, threw back his shoulders, drew himself up to his full height.

He halted and pointed dramatically, a look of sheer exaltation blazing from his sharply glittering eyes.

"You see? You see? I told you this would happen, and now it has!" shouted Roland L. K. Washburn.

13. Virginia

DR. NOBLE St. Vincent Ettmann stared at Buddy, then at Roland, then back at Buddy. Washburn was clad in loose-fitting, casual ward clothes; Satvan, in a plan gray tunic and trousers. Washburn's bearing was stiff and militaristic, seeming to add inches to his stature and authority to his presence. Satvan's slouch made him look shorter and softer. His air was unassuming, almost timid.

Yet—they were the same man. There could be no denying it. The same features, the same brown eyes and dark sandy hair, the same body conformation behind the different bearing of the two. They had to be the same person. Or twins. Maybe they *were* twins.

Dr. Ettmann drew his own shoulders back, fingered the rust-colored nylon-knit tie that he favored with his herringbone jacket. "Ah—we'd better settle this right now. Will you come along and submit to fingerprinting, Mr. Washburn?"

A curt nod.

"And you, Mister, ah, Satvan?"

"Y-yes. Sure, Dr. Ettmann." He turned slightly. "Hello, Timmons. Uh, Simon. How are you? Uh, Tara, have you met Dr. Ettmann and Mr. Timmons?"

Tara said she had.

"Ah—Miss Sakti," Ettmann addressed Tara, "would you, ah, accompany us also? Maybe you can offer some assistance. Some clarification. We, ah, this entire procedure, our entire program of counseling and therapy, has been built on the theory of the multiple personality, grand hysteria. First formulated by Morton Prince, you know."

He fluttered his hands, flipped the end of his tie, then looked down at it and dropped it, flushing. "The, ah, commitment order, the court action, you know, was based on the, ah, belief that Roland Washburn and Buddy Satvan were two personalities inhabiting a single body. Ah—alternately, you see.

"Separate persons in a psychological sense, but physically one. And the objective of therapy has been to promote, ah, the reintegration of these personalities into the single, complete *persona* which had originally produced them. You see?"

Tara said, "Yes," pale, holding Buddy's hand, watching Roland Washburn. *Were* they the same? Their appearances. . . . Yet, how could two men be one man? She shook her head and waited for Ettmann to resume his explanation.

"But—but if they really *are* two separate persons—if they *really* are two separate persons—if they. . . ." He trailed off into blank silence, then faced the two men alternately and repeated, "Would you, ah, come with Timmons and me and, ah, come to the administration office, to the admitting office, and we can, ah, get sets of fingerprints from you both."

He led the way and they followed, Washburn and Satvan marching warily side by side, Timmons and Tara Sakti following. They arrived at the admitting office and Timmons took print sets from Washburn and Buddy. Then they made their way to Ettmann's office. Timmons brought in extra chairs and they all sat except the attendant.

Ettmann held the patient's dossier and the sets of fingerprints. There were three in all, the two new sets and a card he had pulled from the manila folder. Turning his eyes from one set of prints to another, brow creased in puzzlement, Ettmann stared at the three sets of fingerprints. Finally he scribbled a few notes on the two new ones and slipped all three back into the folder. He pulled the glossy photos of Satvan and Washburn and looked from them to the men opposite him. Tara Sakti's chair was between Buddy's and Roland's.

"We'll. ah, have to get these verified by an expert," Ettmann said at last, "but they look identical to me. I don't see how this can be. Clearly you two"—he switched his gaze from one man to the other—"can't be the same person. Yet we have the entire history of the Satvan-Washburn personality alternation, and these fingerprints appear to be, ah, to be identical."

A lengthy silence settled over the group. They sat, Tara watching Ettmann, Ettmann looking alternately at Washburn in his ward clothes and Satvan in his gray tunic. Washburn and Satvan were stationary in their chairs, eyes locked on each other.

Finally Buddy broke away from the silent confrontation and turned toward Ettmann. "I've had a very strange experience, Doctor," he said softly. "I was—the last I knew *here* was that I was trying to concentrate on my work, getting something done on *Diamond Sutro,* you know. And—and I think I blacked out, you know. Roland"—he looked away from Ettmann, straight at Washburn, then back to the doctor—"Roland came out, then. I think he was coming out, anyway. I—kind of lost control, the way it happens each time. I think I kept a little awareness, though, just a tiny glimmer from far in inside.

"Roland was, ah, very upset. I could tell that. And he started to shout and to carry on and—"

Roland Washburn cut him off. "Shut up, you soft fool! You know nothing about me or my activities!"

Dr. Ettmann made a placating gesture with both hands, holding them toward the men. "Please, ah, please, Roland, if you'd just let Buddy, Mr. Satvan, tell us what happened to him. This is, ah, this is really such an unusual situation, we, ah—in fact, it's quite unprecedented.

"If Buddy could tell us what he, ah, experienced, then I'm sure we would be very pleased, ah, more than eager to have your comments." He reached into a pocket of his soft tweed jacket and pulled out a pair of horn-rimmed glasses and slipped them on. "If you, ah, is that. . . ."

"Very well, doctor," Roland said stiffly.

Buddy looked from Washburn to Ettmann, then said "Well, ah, quite suddenly I found myself in a strange, remote place. With a group of very unusual beings. People. Ah, beings. But you see, I wasn't out when this transition happened. I think that Roland was. Ah—but, ah, the *me* Roland, you see, Dr. Ettmann, not *this* Roland."

He pointed at Washburn. "It's all very. . . ." Buddy shook his head and became silent.

Dr. Ettmann propped one elbow on his desk, rested his forehead on the opened thumb and forefinger of his hand. After a moment he looked up at Roland. "Hmm? Mr. Washburn?"

"Sheer nonsense. I listen to this man's maunderings, Dr. Ettmann, with a deep sense of repugnance. I am only pleased that he appeared here to establish once and for all that I am not in any manner or degree the same person as Buddy Satvan. I have no idea what his wild story of purple monsters from outer space—"

"Yakshis."

"So be it. All a pack of degenerate nonsense. Lies and insane babbling. I suggest that you put this man where he belongs, right here in this institution. Timmons here—Timmons, I demand that you prepare my belongings for my immediate departure. Dr. Ettmann, you must complete my discharge papers. And, Timmons, I will require a limousine as well. Summon one at once."

Ettmann made a placating gesture again. "Mr. Washburn, please. You were committed here by the court. I cannot discharge you without court approval. And we have yet to settle this, ah, this rather puzzling, not to say embarrassing, situation between yourself and, ah, Mr. Satvan here."

"Mr. Satvan," Washburn snorted. "Panderer to degenerates and morons!"

"That isn't so! Buddy does a wonderful job!" Tara broke into the exchange, turning now toward her employer. "Tell him, Buddy, what's the real purpose of *Diamond Sutro.* Why it's important to people!"

Buddy pushed his hair back from his forehead. "Well, ah—"

"If you will, Mr. Satvan. If we can achieve some better degree of understanding between the individual personalities, between Satvan and Washburn so to speak. Of course since you really are separate persons. Or appear to be. Ah—" He stopped himself.

After a brief silence Buddy complied, addressing himself to Roland Washburn. "Well. I don't think you really understand *Diamond Sutro,* Mr. Washburn. Ah—Roland."

"Of course I do! A lot of worthless tripe, filling people with escapist pap. Part of the plan to distract them from the forces that are working against them, forces which they will someday recognize as their real enemies, and smash. As they should have been smashed thrity years ago!"

"No," Buddy replied quietly. "I don't think you see the situation that the average person is in, in this country. In this society of ours. There's nothing sinister or dramatic threatening the ordinary man or woman. It's—"

"It's an international conspiracy!"

"No, Roland, it is not." Buddy shook his head slowly from side to side. He reached with one hand and squeezed Tara's. "You look at the average working man, what are his problems? Nothing acute that he can grapple with. There is no villain that he can confront, that he can come to grips with. The average person who reads *Diamond Sutro* is some factory worker in, oh, maybe Topeka or Buffalo or Galveston. You know.

"He, oh, maybe he operates a lathe for a living, making parts for die stamping machines that makes household appliances. He's forty-two years old. Well, they have all sorts of demographic info at the syndicate office, lots of details, but this is an average, okay?

"This reader's been working at that lathe since he graduated from Topeka Central High School twenty-three years ago. He married a girl he knew in school and she's kind of dumpy and dowdy now and he probably loves her in his own way, but he's been bored with her for at least the past fifteen years. And he's no bargain himself, he's getting bald and he's got a beer-belly and she's as tired of him as he is of her."

He shifted in his chair and caught his breath before the resumed. The others were watching him, waiting for him to go on.

"He doesn't understand his children and he can't control them. His boss puts him down every day at work. One of the guys in his car pool irritates him, but he doesn't know what to do about it because if he quits the pool he'll have to drive every day and then his wife won't have the car for shopping."

Buddy stopped and caught his breath again.

"His mother-in-law has been annoying him for as long as he can remember.

"He's carrying a murderous tax burden, he's paying a fortune for his mortgage, and every time his income goes up ten percent his expenses go up fifteen, and he can't figure out what to do about *that.*

"His daily life is, he gets up and goes to work all day and come home and eats dinner and watches TV and goes to bed. His s-sex life is infrequent and hardly worth the trouble anyhow.

"He goes bowling every week with the same guys he has for ten years, never rolls over one fifty. Saturdays he mows the lawn in summer or shovels snow in winter and tries to fix his house because anybody he hired to do it would be too expensive."

Washburn gave a snort of disdain.

"Please," Dr. Ettmann said, "let him go on. This is extremely, ah, instructive."

"O-okay," Buddy said. "I was almost done anyhow. Anyhow, this guy in, ah Topeka, or wherever. I was almost done with him anyhow. You see, he—oh, and Sunday, Sunday morning his wife makes him go to church and he doesn't want to and Sunday afternoon he watches professional football on TV. He just wishes the season would run all year, you see?

"Well, ah, I write *Diamond Sutro* for him. For that guy in Kansas. That's why I do it."

Washburn stood up, pounded a fist into his palm. "This is trash, what is all this trash? What kind of sob story are you trying to peddle here? Dr. Ettmann, are you going to let this fool push his moronic theories on us? It is exactly this so-called ordinary man that you talk about, you fool, who will provide the solid strength and sinew of the Revitalization League! This man of yours is the victim of international bankers and leftist mongrelizers!

"This man must rise! And under my leadership he will!"

Dr. Ettmann stood up and started around his desk. "Please, Roland," he said placatingly. He cast a silent look toward Timmons. "Let's, ah, let's permit Buddy to finish his statement. Were you finished, Mr. Satvan?"

"Almost. You see, doctor, you see, Mr. Washburn, Roland—this is the man who lives the life of, ah, I think the expression is quiet desperation. He desperately needs relief—but who can relieve him from his boring job? From his dull wife? From his car pool? From his mother-in-law, taxes, children who baffle him? What can he do?

"He, ah—this man is the person who joins organizations like the Rosicrucians, you see. Have you ever looked into the Rosicrucians? Perfectly harmless, benign mumbo-jumbo. Our average bored man or woman pays a few dollars a month for so-called secret knowledge. He's *really* paying for glamour, for a sense of excitement in his life. He may live in a drab and badly-built house with a dull wife and go every day to a boring, oppressive job—but he is a Rosicrucian!

"He has the secret knowledge! He is a member of a worldwide, ancient and mystical order! He is a very special man—in his own mind. It may be the only thing in his life that's really valid, the Rosicrucians. The only thing that gives him even a little bit of satisfaction and self-esteem."

He stopped and asked Dr. Ettmann for a drink of water.

"Or if he doesn't join the Rosicrucians or the Masons or the Knights of this-or-that—"

"The Mystic Knights of the Sea," Roland said acidly.

"Yes, yes. Well, or otherwise he gets caught up in something like a flying saucer cult or Scientology—you know about Scientology, Dr. Ettmann, I'm sure. Or, or whatever. He may wind up in a dangerous political movement, because extremists offer easy dramatic solutions to problems."

"And what do *you* offer, little man?" Washburn demanded.

"Well, you see, I thought about my comic strip for a long time before I was ready to do it. I worked as an assistant, I inked for people, I did paste-ups and mechanicals, I did all sorts of jobs. And all along I was learning. And planning.

"What does Diamond Sutro offer his readers? The feeling of mysticism, the distinctive costume, the magical powers. The wealth of his secret counterpart Arnaud Subhuti. Exotic settings. Dramatic adventures. Beautiful, exciting women—remember Crystal Knight, Astoroth Anderson? And wait until you see Aphrité Anubis!

"I offer my readers glamour!

"The same thing that people got from movie stars, once, that the young people get today from their, ah, people like the Beatles, you know. A feeling of specialness. An escape from the *banality* of their lives.

"That's it," he said agreeing with his own conclusion, "that's what my factory worker in Topeka gets. Maybe for just five minutes each day he becomes Arnaud Subhuti or Diamond Sutro, and for those five minutes all of the banality is left behind. Or a woman reader, she can be Crystal or Astoroth or Aphrité Anubis. No supermarkets, no diapers, no *boredom.*

"That's what I offer people!"

He stopped and drank down the rest of the water in his glass and placed it on Ettmann's desk. He was flushed, embarrassed. "I—I'm sorry. I, ah, don't make speeches. But—well. . . ."

"You did fine, Buddy," Tara said. She looked up. "Dr.

Ettmann, you can see what a fine man Buddy Satvan is. And what—what kind of man Roland Washburn is, too. Don't you think you ought to discharge Buddy, or recommend to the court that he be discharged? And let Washburn face up to his guilt?"

The doctor shook his head helplessly. "Miss Sakti," he said, "to quote Mr. Satvan, you really don't understand the situation. Certainly I found his statement moving. It reflects a humane sensitivity that I have to admire.

"But that is not the issue. The issue is—how can we resolve the conflict between the two personalities? And now, how can we resolve the problem of the sudden appearance of a second completely separate, ah, personage, when we thought there was only one? I think the best I can do, as someone responsible to the court, is, ah, detain both Mr. Satvan and Mr. Washburn for the time being.

"Please"—he put up his hands again, trying to soothe—"please, I hope you will both remain here voluntarily. For tonight, at least. I will contact the court in the morning. I must have some legal guidance. There will have to be a determination. The court will have to rule. You can't *both* be responsible for the killing—ah, I'm sorry—for, ah, what happened to Oskar Schrieber. But, ah, who is the man the court remanded to the Institute?"

Buddy let go his long-held grip on Tara Sakti's hand. He leaned forward nervously, about to make a point to Dr. Ettmann—and found himself back on Sravasti!

Pieter Wachtel watched the chilly Dutch winter deepen and darken until the December holidays approached. The young man with the blue overcoat had taken Pieter under his wing. His name was Leon Pisk. Pieter began by calling him Mijnheer Pisk, but this quickly became Mijnheer Leon and then Oom Leon.

Not that Oom Leon was very much like Oom van der Roest. Oom van der Roest had been a fat, hearty man with big moustaches that Pieter liked to watch move as Oom spoke or puffed on his big curving pipe. Oom Leon was thin, with sunken cheeks and dark, lanky hair. He was a taciturn man, his eyes deep and dark, who smoked hand-rolled cigarettes

and spoke with a harsh intensity that sometimes frightened
Pieter.

Still, Oom Leon cared for him, prepared food and saw that
Pieter had enough to eat—most often potato soup, an occasional apple, some bread. Even, although rarely, an egg or a
small piece of meat.

At Hanukkah some of the people in the large hut where
Pieter lived with Oom Leon erected a menorah. Most of the
younger men and women had little to do with the trappings
and observances of their religion, but the old ones kept up the
traditions. Aged men with white hair and long beards wore
yarmulke, tallith and philacteries, burned candles each night
and prayed.

Old Mijnheer Ottenstein, Reb Ottenstein, conducted
services each night at sundown.

Pieter, timid yet strangely fascinated by the activities, found
the rabbi in a solitary moment, swaying and mumbling to
himself. Pieter stood watching, fascinated, until the rabbi
looked up, saw him. "What is it, child?" the old man asked

Pieter didn't know what to say. He stood, awed, in front o
the old man. Then, silently, he reached and touched the old
rabbi's prayer shawl, the white cloth with its blue stripes.

"Eh, you wonder at the meaning of the tallith, boy? What i
your name, boy?"

Pieter told him. The rabbi nodded. "Ah, a good name, that
an honorable name." His eyes, the eyes of the old man, were
faded, cloudy blue. As he spoke to Pieter they seemed at the
same time to twinkle with an aged joy—and to grow moist, as i
with tears.

"God let me help this innocent child to find Him," the rabb
said softly. "Very well, Pieter, what little I can teach you, I will
The tallith is a very old part of our faith. It reminds us of th
covenant made between God and Noah, the sign in the sk
being the rainbow, the bands of color represented by th
stripes of our shawl."

The rabbi told Pieter the wonderful story of the ancien
people, of their wickedness, and God's punishment. It was
strange story. Pieter liked it almost as well as he liked th
stories in his foreign magazine—the stories that he himsel

had woven around the colorful pictures since he could not read the language of the magazine.

Reb Ottenstein told Pieter that if he would come each day, the old man would tell him stories as wonderful as the story of Noah, would tell him the meaning of Hanukkah and other observances, would even begin to teach him the special language of their people.

"Not Dutch?" Pieter asked.

The old Reb shook his head. "No, Pieter, Dutch is a good language, but our language is another, called Hebrew." The old man placed a trembling, spotted hand on Pieter's unkempt hair and mumbled something in the special language, and Pieter went back to see if Oom Leon was in their section of the hut.

He was. Pieter told him what had happened with the Reb, and Oom Leon looked at Pieter oddly, then turned toward the end of the big hut where Mijnheer Ottenstein sat beisde the menorah.

"Come, let's look at your magazine," Oom Leon said to Pieter.

For the first time, when Pieter showed him the precious magazine, Oom Leon seemed to look at it closely. "Hah!" he laughed, reaching into a pocket for a half-smoked cigarette. "English!"

He took the magazine from Pieter. Pieter stood close by, not letting the precious thing out of his sight. "No," Oom Leon corrected himself, "not English. American. How did it ever find its way to Amsterdam? Well, Pieter, I can read a little English. Would you like me to translate some of this for you?"

14. Sravasti

HE blinked, sniffed, squeezed his eyes shut and then opened them again. No question about it—this was once more Sravasti. Buddy was standing on the flat area where arrivals had found themselves in the past. He looked around, saw the two—no, three—Yakshis, presumably Asoka, Nanda, Kal inga.

And standing with them, Roland L. K. Washburn.

Washburn looked at Buddy, mockery in his eyes. "How are things on earth, Satvan?"

Buddy gaped. "How—? You are here too? But you were just with me in Dr. Ettmann's office. How did we both get back to Sravasti?"

"I think you'd better ask your friends the Yakshis," Washburn grated. "But as for me, I've been here all along. I you went back to earth, you've been doing some things haven't seen. I will want to catch up on the situation there. A for things here—it's been very quiet lately, very quiet."

Buddy took an unsteady step toward Washburn. Roland was wearing the gray tunic and trousers of the Yakshi materi al, not the ward clothing he'd worn in the Morton Prince Institute. Other than that, he had undergone no apparent change.

"Are you confused, Satvan?" Washburn's voice again mocked the other man.

"I—I don't understand what's happening. That's all."

"Well, maybe you'd better get a headband and find out from our hosts here. Washburn turned toward the Yakshi nearest himself. A look of concentration appeared on his face In a moment the Yakshi disappeared from the room, then returned bearing a headband. The one that Buddy had with him on earth had been lost somehow.

Now he took the newly proferred strip of metallic cloth and slipped it over his forehead. He turned toward the hovering shadows and concentrated, sending his unspoken question to them. "How can there be two of us—Roland Washburn and me? We were a single person, or two persons sharing a single body. Now we are separate beings. Did you cause that in some way? Am I permanently freed of him?"

The three Yakshis leaned toward each other. Whatever communion they achieved through their headbands, or through the electronic linkage of the machines that maintained them, they still seemed to gain some added com munication, some added strength, from physical proximity to one another.

At last one of them emerged from the group, through the neuronic stimulation of the headbands spoke to Buddy—and, from the look on Roland's face, to him as well.

"It is time that you learned a new fact. This is something that we could tell you ourselves, we Yakshis. I am Nanda, but Asoka and Kalinga know all that I know. You best can learn what you must know from the great machines. You must come with us, lie where we tell you to lie. Your minds may enter the machines. One of your minds did already, but it was a person neither Old Buddy Satvan nor Roland L. K. Washburn.

"Now you both must learn from the machines."

The three Yakshis quivered, danced, led the way from the room. Casting suspicious glances at each other, Buddy and Roland followed. They lay on pallets where the Yakshis directed them.

Buddy felt his mind sliding, not as it did when the other came out and Buddy lost control of his body, but rather as if the locus of his ego were moving, moving from his brain, from his body, down into the circuitry and the extensions of the great computer whose bulk filled much of the volume of Sravasti.

He could sense the presence there of others—of Roland L. K. Washburn as a hard-edged, sharp-cornered manifestation of rigidity and discipline; of the three Yakshis as purple-gray shadows, flitting here and there.

"You see"—the Yakshi voice seemed to penetrate his entire being—"you see how the machines work?"

The three great devices of the star peoples, the computer, the scanner, the transporter, were one great interconnected system. Buddy could penetrate the recorded history of the machines' activities, could see into the recent past as the Yakshis, frightened by the spaceburn phenomenon, had summoned the machines to full activity, had directed the circuitry of the great computer to deal with the menace that threatened the very existence of the universe.

He felt rather than saw the circuitry of the great computer processing billions and trillions of "trits" of information at last arriving at the statistical description of the one mentality in the universe that might—just might!—solve the mystery of the spaceburn. He relived, with the machine, its dispatching of control signals to the scanner . . . the scanner's search of the quintillions of sentient inhabitants of the sidereal universe . . . its discovery of the one, the sole entity in existence that might stop the spread of the spaceburn.

He experienced the flashing signals of the transporter as it functioned, guided by the scanner, commanded by the computer. As the Yakshis, acting as the legatees of the ancient star races, using the mighty machines, came for him in the violent ward of the Morton Prince Memorial Institute on earth.

But how did the machines do their job?

For the first time Buddy comprehended. They did not truly move him at all. Rather, using the pattern derived by the scanner, the transporter built up a duplicate of the scanned object. From the most minuscule subatomic particle to the grand design of the entire entity, the scanner described and the transporter duplicated.

Within a matter of seconds, where Roland L. K. Washburn had stood, eyes blazing furiously in the violent ward of the institute, he was recreated, electron for electron, atom for atom, molecule for molecule, in the building of the Yakshis on the artificial world. But he remained, unaware of the happening, on earth!

Later, when he had insisted on being transported back to earth—the Yakshis, learning of his insistence on clothing, had altered the computer's instructions to duplicate his garb as well as his person—he had remained, unaffected, on Sravasti as well.

On earth he had had new experiences, encountered the girl in the quick-food restaurant, phoned Willy Albertson, eventually returned to the institute and met the original Roland Washburn. By now, of course, the traveller was Buddy Satvan! And the star peoples' machines had summoned him back again to Sravasti, but it was another "He" who returned. The Buddy and the Roland in Dr. Ettmann's office were still there too!

There were thus *four* of him now: two on earth, two on Sravasti. He drew back, not physically but psychically leaving the machine. He sat up, saw that Roland Washburn had done the same, had in fact preceded him and was standing, feet apart, arms folded, sternly awaiting Buddy's return.

"Then you—you've been here all along," Buddy said.

Washburn nodded affirmation.

"When you—I—went back to earth, the other one of us—you—stayed here."

"Precisely."

"Well—well there's so much to do. So much for us to do. We have to—the spaceburn, I mean. . . ."

"We have far more important things than that to attend to. I can see in this machinery an invaluable tool. I have had some difficulty in recruiting members for the National Revitalization League. And those I have recruited have on occasion caused problems. Certain emotional instabilities seem to crop up. Certain unreliabilities of behavior.

"Enough!" He made a fierce, cutting gesture with one hand. "There will be no more need for recruits! I can simply duplicate myself, over and over! An elite corps of Roland Washburns! An entire army—a *nation* of Roland Washburns!"

He turned glaring, eager eyes toward Buddy. "The only problem is—so far I cannot maintain myself in control all the time. And when *you* come out"—he shook his head as if to clear it—"when you come out, you perform acts of weakness and stupidity. You would subvert the Movement. As when you killed poor Schrieber, my deputy. Pah!"

Buddy gaped at him, astounded. "I didn't kill Schrieber. That's what started this whole, uh, this whole mess. When you shot him and then submerged and left me with the smoking pistol when the police came."

Washburn narrowed his eyes suspiciously. "You mean to tell me you really didn't kill him? I thought I could see all your thoughts, you fool. But I never saw that, I wondered about it."

"S-scout's honor, Roland. I didn't do it. I didn't do it. I really thought all along that you did. You know, I can't read your thoughts, except a very little bit, once in a while. You really didn't kill him?"

"Murder Oskar Schrieber? My closest associate? My deputy

führer? Would Hitler kill Goebbels? Of course I didn't shoot him!"

"But then—who did?"

The nearest Yakshi, hovering, bobbing in the air, sent waves of thought to them. "The other. Was it the other self of yourselves? We have told you there was another, another self of yourselves."

The two men looked at each other. "It—it could be. If we were really one person. I mean, ah, if you and I, Roland, were originally one person? And something—something happened. Long ago. On earth. That's Dr. Ettmann's idea, you know."

"Yes." Lips set grimly. "I know."

"Well—well"—Buddy spread his hands innocently—"maybe there are *more* than two of us. If one person can split in two, uh, I don't mean into two bodies, like the machines have done to us, but into two, ah, persons, ah, personalities. . . ."

"Yes? What then?"

"Well, ah, then maybe, don't you think, we—I mean, the original person who became *us*—might have split in *three.* You see? And you and I just don't know about the other one. Who he is. What he's like. What kind of person he is. Even what his name might be.

"And—and maybe *he* killed Oskar Schrieber!"

The voiceless communication of a Yakshi interrupted their dialog. "Ole Buddy Satvan. Roland L. K. Washburn. I hesitate to disturb your—communion. But the purpose of your presence in Sravasti is to stop the spaceburn. Whichever of you can do this, must proceed to do it. Else—all is lost! All!"

"Relax, shad! First I want to get this straightened out with Satvan here!" Roland returned to Buddy. "It still mystifies me how any part of my personality could be the weakling panderer to people who read comic strips. Especially a worthless, bourgeois piece of trash like your strip."

"I thought we—we'd been over all that. Just before now. In—in Dr. Ettman's office." Buddy stood still, thinking. Then, "No, of course not! You weren't there! A different Roland was. And he must be the original—the master copy they made both of us from! And the other Buddy who's on earth. I remember what happened to me when I went back, but you wouldn't know that, would you? Ooh!" He rubbed his face with both his hands, trying to get a grasp on the situation.

When he looked up again he could see Roland, too, visibly struggling with the multiplicity of selves in which they participated. "Listen to this, then. If this peculiar theory is correct—and I have my doubts, it sounds like some new and degenerate refinement of the Vienna Jewish clique—but if it is correct, then there is a Satvan within me, and a Washburn within you.

"You understand?"

Buddy nodded.

"Then if there is also a third personality," Washburn went on, "why does it—he—not manifest himself? If you and I are merely aspects of an original being, and if there is a third self, he would speak up, would he not? Why are we both unaware of him? Why does he refuse to appear?"

He stood silently, as if savoring the dramatic effect of his questions. Then he seemed to undergo a sudden transformation. Before Buddy's popping eyes Washburn's facial expression changed, his body posture altered. The new look on his face was alarming. It was like that of a child, frightened, desperate, cringing in imminent fear of its life. The very torso and limbs seemed to shrink in upon themselves, to those of a small boy.

And then, with equal suddenness, a look of self-possession replaced the panic in the face. A confident, manly bearing succeeded the body tone of the frightened child. But this was not the rigid, militaristic bearing of Roland L. K. Washburn. Nor was it the soft-visaged, easy-going Buddy Satvan. This was another man!

"Who—who are you?" Buddy squeaked.

The stranger seemed to shudder slightly, adjusting to his own emergence. "My name is Auburn Sutro. I operate a mining engineering consulting service out of San Francisco. Folsom Street. But you—you seem to look a good deal like me. And—and this place. . . ."

He stood gazing around himself. "I have been here before." He turned to a hovering Yakshi. "I know you, you shadow-folk. I've been here before!"

"You have, yes," the Yakshi pulsed.

"I—I thought it was a dream. But it wasn't. It was real. Oh, my God, it was real!"

Buddy reached with one hand, put it concernedly on the other's sleeve. In a way it was like touching himself, yet he felt as if he didn't really know the other man. "Your name. You said your name was Auburn Sutro? Of San Francisco?"

"Yes. Why?"

"Ah—w-well, I'm Buddy Satvan."

"Yes? Do I know you?"

"Well, I write the *Diamond Sutro* comic strip. Draw it sometimes, too. Right now my assistant Willy Albertson is running the strip from my tapes."

"I don't understand. What is the relevance of that? If we are really standing in an artificial contruct created billions of years ago by races probably long extinct by now . . . somewhere in the very center of the universe . . . and the universe is being destroyed, will be destroyed unless we can prevent it—

"You want to talk about comic strips?"

Buddy stammered and shook his head. "You, no, the hero of my comic strip is named Sutro, too. And his secret identity, one of his secret identities, is a scientist who lives in San Francisco. On Nob Hill."

"Sorry, my friend. I wouldn't live on Nob Hill if I could afford it, which I can't. I don't even live in the city. Mill Valley, I come in on the ferry every morning." Something clouded his self-confident expression. "Or I did when I was able to."

The two men stood facing each other, momentarily at a loss. From the Yakshi came a message, mentally communicated to them both. "If you would follow. You need not be uncomfortable. You need to be nourished."

"Eh—likely so. Well, Satvan, what do you say?"

Before Buddy replied the Yakshis did. "Follow, we will show you a room where you can sit. And then merely direct your thoughts, use your headbands to summon what you wish from the machines."

The Yakshis bobbed, glided away. The two men followed. In a few minutes they were seated. Buddy held a cup of tea; Auburn, a Manhattan in a crystal highball glass.

"You—you and I," Buddy began over, "and another man, Roland L. K. Washburn—"

"What?" Auburn Sutro interrupted, "Roland Washburn? That rabble-rousing nazi! What are you saying? That he and I—and you and I—?"

"Yes," Buddy affirmed, bobbing his head. He stopped and sipped his tea, its hot feel and familiar taste comforting him. "According to Dr. Noble St. Vincent Ettmann. Washburn and I are the same person. Ah—fragmented personalities, he used to say, produced by a trauma that affected the original personality who was you—me, that is. At least, I always tried to believe that I was the original, ah, person. That Washburn was the product of the trauma.

"Of course he insisted that it was the opposite. Or mainly, Dr. Ettmann used to tell me, Washburn denied that he and I were associated in any way. That we alternated in the use of my, uh, our body."

Auburn Sutro shook his head. "Where do I come into all this?"

"I—I don't know. Maybe, ah, you are the original personality. Maybe it was neither Washburn nor me. What—didn't you know anything about either of us? But you must have been—" A sudden chill gripped Buddy.

"You must have killed Oskar Schrieber!"

"Oskar Schrieber? I don't know any Oskar—wait! I think I have heard of him. Some old World War Two nazi? Served a jail term for war crimes, then immigrated to America and hooked up with Washburn and his outfit, that Revitalization League. I always wondered how that fellow even got past immigration."

He continued. *"Hmph.* What about Oskar Schrieber? You're not going to say that *he's* part of me. Of us. Are you?"

"No." Buddy shook his head solemnly. "One of us shot Oskar Schrieber. That's what I'm saying. 'We' killed him!"

"Oh, no, no, no!" Sutro drained his Manhattan at a gulp, dropped the glass from shaking fingers. As it hit the floor it seemed to dissolve and float away through the purple-tinted air.

"I'd been having these blackouts. Sometimes for months at

a time. But I thought it was from drinking, you know, an old San Francisco syndrome. Alcoholics' capital of the world. But I couldn't have *killed*. . . ." He shuddered.

"Not that he didn't deserve killing. Now I remember Oskar Schrieber. He was a prison camp guard. Just a guard, there were hundreds of them, thousands, in the war. But witnesses stood up, pitiful wretches who somehow had survived the slaughter, and gave testimony against Schrieber. The things he did. The joy he took from the most savage of acts.

"But—*I* killed him? Wouldn't I know if I'd shot the man? Does this Dr. Ettmann say that I killed Schrieber?"

Buddy waved his free hand, holding his tea cup steady in the other. "No. I don't think Dr. Ettmann even knows about you. He only knows Roland Washburn and me. We—I was found with Schrieber's body. I had the—the proverbial smoking pistol in my hand.

"But I didn't kill him! I was in Washburn's headquarters. I didn't know how I got there. I didn't know anything about multiple personalities except for a silly movie I'd seen once. I knew that I had these, um, these problems part of the time. But I never dreamed that I was two men in one body."

He gazed at Auburn Sutro, then lowered his eyes again. "Or three men. But—when I told the police everything I knew, they sent me to see the doctor. Took me, actually, they weren't setting me loose. I don't suppose I blame them for that. Anyway, they took me to see Dr. Ettmann at his hospital and then he discovered the truth, I g-guess it's the truth, that Roland Washburn and I are one man.

"There was never a real trial, just a court hearing before a judge. My lawyer was there—my lawyer, Buddy Satvan's lawyer, you see. Also Roland Washburn's lawyer. They didn't even know each other.

"Part of the hearing, I was there. I even testified. The rest of the time—I guess Roland was there. Somehow we, I, got through it. The judge committed Roland and me to Dr. Ettmann's hospital. That's all bad enough. But then the Yakshis took us out of there, brought us here. And there's all of this spaceburn affair.

"And—and now you! How many more of us are there? And can you, can we save the universe?"

Sutro began to laugh.

"Wh-what's so funny?" Buddy demanded.

"Can we save the universe?" Sutro repeated. "What melodrama! What suspense!"

"B-but—b-but th-that's what the Yakshis say we have to do!" Buddy stammered.

"I understand that." Aubrun Sutro leaned forward in his chair. For a moment he looked away, signaled a hovering Yakshi with one hand. "In any case," he said, "do you think I could have another Manhattan? Just a trifle drier this time. Hold the cherry."

"What? What?" Buddy pleaded.

"Dear friend," Auburn Sutro purred, "it looks to me as if we are both absolutely over-the-side lunatics. But as long as that's the case, I propose to relax and enjoy it!"

He reached for his fresh drink, murmured, "Thank you ever so," and over the edge of his glass saluted Buddy with a raised eyebrow and took a hearty swallow of his highball.

For a few days Pieter visited Reb Ottenstein each morning. Most of the people in their hut—most of the people in the Westerbork camp, in fact—were required to perform useful labor. It was part of the great plan. No parasites were to be tolerated.

A few exceptions however, were permitted: the sick, the aged, and the few children in the camp who were regarded as too young to work.

Pieter's new Oom Leon worked every day, but both Pieter himself and his friend the rabbi were excused: the one, as too young; the other, too old. The rabbi told Pieter wonderful stories of Jews in olden times, of their great heroes, great leaders and teachers, of the prophets. As long as the Jews kept strong their faith in God, they were protected. They were triumphant. When they strayed from the path of righteousness, from the Law, from the One God; when they followed after other gods and after the pleasures of the flesh, then the One God deserted them. And when God deserted the Jews, woe unto them!

People came to the camp and went away from the camp. Sometimes Pieter wondered if even his own Mamma and Paps were somewhere in Westerbork. He asked Oom Leon, but Oom Leon said he was quite sure that Pieter's Mamma and Paps were not in Westerbork. Maybe elsewhere. Maybe—if they had ever been in Westerbork—they had been transported to the East.

Transports departed every Thursday for the East. People from the camp boarded railroad trains, each person allowed to take along one suitcase or parcel, and the trains left for the East. But somehow the Westerbork camp never became empty. The hut in which Pieter lived, his cot beside that of Oom Leon, lost people in almost every week's transport to the East. But new people also arrived—from Amsterdam mostly, but also from Rotterdam, from Delft, from the Hague.

Pieter asked where the trains went. Oom Leon did not know. "Maybe Palestine," he said one evening when Pieter asked him. Pieter asked what Palestine was. Oom Leon said it was a beautiful place where someday all the Jews would go. It would be their own land.

Pieter asked Reb Ottenstein about Palestine. The rabbi told him that it was the land of the prophets, where Israel had known her holy days, where someday Jews would again bend the knee to God. Pieter asked if the trains that went to the East took Jews to Palestine. The rabbi didn't know. Would Pieter like to begin the study of the Hebrew language, the rabbi asked.

The next-to-last day of Hanukkah was a Thursday. Pieter rose and had his breakfast, then went to see Reb Ottenstein. The old Jews who stayed around the rabbi's part of the big hut were weeping. Pieter looked at them. He knew several of them by now. He asked them what had happened, where was the rabbi. One of the old men, tears running down his face, told Pieter that the rabbi had been transported.

Pieter smiled happily. "He has gone to Palestine, then! That is the Jews' own country."

15. Hathor

IMAGINE, if you will, a complete world without a single intelligent creature upon it. Perhaps as the earth was before the appearance of man. There are mountains, valleys and deserts, rivers and seas and mightily heaving oceans, grass-covered plains and tall whispering forests, fishes and beasts, creeping reptiles and flapping fowls but—no man.

The air is clear as it was on the day of creation; the water is as sweet as fresh pure rain.

Behold: Hathor!

The ether-ray ship *Isis*, graceful and unscarred by her encounter with the searing flames of the sun itself and the claws and fangs of the solar salamander, was visible to an ridescent ichthyfalcon as that gorgeous but terrible creature ored from its subaqueous den into the chill, crystalline air bove Hathor's mightiest ocean.

It was night. The atmosphere was invisible, the contellations brilliant and glittering against the velvety blackness f space.

The iridescent ichthyfalcon, one of the magnificent life orms native to Hathor, made its way over the featureless sea y means of celestial navigation, Mother Nature's own adaptaion of the unchanging stars and the slowly precessing planets o aid one of her creatures in its nocturnal hunt. But tonight he iridescent ichthyfalcon's bright, faceted eyes were stounded to see a new and unfamiliar light moving across the odiac.

It was the ether-ray ship *Isis*. On board the ship were the ncomparable Aphrité Anubis, the most beautiful woman live and daughter of the archfiend of the modern world . . . nd Aphrité's companion Arnaud Subhuti, the world's reatest scientist. Kidnapped and drugged by Aphrité's maiacal father, Subhuti had been taken first to the mad genius's ecret Andean laboratory where five of the world's outstanding intellects labored, drugged zombie-slaves of the arch-fiend.

But this was not to be the fate of Arnaud Subhuti. Anubis wanted the greatest of all geniuses as his associate and agent, not as a mere volitionless zombie. Using a drug to weaken the will of the scientist, Dr. Anubis had brought forth the voluptuous, ruby-irised Aphrité to work her wiles upon Subhuti. Together they had been dispatched by Dr. Anubis in the ether-ray craft to his top secret hideaway and scientific base hidden in a giant glass dome deep beneath the Sea of Charon on the planet Hathor.

Also—unknown to Dr. Anubis as to the rest of a trusting but uninformed world—Arnaud Subhuti was more than a great scientific thinker. He had other identities, secret selves known to no other. One of these—undoubtedly one of the world's most carefully guarded secrets—was that of Diamond Sutro.

Diamond Sutro, the Champion of Righteousness, He Who Proclaims the Truth, the Greatest of All Heroes.

Diamond Sutro, whose stern visage and mystic talisman strike terror into the hearts of evildoers everywhere! And this very Diamond Sutro who was the supreme nemesis of Dr. Anubis and his evil ambitions, Anubis had taken to his Andean base and from thence dispatched with his daughter the ruby-irised Aphrité to the secret planet Hathor! An ironic joke on the evil mastermind, this!

Now as the graceful, lucite-walled ether-ray ship *Isis* settled into orbit above the planet Hathor, her two occupants gazed downward through transparent walls. The tiny ship skimmed the upper edges of atmosphere, her vermillion ether-ray envelope flaring and glowing as she moved into the night half of the planet, then fading in the clear sunlight as she crossed into the daylight.

The gorgeous Aphrité Anubis now sat in the pilot's chair of the superscientific ether-ray ship. Her eyes flicked from dial to viewscreen, their ruby irises reflecting the quivering needles and flashing computer readout tubes. Graceful feminine fingers, capable equally of the most exquisite tortures or pleasures, flew from toggle switch to vernier nob. At the crucial moment, as the *Isis* sped across the glimmering water of the sea of Charon, Aphrité turned her intense features toward the tall, slim man seated beside her.

"Hold tightly, Arnaud Subhuti," she shot urgently at him.

The only reply was a grim smile. Subhuti had faced danger and death itself in every corner of the earth, from the mountain fastnesses of high Tibet to the terrible ice fields of the poles to the deadly canyons of the world's great metropolises. Often that death had been the final prize in an unending contest between himself and Aphrité's fiendish father.

No fear affected Arnaud Subhuti!

"Go on," he gritted in a firm, reassuring tone, "do what is to be done!"

"Very well!" Aphrité's ruby-irised eyes flashed with excitement. To this woman danger was a veritable drug!

Once more graceful fingers flew. The vermilion sheath that glowed and sparkled around the *Isis* flared into new brilliance. The little Lucite-hulled craft shot into a sudden, screaming arc high in the atmosphere of the planet Hathor. Then, spinning like a maddened drill, the *Isis* settled back on its tail, plunging with white-hot speed down, down toward the lapping wavelets of the Sea of Charon.

With a mighty roar the ether-ray envelope of the ship met the white-capped waters of the Sea of Charon. *Isis's* gracefully tapered nose disappeared in a towering funnel of green-white spume. For a few seconds the usually peaceful waters seethed and boiled at the violence of the entry.

Then the spume fell back, the heat of the ship's entry was dissipated through surrounding currents, and the Sea of Charon, as seen by any flying creature, was its normal, tranquil self.

Within *Isis* Arnaud Subhuti looked through transparent walls, marveling at the incredible marine life of the Sea of Charon. Schools of brilliantly colored submarine squirrels flashed by. A giant sea bat fled screaming, its fangs and claws no match for the heavily tempered walls of *Isis.* A gargantuan creature resembling some mad cross between the afghan hound and a monster kraken swam parallel to *Isis,* staring at the ether-ray craft's occupants in chillingly intelligent curiosity before disappearing with a stroke of its mighty tail.

And now, beneath the transparent ship, a glistening dome became visible. Aphrité took the hand of Arnaud Subhuti and pointed downward. "Our goal," she murmured.

Mighty hatches swung wide at the approach of the ship. *Isis* floated ballerina-like into their gaping maw. The hatches closed. Titanic sea-locks sealed and unsealed, pumping air into the chamber, forcing the green waters out.

"We are here," Aphrité said. "This is my father's mightiest bastion—his most carefully guarded secret—his ultimate headquarters and final refuge!"

"Strange, Aphrité, that he should have you bring me here!"

The woman's expression grew serious. "He meant me to bring you here as my love-slave and his own loyal lieutenant—or not at all!"

A signboard flashed on the wall of the sea-lock. CHAMBER EMPTY! EXIT FROM SHIP PERMITTED! SCUBA GEAR NOT REQUIRED!

"Come!" Aphrité gasped. "You will see my father's triumph: the City of the Styx!"

Arnaud Subhuti stood waiting while Aphrité punched the combination on the ship's control panel that caused its entry ports to swing open. A moment later the two travelers stepped down the ether-ray craft's ramp, strode with echoing footsteps across the puddled stone floor. They reached another doorway, Aphrité rapped out a code on a flush-mounted panel and they stepped through into the City of the Styx, the doorway sealing itself behind them.

The eyes of Arnaud Subhuti had gazed upon the wonders of the world, in ancient times before the antediluvian holocaust that had cast both himself and his archfoe Dr. Anubis into the irreversible stream of time, and in the modern era of superscientific wonders. Those eyes had seen the great stone monoliths of ancient Antarctica, marvels of which no modern mind has more than dreamed in the wildest of fantasy or nightmare. They had seen the inside of forbidden lamaseries, the heart of nuclear reactors, the flashing crystallization of subatomic molecules.

But never had they seen the likes of the City of the Styx.

Massive carven structures with looming faces that leered and snickered grotesquely. Human—and inhuman!—figures that seemed to writhe with a kind of frozen half-life. Pleasure domes, laboratories, dizzying towers that raised their heads above fleecy clouds which danced and drifted overhead.

Automatic vehicles that lumbered or skittered through broad, stone-paved streets, boulevards thronged with cargo-bearing unicycles and silent, mysteriously powered transports.

Shimmering above it all like a titanic soap bubble blown by some gargantuan child was a thin, transparent dome that held the city in its center, protecting the buildings and thoroughfares and vehicles from the crushing pressures of the Sea of Charon above, that kept the waters and the denizens of that sea from filling the city and turning it into a Hathorian lost Atlantis.

And yet—not one living being did Arnaud Subhuti encounter. Guided by the beauteous Aphrité Anubis, the breathtaking woman so touchingly proud of her father's achievement, Subhuti looked for evidence of man, woman or child, beast or bird within the City of the Styx.

And saw—none!

Standing before a massive, barbarically splendid temple, he halted. He faced the flame-robed Aphrité. "Is there no one in this entire city? Are we two the only living beings beneath that shimmering dome?"

The ruby-irised Aphrité looked up into Arnaud Subhuti's cool, blue-gray eyes. "We are," she nodded. "We alone inhabit this city. Save for the wild beasts, Arnaud Subhuti, we alone inhabit all of the planet Hathor! We could be—another Adam and Eve, Arnaud Subhuti!"

"But why? Why did Dr. Anubis send us across all the millions of miles of space that separate earth from its transsolar analogue Hathor? What can we do here that could not be done at Mt. Huascaran, Dr. Anubis's terrestrial headquarters and secret laboratory?"

Aphrité laughed. "Nowhere on all of earth did my father trust you to complete your greatest invention, the ZINGARR! No point on the face of the planet would be safe from the intrusion of my father's mortal nemesis, the great Diamond Sutro!

"But here on the planet Hathor, nearly two hundred

million miles from earth, alone in the City of the Styx, you can complete your work in total security. I shall be your assistant. Diamond Sutro, we can be certain, is safely at home somewhere on earth, chasing down some crew of petty bank robbers or rescuing the victims of an Asian typhoon."

Arnaud Subhuti smiled thoughtfully.

Suddenly the incomparable Aphrité threw her arms about his neck. "Say you will do it!" she cried. "Not for my father, Dr. Anubis! Do it for yourself! Do it, if you will, for me—because I have learned to love you, Arnaud Subhuti!

"Complete the ZINGARR! Then I will return to earth with you—or I will go willingly anywhere in the universe you wish to take me!"

Subhuti brushed her soft, flowing hair with his hands. His eyes were fixed on a grotesque, carven face that bore a chilling suggestion of the head of a jackal. "If you are willing, Aphrité—with no strings attached—I will do it! I will complete ZINGARR! And then—we shall see!"

She led him to the greatest of her father's laboratories. Never in all of his travels on earth—to the most advanced research facilities of Alamogordo, Jodrell Bank, Ulan Bator, Novosibirsk, nor even the ancient and long forgotten chambers now buried miles beneath the bedrock under crushing tons of Antarctic ice—had the scientist Arnaud Subhuti seen the likes of the master laboratory of Dr. Anubis in the City of the Styx here on the planet Hathor!

"How was this built?" he asked.

"Mostly by my father himself," Aphrité responded. "Not without assistance, of course. I worked with him. Some of his zombie-slaves were here: They remember nothing of Hathor of course. Their minds are totally controlled by my father. He can give them false memories or wipe out recollections at his whim!

"And there were robots. As you are aware, my father is the world's leading cyberneticist—"

"At the risk of immodesty—" Subhuti interrupted.

"Of course!" A strange expression crossed the beautiful features of the flame-cloaked Aphrité. "Of course, Arnaud Subhuti almost alone of the world's living scientists rivals Dr. Anubis in sheer brilliance!"

"And the other?" Arnaud Subhuti pressed her. "What of the one known as Dr. Goodlaw, He Who Proclaims the Truth?"

"You mean Diamond Sutro!" Sudden rage filled the beautiful features of Aphrité Anubis. "Never mention that name to me again! From the day of my birth I have been trained to hate Diamond Sutro and all that he stands for! He alone has stood between my father and the attainment of his every ambition!

"His powers are immense, mysterious, mystical! Compared to Diamond Sutro any ordinary man, even you, my beloved Arnaud Subhuti, even you are dwarfed to puniness. I hate Diamond Sutro! My greatest desire would be to see him destroyed!"

Arnaud Subhuti stood, white-clad in his scientist's garb, calm and strong throughout Aphrité's tirade. Now, his arms crossed, he said solemnly, "I doubt that Dr. Goodlaw is all as bad as you seem to think, Aphrité. Perhaps your father's indoctrination of you has produced a somewhat—distorted—impression."

As he spoke a smile flickered across his thin, almost ascetic countenance. Aphrité did not answer. Finally the scientist continued. "Very well. With your assistance, I shall complete ZINGARR!"

They set to work.

Later, after days of experiment and nights of study, after painstaking labor directing the laboratory robots and risking their own lives at crucial moments, the long-awaited time arrived.

Arnaud Subhuti carefully lowered an electro-photonic matrix he had been calibrating against an ergometric scerplex. With one hand he shoved back the spectro-phoretic goggles that had protected his cool, steely eyes from the raking glare. With his free hand he brushed a trickle of perspiration from his brow. Those few drops were the only evidence of the strain and the risks he had uncomplainingly faced throughout the course of the perilous experiment!

He turned to Aphrité Anubis. During these past hours she had been neither the most beautiful woman in the world nor the daughter of Professor Anubis, the world's most dangerous fiend. She had been the laboratory assistant of Arnaud Subhuti—this and this alone!

And she had performed brilliantly.

"It is done!" Subhuti proclaimed gravely. "ZINGARR is completed!"

"I'm so proud of you, Arnaud Subhuti," whispered the gorgeous Aphrité. A smile of peace flickered around the voluptuous lips that had maddened regiments, and she fell, fainting, into the arms of the scientist.

He carried her tenderly to a low couch that stood against one wall of the laboratory—a momentary resting place provided for the workers, but one that neither had used for so much as an instant's respite during all the grueling hours of their intense efforts. Now he placed her gently on its plush cushions, and went to bring her a beaker of *aqua pura* that she might sip of it and recover a little of her strength.

She accepted the water gratefully, clinging to his white-sleeved arm that held the beaker to her lips. Then she lay back on the couch. "What now, Arnaud Subhuti?" she asked. "Shall we return with ZINGARR to planet earth, to my father's secret laboratory and headquarters in the Andes of Peru?"

Subhuti shook his head. "Before we do anything we must test our invention."

"Our invention," she repeated in a soft whisper, "our invention. You make it seem as if I had contributed more than a menial assistance. My father would never make such a statement. In his laboratories it is always *his* invention, *his* discovery, *his* fame, and *his* achievement!"

"Judge him not too harshly, Aphrité. Your father's goals are warped, his objectives evil, but he is still a brilliant scientist. And someday, with kindness and rehabilitation. . . ." He raised her gently to her feet, led her to the laboratory bench where the final working model of ZINGARR stood, its power and precision gleaming from every lens and relay, every circuit and miniature reactor. "I must run the risk of the first test," he said, "that is ever the creed of the true scientist."

"What are you going to do?"

"Through ZINGARR it is my intention to contact neuro-astrally the literal center of the universe itself! Stand back, Aphrité—what follows now carries with it a terrible risk!"

He adjusted the controls, pressed the master power switch of the device. Its indicators flared into urgent life. Arnaud Subhuti stood rigid, every neuron in his body tensed. After a few seconds the lights on ZINGARR winked out. Subhuti shuddered, staggered once. Aphrité caught him, led him now to the very couch where he had so recently placed her.

She stood over him, concerned, terrified that he might have been injured in some way. Before she could act, however, the scientist spoke. "It works," he mouthed solemnly. "ZINGARR works. I have made contact with the center of the universe itself, with a place called—Sravasti.

"And I have learned that the universe is—imperiled!"

"No!" The beautiful Aphrité blanched, her ruby irises and vivid tresses contrasting all the more vividly with her pale, creamy complexion. "What can we do?" she cried.

"We shall do the only thing we can in this moment of mortal danger to all of creation! We will travel to the center of the universe, to Sravasti! There we will meet the men and the other, stranger-beings who dwell amidst the wisdom of ancient star races! Come—there is no time to be lost!"

"But—but—how can we travel there? In our ether-ray ship *Isis*? It would take too long!"

"Aphrité!" Arnaud Subhuti stood before the beautiful woman, his deep gray eyes boring into her unique ruby-tinted orbs. He took her hands in his own, felt them cold and trembling. "You have learned to trust me, have you not?"

"Yes," she whispered.

"Then you must trust me once more. You must trust me against all that your father has taught you from your infancy onward! In return, Aphrité, I shall entrust you with a secret known until now by no one! No one—not even Crystal Knight, nor Astoroth Anderson, not even my closest aide Rod Cohen!"

She stepped back from him, her eyes wide. "Yes! Anything!"

Arnaud Subhuti opened the collar of his white laboratory smock. Solemnly he reached within and withdrew a glittering rococo talisman which hung from a heavy chain of pure beaten gold. He raised the talisman to his lips reverently, then held it before him where both he and Aphrité could see its scrollery and the great gleaming stone mounted in its center.

"The talisman Vajrachedika," he said quietly. "The most ancient amulet, known as the diamond-cutter, the penetrator of the impenetrable." He raised his eyes from the glittering jewel to those of the beautiful woman who stood before him. "Do you know what this jewel means?" he asked her. "Do you know the meaning of the Vajrachedika talisman?"

"I do," she hissed. "It means that my father has been outsmarted. It means that you are an agent of his supreme nemesis—Diamond Sutro!"

Arnaud Subhuti smiled thinly. "In a sense—yes. But more than that. It means that Dr. Anubis' petty ambitions for the conquest of the planet earth pale to nothingness against the menace that threatens the continuity of the universe itself. I will show you what the Vajrachedika talisman means, Aphrité Anubis!"

He strode to a place alone in the center of the laboratory . . . stood with legs apart, one hand holding the glittering amulet high above his head. He shouted the mystical word *Parama!*

Suddenly the room was filled with a blinding, dizzying glare of dazzling diamond-blue light. A sound like the opening of a crack in the very fabric of existence echoed and re-echoed in the terrified ears of Aphrité Anubis. A strange odor like that of lotus-petal incense filled the air.

Arnaud Subhuti was gone.

Where he had been there stood the Champion of Righteousness, He Who Proclaims the Truth, the invincible Dr. Goodlaw—*Diamond Sutro!*

"Come with me, Aphrité Anubis," he commanded in rolling bass tones. "We are needed far from here!"

"But—but how?"

"Diamond Sutro has no need of spaceships or ray machines! I travel instantaneously to any point I choose! I shall travel to Sravasti and I shall bring you with me, using only the power of the Superiority of Unformulated Truth!"

"The Superiority of Unformulated Truth!" Aphrité gasped. "I've heard of that! But Diamond Sutro is invulnerable to harm. I am a mere mortal! How can I travel through space without a spaceship?"

Diamond Sutro threw back his head, stood with feet apart,

hands on his hips, and laughed loudly. His was a laugh whose heartiness had struck fear into the souls of evildoers and brought joy to the souls of the innocent the world over. His eyes sparkled, his teeth shone, the muscles of his mighty torso rippled.

As suddenly as the laughter had come, it departed. Diamond Sutro fixed the flame-cloaked Aphrité with a gaze that held its object frozen entirely within his power. "I shall wrap you in the Unreality of Phenomenal Distinctions, Aphrité. So protected, no harm shall come to you! You shall be as safe with Diamond Sutro as is an innocent babe at the bosom of its mother!"

So saying, Diamond Sutro flung out one arm, finger extended.

"Wait!" Aphrité cried. "When we reach—Sravasti. . . ."

"Yes?"

"Will you—reveal your true identity to the people there?"

"In Sravasti there dwell Yakshis, artificial beings projected electronically by the machines of the great ancient ones. To them, I shall be known as Diamond Sutro.

"But there are others in that place, mortals drawn from the earth by the great machines. Them I shall approach in another guise. I shall use the identity of—Renaldo Warbuckle, radical rightist law professor at the San Francisco Municipal University and Kommandant of the Fraternal Order of the Fylfot!"

16. Westerbork

IT was a few weeks after Reb Ottenstein was transported to the East that the new boy arrived and replaced Pieter Wachtel. No one saw it happen, not even Oom Leon Pisk. At night the people in Pieter's hut had sat around smoking and talking, talking low, long into the night, about what happened when you were transported to the East.

There were many theories. Some held that the Germans were indeed establishing a Jewish state in Palestine. It would be logical, would it not? They clearly wished to rid Europe of Jews, that much was crystal clear. Rounding up Jews and placing them in camps like Westerbork could be nothing more than a temporary means.

The war was going on and on. The Jews in Westerbork had at first hoped for a short war. They were being interned only for the duration. Was it not true that friends and relatives were allowed to send in parcels, money, even to visit occasionally? Was it not true that on even scarcer occasions residents of the camp were allowed to return to Amsterdam or elsewhere on furlough?

But the war was not going to be a short one, that became more clear with each passing month. Shortages worsened, food and clothing and transport became more difficult and sparse. Fewer German aircraft appeared overhead moving westward to attack enemy bases in England. More and more enemy planes appeared, droning overhead, roaring eastward to attack German rear areas and industry.

The war was not ending soon.

Maintaining a camp like Westerbork was expensive for the Germans. They had to tie up transport and weapons and troops to guard the inmates. The Germans left most of the administration of the camp to its residents. To a selected elite of German Jews like Schlesinger and Spanier and Lippmann and to a number of Dutch Jews as well, buying their services with extra privileges and with deferment from transportation to the East.

Even so, it was expensive to run a camp like Westerbork. The Germans would rather use their troops for fighting the enemy. Thus it was logical for them to transport Jews to Palestine and there to give them their own state.

Others disagreed. The Germans had no interest in a Jewish state in Palestine or on Madagascar or anyplace else. The Jews were labor for them. The Jews were transported not to Palestine but to labor camps in Germany and Poland and Rumania, and worked there until they dropped.

That was why there was a constant need for more, not to be transported to Palestine but to replace workers in the labor camps in the East when they dropped. That was why no one ever received mail from the East, from Palestine or anywhere else. You could receive letters and occasional packages from Holland, but once Jews were transported to the East, they were never seen nor heard from again.

Maybe they were killed.

Who said the Jews were killed? Some cynic. Some embittered young man. The deep-eyed, sunken-cheeked young man, Leon Pisk, the cynic of the blue overcoat. Sure, the Germans wanted to get rid of the Jews. They didn't want a Jewish state to rise some day and challenge the New Order. Not in Palestine, not anywhere!

Nor did they want the Jews for labor. They surely wouldn't mind working the Jews for a while—starve them, beat them, force them to strain to support the German war machine like the Israelites slaving in Egypt for the pharaoh. There was an irony for you—five thousand years from pharaoh to führer, and still Jews slaved and died for the oppressor. The more things change the more they stay the same.

Only, where was Moses this time?

Face it, Pisk the cynic growled between puffs on his crude hand-rolled cigarettes, Jews who were transported to the East were transported to death camps. That was the only solution to the Jewish problem that would satisfy the pharaoh. That was good and complete and final. Face it, Pisk insisted, transported Jews were dead Jews and in due course all Jews would be transported.

He gave away the butt end of his cigarette, and from wherever he kept papers and precious tobacco he extracted more and rolled another cigarette for himself, laughing all the while quietly and bitterly.

Pieter Wachtel lay unmoving on his cot throughout the debate. The hut was cold and shadowy. He huddled deep beneath his blanket wearing his clothes even in bed, his precious American picture-story magazine clutched to his chest. It was tattered and faded, but Pieter never left it out of his possession, not ever.

He lay and listened to the voices and the theories, the arguments and the reasoning. At last he heard the voice of Oom Leon, his own dear Oom Leon who cared for him and told him what the strange writing in his magazine meant in Dutch. Oom would tell them, Oom would set the debaters and the theorizers to right. Pieter waited and waited and at last he heard the voice of Oom Leon. He hung on every word, not budging a single toe, not making a single sound, and listened.

When Oom Leon finished his argument Pieter found himself slowly sinking. He was still in his cot, his magazine clutched to his chest, his blanket pulled over him head and eyes and all. And he was sinking. There was a blackness around him, blacker and deeper than the darkness under the blanket, and there was a silence. The voices that he had listened to, the voices of Oom Leon and all the others, grew fainter and fainter and more and more distant. Everything was going away. The bed and the hut and Westerbork were going away. Oom Leon was fading away as Reb Ottenstein had faded away, as Oom van der Roest, Tannie van der Roest had faded away, as Mamma and Paps had faded away.

It wasn't that Pieter was going to sleep. This was a little bit like going to sleep, but it wasn't exactly the same thing. It was just darkness, darkness and darkness.

In the morning the new boy awoke in Pieter Wachtel's cot. His name was different from Pieter's and he spoke differently—still in Dutch, but oddly, almost as a German boy would speak Dutch—and he was not Jewish. He was not Jewish!

Leon Pisk kept saying that the boy was Pieter Wachtel, but he wasn't. He stamped and shouted and demanded to see Untersturmführer, Obersturmführer, any guard, any German—but he must see an Aryan! Finally Pisk took him to the camp hospital. It was staffed by Jewish doctors and the joke ran that even the SS guards came for treatment of their ailments because it was the best hospital in all of Holland.

The doctors took the new boy and put him in bed. He insisted that he was not ill, it was all an error—or worse yet, a plot, a hoax! To claim that he was this Wachtel, this Jew. Disgusting!

They kept him for a few days, then said there was nothing wrong with him. He was clearly not faking. He wasn't Pieter Wachtel, that was all, he was really not Pieter Wachtel. They examined him and found that he was circumcised, but that wasn't proof of anything. Some Aryans were circumcised, it was a fad, or had been before the New Order, a fad probably started by Jewish doctors.

Finally they had him taken to the section of the camp set aside for baptized Jews, Christianized Jews. And for *Weiss-juden,* white Jews, non-Jews who had sheltered or aided or openly sympathized with Jews. He was given a cot in a hut where a Christmas tree had been erected, and a manger with the Christ Child at one end of the hut.

There were a few children in the hut, a great many adults. One couple saw the new boy enter. The woman dropped a pot she was cleaning. Her husband looked up from the empty pipe he was turning in his hands. Together they ran to embrace the child.

He didn't know them.

He stayed in the hut for another month. Christmas came and passed, a melancholy event despite attempts to brighten the hut and make the children's festival, at least, a joy-filled time.

January was cold and damp, wet snow fell and was packed onto frozen dirt around the huts. The days were short and dim, the nights long and black. Small-scale factory work had been initiated in the camp. Westerbork was not a rest camp, nor a winter resort. All inhabitants must earn their keep.

Still, transports left each week for the East. New residents arrived at the camp: mostly Dutch Jews but also a scattering of Germans, and also occasional Turks, Gypsies, others.

The final transport of January included the complete population of the hut where the new boy lived. Everyone was allowed to carry a small sack or suitcase. They got to ride on a train. It was really not uncomfortable. The new boy was quite thrilled. Perhaps they were going to the German fatherland. He was a pure Aryan. He would be going home.

Word was passed of the destination of the train. Not Germany after all. Poland. Some of the people in the car had heard of the place they were going. It was called Auschwitz. No one knew just what they would do at Auschwitz in Poland—probably they would be put to work. The German war effort needed more and more production, and this in the face of military setbacks and heavy bombing raids.

Yes, surely they would be put to work. Even the children, the new boy thought. Well then, he could make a contribution to the Cause. If only he were a few years older—some of the soldiers they saw nowadays were hardly more than boys themselves. If only he could become a soldier! Well, at least he could work in the factory at Auschwitz in Poland helping to make supplies for the Reich's heroic soldiers to use against their decadent enemies. That was something he could be proud of even if it wasn't as good as being a soldier himself.

Tara brought a pot of coffee from the kitchen and poured cups for herself, Buddy Satvan and Willy Albertson. "I suppose I'm being very unliberated," she said, "but in my own house I figure it's a good-host-personly thing to do."

They all had to laugh at that, and then Willy Albertson, Adam's apple bobbing, said, "It's good to have some coffee before you go to a meeting with Arch Cantrowicz and Burt Bahnson. You know how they are with the bottle!"

They had another laugh, then Tara said, "Well, I think we should prep ourselves for them up here"—she tapped her temple—"as well as in our bloodstreams. Burt's a good editor, but Cantrowicz has him under his thumb. And I don't trust *that* guy as far as I could throw Grant's Tomb."

"Don't be such a gloomy gus, Tara," Buddy responded. "Arch is a good fellow despite his faults. Besides, everything seems to be going so well now for a change. I'm sure it has to be all right."

Willy took a sip of hot, black coffee. "That's right. I guess it is. Not that I really understand everything that happened down there in Virginia. Do you think one of you could go over it again for me? I was sitting up here in New York working on the strip, when first I got this strange phone call from Buddy, and next thing I knew you were both back in town. So I left Ivy to finish the new inks. And—"

"And here we are." Tara rattled a spoon in her saucer, picking it up and gesturing with it. "Buddy turned up and proved, once and for all, that he and that beast Washburn are two separate men."

"But then I'd think they would have kept Buddy in the booby hatch—uh, sorry, Buddy—and turned Washburn loose. Not the other way round. Wasn't Buddy the one with the gun in his hand when the cops arrived? I mean, after Oskar Schrieber got offed? So how come they kept Washburn and turned Buddy loose? I mean, not that I'm not glad you're out, Buddy, you understand."

Buddy grunted. "Sure, uh, sure. Yes. But you see, Washburn had been both himself and me. So had I, in fact, And—"

"I'm sorry, I just can't follow that."

"Well, kind of like Diamond Sutro and Arnaud Subhuti and that maniac Renaldo Warbuckle."

"But that's a comic strip, for cryin' out loud!"

"I know. I didn't mean it was exactly, uh, the same. But anyhow, everybody thought we were different personalities in the same body. And that was the *body* that had the smoking gun in, uh, its hand. Washburn and I kept cycling in and out of phase. But whoever it was, whichever personality, you see, it was still *that body* the judge ordered locked up.

"And I'm not that body. Not anymore."

"Yeah. Okay, I guess." Willy rubbed a long finger against the side of his thin nose. "And all of this business about outer space and electric people—what's that all about?"

Tara broke in. "Let's leave that aside for now. It was obvious to Dr. Ettmann that Buddy was *not* his patient. He checked with the court, and they said it would be okay until they settled things finally, to let Buddy go free. Provided he wouldn't travel any place other than New York to do his work, or back to Prince Morton County. And I had to promise to stay with him and take responsibility for him."

"I appreciate that, Tara. It's a real help."

"But—what about this business of changing from one to the other? Like Diamond Sutro. How about that, Buddy, Tara?"

Buddy shrugged. "I don't know. I haven't changed any more. Not since what happened, uh, happened. And neither has Roland Washburn. Last I knew he hadn't, anyway. So maybe we're permanently split. I don't think Dr. Ettmann would like that idea. But I do. A lot!"

"Okay, I'll take it on faith, what I don't understand. Which is most of it." Willy looked at his watch. "We ought to be leaving pretty soon."

Tara stood up and began gathering cups. "Before we go, Willy, I want you to tell Buddy everything you told me earlier. Buddy, you'll see your old friend Archibald Cantrowicz isn't quite the innocent boy you think he is."

"I never said he was." Buddy shook his head. "He couldn't be and run the syndicate the way he does. It's a tough, competitive business!"

Tara snorted. "Sure it is. But there's such a thing as ethics, even in this business. Or there ought to be. There's such a thing as minimal human decency. And your so-called friend Cantrowicz—oh, you tell him, Willy."

Albertson leaned forward earnestly and poked Buddy's round, fleshy knee with a long, hard finger. "Cantrowicz is dropping you. Unless you can maneuver him out of it, he's going to take *Diamond Sutro* away from you. He already offered me the job. Or rather, had Burt Bahnson do it for him. I told him no, and he said he'd get somebody else and fire us both. He said maybe he'd give the strip to Ivy Lawton."

"Ivy?" Buddy's eyebrows shot upward. "She's good but she's just a beginner. What's she ever written? Is he going to buy outside scripts and give 'em to Ivy to draw up? I mean—"

Willy shook his head. "Whatever the details."

"But why? Tara, Willy, why? We've been keeping the strip going even while I was away. You told me we've been picking up papers—and most strips are losing nowadays. Now that I'm back we should do better than ever!"

"It's the TV money, Buddy." Willy Albertson stood up and walked across the thinly carpeted floor. He stopped and looked out the window, down into West Seventy-third Street. Then he looked around at the others.

Tara had finished what she was doing, and sat opposite Buddy. She was holding his hands in hers. "It's the old story, Buddy. You know. The Katzenjammer Kids. Siegel and Shuster. Creators aren't anybody special, they're just talent that you hire and fire."

"I don't—I still don't see—I mean, sure, let's do the TV deal. That's grand. We'll reach a bigger audience than ever. Can't you just see it—maybe Paul Newman or somebody as Arnaud Subhuti. *Parama!* Turn loose the special effects crew!"

"No, Buddy." Tara turned desperately away. "You explain Willy, the way you did to me."

Albertson came back from the window and stood over uddy and Tara, his lanky form looking awkward as ever. ccording to Burt Bahnson and Cantrowicz both, the TV eople are scared of you, Buddy. Not you personally. They're ared of publicity. You know how goosey TV is about anying controversial. They love *Diamond Sutro,* and they're hot r a two-part movie and a regular series for sure if the movie raws flies."

He shoved his hands into pockets in his baggy, pleat-topped ousers, then pulled them out again exposing an inch of ocket cloth and squatted on the rug beside Buddy and Tara that their eyes were all at one level. "Your name is tied in ith this Schrieber killing and Roland Washburn and his scist bunch, and the TV people are frightened of getting ny kind of flak, any bad publicity, because of you.

"So Cantrowicz wants to dump you to get the TV money. e doesn't have anything against you, you're just in his way so u're goin' to get run over by a steamroller if you won't move ide!"

Satvan withdrew his hands from Tara Sakti's and rose slow- to stand near Willy. "I see." He shook his head. "I didn't nderstand. But now I do." He looked sadly at the others. Well, I guess all we can do is go over there and try to talk him ut of that."

"Fat chance," Albertson grunted.

"Willy," Buddy said, "is Tara included in this? No, never ind, don't even tell me. I want her there. Tara, will you come long and participate in this so-called meeting?"

She grinned and slipped her arm through his.

At the syndicate offices they found Arch Cantrowicz and urt Bahnson waiting for them. Burt jumped out of his seat nd threw his arm around Buddy's shoulders. "Glad to see ou, Buddy. Man, you're looking fine! They couldn't knock e spunk out of our old Buddy, anybody can see that!"

Cantrowicz leaned across his desk to shake Buddy's hand. Delighted to see you, Satvan. I have to say, it's remarkable the ay you've kept up your work, hospitalized and all, emarkable. I suppose Tara and Willy get part of the credit,

and that little girl, what's her name? That little inker that Wil
found. Very talented kid. Bright future. What's her name
Buddy waited until Cantrowicz released his hand, the
found a chair and sat down. The others had already done s
"I came in to see you because Tara said you'd called th
meeting. It's good to be back, and—Burt—maybe we can g
together and talk about the upcoming sequences in the strip."
Bahnson looked uncomfortable.

"Satvan, you've made an outstanding contribution
Cantrowicz interjected. "I think your going to go on to c
even greater things, that's why I'm so pleased that you're o
of the hospital. I'd like you to work up some new proposa
and submit them to Burt. You'll have the full backing of th
office."

"Proposals?" Buddy asked.

"Of course." Cantrowicz leaned back in his chair, tugged a
the metal door-pull on his cabinet, brought out a bottle an
glasses. "Frankly, Satvan, I'm afraid that *Diamond Sutro's* bee
getting a little bit stale lately. Nothing serious. But I'm sur
you can do better. Maybe you've just outgrown the strip, eh
But I'm sure you can do better, You ought to take a little re
now and come up with some new ideas, talk 'em over wit
Bahnson, see what you can work up."

"I thought you said *Diamond Sutro* was doing well. Haven
we been picking up circulation?"

"Well, yes, it's been doing well. But it's kind of stale, too. S
we're taking you off it and we'll give you something else to d
You won't find yourself on the street, we don't operate tha
way."

"You're firing me?"

"Of course not! One of the leading comic-strip talents in th
country! Creator, writer, artist—we wouldn't fire a triple
threat man! Besides, you're on contract to us, with option
We need what you have to offer, Satvan."

"Then you're not firing me. Okay, I'll go on with *Diamon
Sutro.*"

Cantrowicz shook his head slowly from side to side, a look o
consternation on his face. "For a smart man, you sometime
act remarkably dense, you know that? I said we'd find some
thing for you to do, but not *Diamond Sutro.* I told you the stri

s getting very stale lately, it's dying on the vine. We have to escue it before people notice. But you can do something else or us. There's work for you. Doesn't—Burt, doesn't Jensen, lidn't Jensen say he was looking for an assistant on *Big Pro?*)on't you think Satvan has the versatility to do a sports strip? I hink he could do it. Keep Jensen's name on it, of course."

"What are you talking about?" Buddy choked. "You want ne to become Walter Jensen's *assistant*? I created my own eature, it's one of the biggest successes the syndicate has, it's ;aining papers every quarter, and you're squashing me down o assistant on a damned beefcake feature?"

"Calm down, Satvan!" Cantrowicz commanded. He stood ıp, tossed off his drink and refilled his glass. The room was ompletely silent except for the breathing of the people present. Finally Cantrowicz said, "I don't know why it is that ou comic-strip people are all so paranoid. I've never seen nything like it in any other field. You always think some-ody's out to screw you. What's the matter with comic-strip eople?"

"This all has to do with the TV money, doesn't it?" Buddy lemanded. "You're scared stiff that my name is controversial o you want me off the strip, is that it? It is, isn't it?" He turned ngrily to Burt Bahnson. "Is that what's going on?"

Burt reddened. "Well, there was some talk. I mean, nobody eally said anything, but out at the studio they all kind of, ah, mplied. . . ." He shook his two hands as if he'd just discovered hat the towel dispenser in the washroom was empty.

"I'll tell you what." Arch Cantrowicz came over and leaned lown to put his face near Buddy's, his left hand clutching the rm of Buddy's chair, his right holding his drink. "You're eally being an unreasonable, stiff-necked son of a bitch, you now. I'm really trying to help you and you show no gratitude vhatsoever. Now look."

He leaned back, straightened up. "If it's so damned im-ortant to you, you can keep doing *Diamond Sutro*. You can ust ghost the thing, we'll say that you're retiring, Willy takes ver the strip and signs it, and you go on helping him out the vay you've been. Christ, he's been doing the strip for months ıow, he deserves his name on it.

"Here, Bahnson." He turned from Buddy. "Go get that

stupid PR bitch what's-her-name in here. We're going to g
out a press release on *Diamond Sutro.* Get that dumb what'
her-name."

Bahnson disappeared, then returned with a young woma
in tow.

"Yes, what's your name?" Cantrowicz demanded.

"L-Loris Kern."

"Okay, Loris. This is Buddy Satvan. He used to do *Diamon*
Sutro for us. He's retiring from the strip as of today because o
reasons of personal health. Here's his assistant, he's takin
over the strip, do a release and get some photos to go with i
We need it today.

"Okay, everybody out of here! Get out of my office, I'm
very busy man today, I have a lot of other things to do than t
worry about paranoid pencillers. Hah! I like that! Paranoi
pencillers! I said get out of here, all of you."

"Worthy of Spiro T. Who," Bahnson growled in an un
dertone. Then, aloud, "Come, we can use my office. Loris
maybe you'd better go get a copy of our boilerplate on Budd
and on the Sutro feature and we'll go over it, update the cop
and such."

Before they got to Buddy's office Tara Sakti said, "Buddy
are you going to let them do this to you?"

He grinned bitterly. "Maybe I should go home and work u
my serious strip, you remember I was telling you about it? Bu
I hate getting shoved out this way. Damn it, those syndicat
contracts, they own the strip, they own the characters, I'n
lucky they let me continue even with my name off it."

"Don't you even think you ought to check with your lawyer
Buddy? You're not going to give up without a fight?"

"I don't know." He shook his head and studied the toes o
his shoes.

They sat around Bahnson's crowded desk, Loris Kern th
last to arrive. "I've glanced over the boiler plate," sh
announced. "It looks very good, actually. Might need a littl
updating, though. I'll need more bio on you, Mr. Albert
son—"

"Willy."

"And, ah, Mr. Satvan, it gives a pretty complete rundown o
you from, ah, 1946 onward, I guess that will do. Just doesn'

give your place of birth and early childhood. You weren't *born* in 1946, were you? That would make you, ah—"

"No. I immigrated."

"Oh." A moment's silence. "I didn't know that. That adds an interesting touch. America the land of opportunity, I lift my torch beside the golden door, that kind of thing. That's really very interesting." She had uncapped a felt-tip pen and was scribbling notes. "You came here from—?"

"I don't think that's very—I'd really prefer"—he made an odd sound and then resumed— "I came from Germany."

"Oh, you were a war orphan? That's very sad. A German war orphan."

"Dutch."

"Oh, but you spent the war in Germany. That must have been very—"

"I spent the war in Holland. Most of the war. And in Poland. I came here by way of Germany." He stood up. "Tara, can we go back to your place? Please!"

Willy Albertson rose to his feet and took a gangling step. "I'll bring you up to date on the strip, Miss Kern. Or do you prefer Miz? And you need some background on me, huh? Listen, this is a noisy place and Burt needs his office back. Let's just the two of us go someplace and find a nice quiet bar where we can talk and I'll tell you everything you need to know.

"Buddy's gone now anyhow. Come on."

Back at Tara's apartment Buddy roughed out panel breakdowns while Tara made dinner. They had a cocktail together, then a light supper with quiet music playing. Afterward they took a walk in the neighborhood window-shopping, contemplating and rejecting all the movie shows nearby, finally returning to the apartment.

In bed still later Tara said, "I didn't know about that, Buddy."

"About what?"

"About the war and all."

"You're too young to remember."

"I mean, about you, and being from Europe and everything."

Buddy stared into the darkness for a long time. Finally he

said, "I don't really remember it. I was very young. And it isn't very relevant to, ah, to the here-and-now. All right?"

"All right, Buddy, I'm sorry I pried."

"No, it's all right. I'd just rather not—" He waved a hand in the darkness.

Tara caught the hand as it fluttered overhead and guided it downward and under the covers of the bed.

17. Auschwitz

LATER he could not recall how long the train trip had taken. They were locked into their coaches and told to settle themselves for a lengthy journey. The train stood a long time before it began to roll, and when it did the motion became a steady rhythmic swaying that lulled him into periods of half sleep in which fantasies arose and mingled with his surroundings to form partly chosen dreams.

Then he would awaken at some lurch or bump of the coach, the dream images and the real jumbled hopelessly. He would look around, rub his eyes, then settle back into a renewed doze and wander away into the other world of intermixed randomness and choice.

Hours? Surely more. Surely the journey lasted for many days, perhaps for weeks.

It was a strange experience for the new boy: blond, blue-eyed, of pure Aryan stock, he was taken in tow by a couple of *Weissjuden* from Amsterdam, Mijnheer and Misiz van der Roest. It was very confusing. At first they insisted that he was a boy named Pieter. He knew he was not, had never heard of this Pieter whom the *Weissjuden* had known both in Amsterdam and in Westerbork.

Finally they accepted his true identity. He was still not happy about having to travel with them, but at least they were of Aryan stock themselves, even though of suspect sympathies.

He appealed to the train guards several times. They were guards from the camp at Westerbork who traveled along with the transport. Some of them listened patiently to his story, others were less willing to hear, but none of them offered help.

There was little food on the train, very little drinking water, few sanitary facilities. Each passing day the cars became stuffier and more uncomfortable.

Finally the train pulled to a halt. The train guards from Westerbork were removed and replaced by black-uniformed *Schutzstaffel* armed with pistols and truncheons.

Misiz van der Roest tried to envelop the new boy, as if she could absorb him through her dress into her lessened flesh, but he squirmed and shoved his way to freedom, ran to the end of the car and stood at attention in front of the *Schutzstaffel.*

The man looked down at him, seemingly puzzled by the boy's approach. In German that he had practiced in his mind since Westerbork the boy started to explain that he was an Aryan erroneously shoved in among these Jews, and should be removed and returned to the fatherland.

The *Schutzstaffel* studied the boy, reached down and lifted the front of his blouse, drew out of his waistband a tattered, brightly colored magazine. The *Schutzstaffel* turned a few pages, looking at the pictures, then with a snarl of rage tore the magazine to shreds. He raised his truncheon and swung it at the boy's head.

The moment seemed to be frozen for the boy.

The face of the *Schutzstaffel* came into focus, contorted with rage: He had a long, pointed nose, high, protruberant ears, and the snarl that twisted his lips exposed glistening canine teeth. The truncheon was moving through the air, coming toward the boy. It moved with a majestic deliberation so that he could make out every feature on it, the leather wrist strap, the tough, textured surface; yet he could not dodge out of its way.

He heard the woman scream. She might have been Misiz van der Roest. Then there were other voices, angry shouts of men, screams of more women, cries of Jewish children.

The truncheon came closer and closer, yet seemed to be

moving ever more slowly. The new boy saw everything from a greater and greater distance. He was fading, sliding away from the truncheon and the *Schutzstaffel* and the shreds of the torn magazine, sliding away from the transport train. Everything was growing tiny and remote and his ears no longer brought him the sounds of screams or cries but only a high ringing.

The baby awoke on his mama's lap. He knew he was a baby, he couldn't even talk yet, but he knew how to walk and he could understand a lot of things. His head hurt and his mama was trying to comfort him and to clean a place on the side of his head where it hurt very badly.

He knew they were on a train. He could hear the click of its iron wheels on the rails and the occasional screech of its whistle. He started to move and he saw his mama's face coming down toward him, tears running from her eyes, and he heard her saying *sssh, sssh* to him. He liked trains and it might be fun some day, when he was a big man, to drive one.

Machines were so splendid, so powerful. The master of machines was a splendid man indeed. Not like his papa. Not that his papa was other than splendid either, with his big mustache and his beautiful carven pipe, but a cheese seller—what was a cheese seller as against a master of machinery!

He lay in his mama's lap until the train stopped, and a man in a black suit shouted something and everybody climbed off the train. He saw his mama and papa reaching for luggage, old tattered suitcases, but the man in black shouted, *"Nein, Nein,"* at them, and they left their belongings and simply walked from the train. His mama tried to carry the baby, but he knew how to walk and struggled from her arms and trotted along, looking at the train seats, holding his mama's hand.

Outside of the train they walked in a big yard. They stood in front of a man with a black suit and a shining glass in one eye. The man wore white gloves on his hands and had a stick. He looked at the people as they lined up, sometimes poking his stick in their chests, and pointing, to this side, to that side, to this side, to that side. The baby went with his father.

They marched for a little while. The baby thought that was fun except he felt cold and tired, and he was happy when they stopped. People came and made them all get undressed, and then they all had their hair shaved and they all took showers and people gave them new clothes, suits with black and gray stripes, and everybody had to get dressed again.

A strange man tried to help the baby get dressed, and he realized that the man was his father, his mustache had been shaved off and the baby began to cry.

They went into a big building and everybody started to look around. People talked to each other a little. There were wooden beds stacked up three high. Every bed already had somebody on it. Some beds had two or three people on them. They were all dressed in gray and black stripes, and a lot of them were very thin. Some of them hardly moved at all.

The baby's papa found a place for them on a bed that only had one person on it. Now it had three. The baby went to sleep.

In the morning everybody had to go outside and line up. It was very early and very cold out. The baby looked around and saw that there were no other children near him, and no women, only men. A man in a black suit came over and shouted at Papa. Papa started to answer and the man hit him with something and papa fell down. The baby was frightened and stood watching with wide eyes.

The man in the black suit started kicking and punching Papa. He would kick him as long as he lay on the ground and when he tried to get up the man would punch him again until he fell down. Finally Papa stopped moving.

The baby started to cry. Then the man wearing the black suit bent over and picked him up. The man reached into a pocket of his suit and brought out a piece of bread and gave it to the baby. Then, while the baby munched on the bread, the man carried him to another place where there were lots of children and a few grown-up women.

The man put down the baby and talked to one of the women. Some of the other children came running over and grabbed his piece of bread. The baby started to cry again, but the other children paid no attention to him. They struggled and fought over the piece of bread.

After that the baby lived with the other children. The women helped them to play games every day and taught them things. Every afternoon they were allowed to sit together in the courtyard and watch and listen. An orchestra would set up chairs and instruments and play music in the courtyard every day.

Sometimes the baby thought he could hear other sounds going on, people shouting and screaming, but the music was louder and much prettier than the screaming so he listened to the music. It helped him forget that he was always hungry and almost always cold.

People arrived and left each day. There were buildings nearby that somebody said were showers. The baby thought that a warm shower would feel nice, but he was not picked to go. Mostly grown-ups got to take showers, but some children did too, usually those who had grown too weak from hunger or sickness to care for themselves. People who took showers never came back, and the baby wondered where they went after they took their showers.

There was another building nearby, with very tall smokestacks that never stopped smoking. When the smoke blew toward the place where the baby lived, it smelled like cooked meat and made the baby very hungry. He thought that maybe meat was being cooked for the children and the grown-ups in the striped clothing, but they never got meat to eat, only bits of bread and thin vegetable soup with sometimes a piece of potato in it.

At times the baby had very strange dreams. Every day he heard voices from a loudspeaker and everybody knew what to do because the voices told them. Sometimes in his dreams he would hear the voices too, and the courtyard music and the screaming. Other times he would see faces, especially his papa's face and the face of the man in the black suit who kicked and punched his papa and then gave the baby bread. The man had a line on his forehead and a funny-shaped ear. The baby saw that line and the funny-shaped ear in his dreams often, and saw the man punching and kicking papa and then giving him a piece of bread.

The baby used to look at the other children and at himself. He would roll up his sleeve or a pants leg and look at his arm or his leg. He felt that he was growing very strange. His arms and legs were very thin. They had been thin for as long as he could remember but they were much thinner now. His elbows and knees stood out like big lumps.

He was weak and sleepy most of the time, and lay on his bunk a lot. When he went outside to listen to the courtyard music he saw that the skies were not so gray anymore. He was not as cold as he had been. Some people said that spring was coming.

One day he was awakened by a lot of noise, loud bangings and thumpings coming from far away. There was a lot of excitement all around, people standing in groups and talking and waving their hands, men in black uniforms running and shouting. Then most of the men in black uniforms ran away. The baby heard the voice from the loudspeaker shouting, saying the things that it said every time that people had to go into the courtyard.

All of the children who could still move crawled off their bunks and started for the doorway of their big room. The women who took care of them went along, one in front and one in back. The baby could see the front of the line. He saw a man in striped clothing run up to the woman and shout at her. He heard her answer, then the man said something again.

The woman turned around and started pushing the children back to their bunks, shouting at them to be quick, quick, and to be quiet, very quiet. The baby crawled into his bunk and lay still and quickly fell asleep.

When he woke up there was a strange man wearing a brown uniform sitting beside him. The man had been feeling the baby's chest. When the baby woke up and looked at him the man smiled and picked up a bowl of soup and began to feed the baby. He ate some soup, then looked around and saw a lot of men in uniforms he did not know. They had strange looks on their faces and some of them were crying. They had a big pot of soup and bowls and were feeding the children who were still alive.

* * *

In the place called Sravasti the Yakshis Nanda, Asoka and Kalinga watched the confrontation between Roland L. K. Washburn and Buddy Satvan. The two men now understood the nature of the scanner/transporter devices. Washburn—*this* Washburn—had been scanned and transported from the violent ward of the Morton Prince Memorial Institute. He was the first human to reach Sravasti; his recollections were those he had formed up to the moment of transit and those of his experiences on Sravasti.

Satvan was a later duplicate. As Washburn had been scanned and returned to earth—arriving there as Buddy Satvan—so he had been scanned and transported from earth yet again. *This* Ole Buddy lacked the memories of Washburn's experiences on Sravasti since Buddy's return to earth. But he possessed recollections of his activities on earth which Washburn lacked.

They stood facing each other near the entrance to the building which gave access to the great machines and to the massive components stored within the core of the artificial world.

"Well," Washburn asked sardonically, "how are things on dear terra firma, Satvan?"

Buddy explained his experiences in Virginia. Then he said that he had returned to New York to work while Washburn remained under the care of Dr. Noble St. Vincent Ettmann. No point in going into his problems with the syndicate.

Washburn stood for a moment as if pondering. Finally he said, "So I remain locked up on earth. Yet here I am free, and I could return to earth if I chose. Or—send a duplicate of myself, anyway. I could"—his face brightened—"I could send an army of Roland L. K. Washburns to earth. I could monitor them through the star people's scanner, send instructions with each additional duplicate of myself. I could receive reports by summoning—no! I wouldn't want a lot of Washburns on Sravasti. One führer is enough. But I can still monitor by scanner and communicate by duplicate.

"Imagine! An entire army of Roland Washburns! Hard men, stern, disciplined, ruthless! In a few days we could take over Prince Morton County! Soon, all of Virginia! Then America! Eventually the world! The world will be mine!"

Buddy looked at the Yakshis. They stood in their place, watching the two men, taking no part in their conversation.

Buddy looked back at Roland Washburn. There was an air of exaltation about him. Buddy said, "Roland, uh, there's one problem to your plan. Uh—Roland?"

Washburn looked at Satvan as if called unwillingly from a favorite dream. "A problem?"

"Well, if I understand our situation right—I mean the things that Dr. Ettmann says—"

"Ettmann, that fool! Probably a Jew as well! But what does he say?"

"Why, ah, even if a whole army of you return to earth . . . well, you see, some of them will be me not you. You see what I mean? And this third personality, whatever his name is, the engineer . . . some of them will be him, too. We'll be one-third Roland and one-third Buddy and one-third, ah—"

"Auburn Sutro!" Washburn looked thunderstruck. He held his head in his hands, then said, "I think I'm going to ask these weirdo's to hook me up with that computer of theirs again. Maybe I can work something out." He gave Buddy a look half sneering, half patronizing. "Good of you to bring that to my attention. You have a use after all."

He started toward the building. "Are you coming along, Satvan?"

"I think I'll stay out here for a while. I'm—a little confused myself. I want to think about things." Buddy watched Roland Washburn disappear into the low structure. The Yakshis seemed hesitant, hovering between the two men, but finally drifted after Washburn as well.

Buddy sat heavily on the ground, settling himself cross-legged with his elbows on his knees. What would Diamond Sutro do in a situation like this? Buddy couldn't decide. Probably use some mysterious power like the Veneration of the True Doctrine. Or the Real Teaching of the Great Way. Buddy ran through a catalog of the cartoon hero's abilities. The Convocation of the Assembly? The Integral Principle of Perfect Tranquility? The Delusion of Appearances?

What could an ordinary little man do? The universe itself was imperiled. His own psyche—for all that he *felt* like a normal person—had been somehow shattered in the distant past. The scanner/transporter had created duplicates of him and there were now at least four of them in various places, either sliding in and out of their various *personae* or . . . or stabilized as Buddy or as Roland or as Auburn Sutro.

He tried to sort them out. There were a Satvan and a Washburn here on Sravasti. There might be another pair back on earth. And the other self, Auburn Sutro the engineer? *Were* there any of him around? Or was he submerged in each Buddy and each Roland, likely to emerge at any time, displacing another personality, sending him tumbling back into the black limbo of psychic extinction.

It did sound like a problem for Diamond Sutro. Too bad he existed only in the funnies.

Buddy sighed. He leaned back, thinking for a moment about Tara Sakti as well. Could he ever get back to her on earth? No, he shook his head: if he used the scanner/transmitter it would only place a duplicate of him on earth. And there was one already there. And *he* would still be *here,* on Sravasti!

But he could use the machines to bring a duplicate of Tara to Sravasti. Would she be only an image, or would she be real, he wondered. Well—she'd be as real as *he* was. He kept thinking of himself as the original person, but in fact his real original was the Roland Washburn still locked up in Prince Morton County, Virginia.

That man had been duplicated onto Sravasti, and that was the Roland he'd been talking with only a few minutes ago. And *that* one had been duplicated back onto earth, transforming into the Buddy who had traveled from Virginia to New York. And *that* Buddy—his head was beginning to spin!—was the one who had been duplicated back here to make *him.*

He was, therefore, a third, ah, level duplicate of himself. Yet he had a full set of memories stretching back to—to what? He pressed his hands to his eyes where he sat, trying to remember. The farthest back he could cast his recollection was a chaotic sequence of events in Europe in 1945 or '46. Soldiers and doctors sorting people out, some of the people simply wandering away, others being herded into camps to await transportation to their homelands.

The children presented a particular problem. Most of them were orphans. Some were so young—or so shattered by the ar—that they could hardly speak, didn't know where their omes were or even who they were. The lucky ones were dopted by European families or taken along by soldiers oing home. The unlucky ones wandered like animals, living n the offal of war-crushed cities.

He had been lucky. No parents were found, no family at all. Ie didn't know his name. He did not speak. But the women ho had been in charge of the children's block said that he was utch. He was sent back to Holland, adopted out of an rphanage by an American soldier on his way back to his ountry. He was taken to America, loved, fed, raised.

His body grew normally—but inside his head there crawled he tortured psyches of four crippled children, four fragmented personalities.

The original had been Pieter Wachtel, the son of bourgeois msterdam booksellers, the foster-child of cheese merchants, he ward of a concentration camp cynic and intellectual. This ad been the first personality to submerge, the most deeply uried, the one least often seen, the one most thoroughly idden. No one knew Pieter Wachtel anymore.

Then had come the strange trio: the artist, the führer, the nining engineer. He who could summon the supernatural ero to save him from his oppressor; he who could triumph ver oppression by building the implements to destroy or to lee.

Nor was that the end, for of the three, he—Buddy Satvan—ad created no mere adventurer, no detective or spy or thlete, but another triplicated personality, its aspects orresponding to the three fragments of the original hattered personality, its images corresponding to the three ivals as they might have been seen in the distorting, xaggerating mirrors of a carnival house.

That meant there must be some crossover among the three najor personalities, else how could Buddy Satvan mirror both he führer and the engineer in the alter egos of Diamond utro? Somehow there was a sharing of awareness, had been or many years. At least since the creation of Diamond Sutro.

If that was so, perhaps the three major personalities *could* eintegrate themselves—if they agreed to do so. But would hey agree? Roland L. K. Washburn had expressed violent

disdain for the decadent, pandering Buddy Satvan. Budd
despised the militant, ambitious Washburn. And Aubur
Sutro? He was the least communicative, the greatest myster
of the three.

Buddy squeezed his eyes together, closing out the worl
Then he opened them again, gazing abstractedly into the sk
of Sravasti, studying the writhing, amber-edged region o
burning space that must be overcome if only the problems o
the shattered personality could first be solved.

He blinked, rubbed his eyes, looked again and again to wa
in astonishment at what he saw.

18. Beyond Hathor

"YOU see it, Aphrité?"

Diamond Sutro pointed ahead of them, through th
blackness of the intergalactic void. Sources of sidereal ligh
were spaced equally in all directions about them, except fo
the flame-edged gash that ravened and tore at the very fabri
of the cosmos. From that quarter of space came nothing at all.

Aphrité Anubis, the most beautiful woman in the univers
trembled within the mighty arms of Dr. Goodlaw, He Wh
Proclaims the Truth. Together they had traveled the in
credible distances, the uncountable parsecs, from the transsc
lar planet Hathor, propelled by the Superiority of Un
formulated Truth, protected from the frigid vacuum and th
searing radiation of space by the Unreality of Phenomena
Distinctions.

"Diamond Sutro," Aphrité whispered in awe, "never have
imagined such a sight. It's—it's indescribable. I can see th
strange tetrahedral construct ahead of us, suspended b
delicately balanced gravitic beams in a state of perfect stasis a
the ultimate center of the universe.

"The construct which you told me is called Sravasti i
covered with a shimmering globe of invisible monatomic film

hat reflects the glories of the distant galaxies and nearly azzles my eyes. Beneath the shell I can see a few clouds loating above ground covered with snow or vegetation. Most f the world is white, with a strange suggestion of violet to it.

"Weird creatures wander the face of this planet, but there is single building of strange design. This must be the hand-work of the great race you have described to me, O Man of ustice!"

Diamond Sutro nodded in agreement, for the world was recisely as she had described it. Now he dropped feetfirst, he lovely Aphrité still in his arms. His feet met the im-enetrable barrier of film which protected the atmosphere of he planet, but at the precise moment that his golden boots ouched the shell he murmured the secret formula of Free-lom from Characteristic Distinctions and felt his very atoms lissolve. Thus he and his precious burden Aphrité Anubis lipped through the barrier and drifted downward, sur-ounded by a nimbus of pure White Light.

They landed softly on the lichen-covered surface of ravasti. Aphrité laughed the breathless laughter of relief. "I ever dreamed that I might have such an experience. Diamond Sutro, there can be no other like you in all of reation!"

"Probably not," Diamond Sutro replied, "unless in the in-inity of being we are all duplicated."

"No, I am certain." The gorgeous daughter of the world's vickedest scientist ran her fingers over the firm muscles of the vhite-suited hero. "There can be none other such."

"Well, enough of these pleasantries," Diamond Sutro esponded. "We must be about our business." He pushed her, gently but with the strength of the Righteous, to a safe dis-ance. While she stood in speechless admiration he raised the alisman Vajrachedika high above his head and spoke the nystical word that brought about the always startling trans-ormations such as that from the scientist Arnaud Subhuti to he Man of Righteousness, Diamond Sutro.

Parama!

Once more the flash, the scent, the mystification. But this ime, to Aphrité Anubis' wondering eyes there appeared not Arnaud Subhuti but a person already familiar to her, a some-

time ally of her sinister father Professor Anubis: Renald
Warbuckle!

Aphrité' hand flew to her mouth in astonishment and fea
This was the dreaded Kommandant of the Fraternal Order
the Fylfot, the head of the underground movement
radicals and professional hate mongers who strove tireless
to turn liberty-loving America into the dreaded Fourth Reich

Involuntarily the gorgeous woman shrank from the jac
booted and black-uniformed Kommandant. "Renald
Warbuckle!" she exclaimed helplessly. "But—but where
Diamond Sutro? What has happened? Oh tell me quickl
what has happened?"

For a moment she could see only the cruelty and anim
shrewdness that shone from the beady pig-eyes of the blac
uniformed Kommandant. He ran his hand down the leath
shoulder strap of his iron-studded belt, bringing his fingers
poise restlessly on the massive death's head belt buckle. In h
other hand he held a cruel riding crop that he twitched u
easily against his polished jackboot.

Then, unexpectedly, he began to laugh—nor was it with th
cruel, mocking laughter of the Kommandant which Aphri
had heard before and which had made her shudder with
nameless apprehension. No, it was the warm, sympathet
laughter of Diamond Sutro that she heard. Aphrité peere
deeper into Kommandant Warbuckle's beady eyes and sav
shining behind the sadism and ruthless hatred, a look of kin
understanding that could belong only to Dr. Goodlaw!

"Yes, my little one," the stranger said, "you now know th
secret of both Diamond Sutro's alter egos—a secret shielde
from the eyes of mankind, a secret so powerful, so dangerou
that its revelation to the forces of earthly malignity would hav
results more devastating than a legion of criminal madmen

"For Diamond Sutro is not only Arnaud Subhuti the world
leading scientist—he is also Renaldo Warbuckle, Kom
mandant of the Fraternal Order of the Fylfot! In this guise
can penetrate to the innermost councils of the world's siniste
schemers. Men who would take arms against Arnaud Subhut
—who would flee in terror at the very suggestion of th
approach of Diamond Sutro—welcome Renaldo Warbuck
into the very hearts of their councils."

He paused in his narration to chuckle once more. "You remember the Menace of the Muvian Mutations, my dear? It was Kommandant Warbuckle who was contacted by the master Muvian and who provided the information that permitted Arnaud Subhuti to develop the Anti-Mutation Ray and send those slimy horrors slithering back to their subterranean citadel!

"You recall the Arctic Abomination? It was Renaldo Warbuckle who led a secret expeditionary force of the Fraternal Order of the Fylfot across the gleaming floes to combat that frightful threat! The thugs and hoodlums who make up the Order, the bullies and the criminals who swell its ranks, all thought they were engaged in secret maneuvers, preparations for a clandestine invasion of some helpless fledgling democracy!

"Hence, without the expenditure of a drop of decent red American blood, without the public's even being made aware of the danger which hovered over them for those perilous weeks, the Abomination was wiped from the face of the earth."

The weird apparition—the black-uniformed Kommandant speaking with the voice and the mannerisms of the glorious Diamond Sutro—grinned and chuckled warmly. "At the same time, Aphrité, the ranks of the Order of the Fylfot were decimated. Their plans to overthrow our constitutionally chosen leadership and establish in its place a dictatorial regime were set back by years. As those plans shall be, every time they approach readiness!"

"I do see," Aphrité murmured. "Your methods are as brilliant as your righteousness is firm!"

"Quite," replied the Kommandant, the last traces of Diamond Sutro's manner fading from his presence. "Now, my dear Miss Anubis, I suggest that we proceed with our mission here on Sravasti!"

They strode purposefully in the direction of the Yakshis' low building. From that building a gray-clad figure was running breathlessly toward them.

Buddy Satvan drew up, almost screeching to a halt. "You!" he exclaimed. "But—but you can't be real! You—you're Renaldo Warbuckle! And you—you're Aphrité Anubis!"

"Indeed," the Kommandant responded. "You have identified us correctly."

"But that's impossible! You're characters in the Diamond Sutro strip! I know it! I invented that strip! I created you both I sent you from Mt. Huascaran to the planet Hathor! You can't be here, you don't exist!"

The gorgeous flame-cloaked Aphrité advanced and laid a slim, milk-white hand on Buddy's arm. Inches taller than he she smiled down at him, her vivid ruby-irised eyes boring into his watery gray ones. "We came here from Hathor. Diamond Sutro brought me here, using the Superiority of Unformulated Truth to obliterate the limitations of time and space and the Unreality of Phenomenal Distinctions to protect me from the perils of the journey."

"That's impossible, Aphrité—Renaldo. I never wrote you onto Sravasti! You're both still on Hathor, finishing your work, that is, Arnaud Subhuti's work on ZINGARR! Unless"—a distant look came into Buddy's eyes—"Willy Albertson did a sequence after Hathor. But no, that couldn't be either. He doesn't know about Sravasti. And even if he did, you're just drawings, you're just a comic strip.

"You aren't real! You aren't!"

The Kommandant gestured imperiously. "Of course we are real! Get a grip on yourself, Satvan! We permit you to record our exploits for the enlightment of the world! We even certify to the accuracy of your renditions!"

"Oh, no, you're not going to catch me up on that one!" Buddy shook his head. "That's the Shadow's gimmick. Walter Gibson invented that and they've been using it ever since. I may keep a swipe file for anatomy and things like that, but I don't steal ideas."

Aphrité slid her hand up and down his arm. "The undeniable fact is, we are here."

"How did you know about Sravasti?"

Aphrité looked earnestly into his eyes, one hand clutching his soft gray sleeve. "Arnaud Subhuti completed ZINGARR. He used it to contact the Yakshis. You know the Yakshis. They told him about spaceburn so he used the Vajrachedika amulet to become Diamond Sutro and bring me here. Then he changed again, to Kommandant Warbuckle, so we could fool the führer Washburn.

"But you know the truth, of course, so there's no need to try and fool you, Buddy Satvan!"

"Washburn? Why do you want to fool Washburn?"

"Why, he's a bad actor. All the worst parts of you, Buddy!"

Buddy lowered his head to his hands. "I know, I know. He even tried to pin a murder on me. He killed that other fascist, that Oskar Schrieber, while I was unconscious. Submerged. Then he left me there with the pistol in my hand to take the murder rap."

"No, no, no!" Warbuckle shook his head. "Roland Washburn didn't kill Oskar Schrieber. What a foolish idea! Why do you say such a thing?"

"Because he did it! And then he blamed me, he framed me!"

"He did not do it!"

"I did not do it!"

"Oh—of course not. I know that, too."

"But—but damn it all, how can you say that neither of us killed Oskar Schrieber? The gun was in my hand, there were an office full of witnesses to the killing. It had to be Washburn. Or—or our *other* ego? The engineer? Did Auburn Sutro kill Schrieber?"

Kommandant Warbuckle smiled sardonically, his grin a frightful parody of Roland Washburn's customary expression. "No, no, no." He shook his head once more. "It was none of you three, you three poor fragments who did the killing, it was the parent of you all, the little child parent of you all."

Satvan gaped at Warbuckle, thunderstruck, Aphrité Anubis' presence completely forgotten. Satvan said, "Which child?"

"Pieter Wachtel."

Pieter sat in his secure perch, deep inside his head, deep inside his mind. Let the others take their turns, let them face the problems and suffer the pains. He watched, and waited, and if and when the time came to act, he would act. So far, that time had not come, not in thirty years.

Well, that was all right with Pieter. He was comfortable, he was not unhappy, he merely sat and watched, sat and watched.

Roland L. K. Washburn was running the body now. Decked out in his black uniform with the silver frogging and electric-blue armband, making the leatherwork of his belt and boots and holster creak with every movement. He lounged in the plush chair, its upholstery customized to match the trappings of his uniform, black and silver and electric blue, his feet on the edge of the giant mahogany desk with its similarly matched tooled-leather top. All of them gifts from admirers.

Basically the National Revitalization League had to scrape for every penny, but thanks to a handful of well-placed benefactors there was always enough cash to meet immediate needs. And thanks to those same benefactors the League's führer, Roland L. K. Washburn, was able to make the well-turned, impressive appearance that a great leader needed to present.

He flicked an ash from his custom-rolled cigar, wondered fleetingly whether cigar-smoking was in keeping with his proper image, then decided that it was permissible to let down a little bit here in his own office.

He glanced up. Silhouetted against the glass-topped partitions between the führer's private chamber and the League's somewhat tacky general administrative offices sat his deputy, Oskar Schrieber. A veteran of World War II, Oskar had survived the infamous purge that had followed the war.

Oskar had served with the finest combat units. Wounded by the shrapnel burst that forever altered and scarred his face, seconded to guard duty in the camp at Auschwitz, he had maintained the proud *Schutzstaffel* tradition to the very end.

A fine man.

And now, in the country of his adoption, he had risen to be deputy führer, chief advisor to Roland L. K. Washburn. In an almost spiritual way, he provided a link, a succession of legitimacy, from the old reich to the new. When the League had its day in the land, then would Oskar Schrieber have his vindication!

Pieter Wachtel slept most of the time. Frequently for months on end, sometimes for years—while Roland and Buddy Satvan alternated their period of activity, and occasionally Auburn Sutro surfaced to resume his brilliant if erratic career as a mining engineer.

Now and again Pieter would awaken. When he did, he watched, watched, rarely gave a little nudge to one of the others. He was fairly certain that none of them were aware of him. They knew about each other, Washburn and Satvan did, and despised each other.

Auburn Sutro was a little different.

And Pieter Wachtel was very different.

Now, Washburn's dialogue with Oskar Schrieber piqued Pieter's interest. Somehow Schrieber's very presence sent shudders racing into even Pieter Wachtel's deeply submerged psyche. If he felt threatened he retreated deeper into the safe, warm darkness, the blackness, the nothingness. If he felt safer at the moment he would rise a little, and observe the activity taking place. But he still left the action to Washburn or Satvan or to Auburn Sutro.

Now he gave a little nudge. Roland Washburn would never notice it, but his thoughts and his conversation would follow a line that interested Pieter Wachtel.

Pieter listened.

"You know," Washburn was saying, pausing now and then for a studied puff on his custom-blended cigar, "I value you most for your experience, Schrieber. I have many men more clever than you—no, don't dispute with your führer. I am not insulting your intelligence. But it is not, I assure you, your strongest suit."

He drew himself erect in his chair, sliding his jackbooted feet from desk top to carpet. "You are loyal, and I value that highly, Schrieber. But even loyalty—even loyalty—" He leaned his elbows on the arms of his chair, spread his hands expansively.

"Well, there are easily a score of men in the League whose loyalty, whose dedication, stops little short of the fanatical. That's good, that's good, isn't it? A few score now, a few hundred or a thousand soon. It doesn't require a really massive movement to gain power, does it? A few men, selectively placed, totally dedicated to the Cause, to the Party, to the Leader.

"That's all it takes, eh?"

Oskar Schrieber shifted uneasily in his place. He raised one hand, massaged a deformed ear. "I am in agreement, führer. Totally. But—might I ask, to what point?"

Pieter Wachtel gave another little nudge.

"In the old days, Schrieber," Roland Washburn resumed, "you were totally loyal also, no? To the bitter end? When others ran, you were the last to leave your post, were you not? But I wonder, why did you leave? Why even then? Were you not prepared to fight to the death for those ideals in which you believed?"

Schrieber ducked his head for a moment, then looked his leader squarely in the eye. "It was a difficult decision to make, my führer. To die in the glorious Cause—but it was a lost cause—or to play the coward at the end and for another day to live." He smiled crookedly. "There is even a saying to that effect, is there not? In English?"

Washburn ignored the question. "You had those scars even then, didn't you?" He watched Schrieber nervously touch the deep mark on his forehead. "You did, Oskar. You received your scars honorably in combat, before you became a guard. I wonder—did you ever think about the people you were guarding? Innocent people. Children, even. People you beat and starved and eventually killed. Did you ever think about them? Did they have feelings, as they went to their deaths? Do you think they were capable of fear, pain, grief? Did they feel rage at their slaughterers, or dumb despair? What do you think, Schrieber?"

Oskar Schrieber reddened, face and neck and ears, all except for the long scar that stood out a livid white. He clenched his fists. Roland Washburn and Pieter Wachtel could see the tension in his muscles. Schrieber was not a young man, but he was in good health still.

Pieter pushed Roland Washburn aside and rose to his feet.

"Do you remember any of them, Schrieber? As individuals?" He smiled at the man, a strangely childish smile.

"No, I'm certain you wouldn't. How many hundreds of thousands of people passed through that camp? You couldn't be expected to remember individuals."

"People? Sub-men!" Schrieber ground in response. "I don't understand you, Führer, about remembering. Of course I never thought of them. They were filth. Filthy parasitical scum. Jews and Slavs and Gypsies. And worse, their sympathizers and helpers! They were the ones who sabotaged the glorious war effort! That was our big mistake! We should have purified our own nation, our own people, completely, before our conquests we began! If we had done that we would in a few years have ruled the entire world!

"But we shall have another chance! We shall!"

Pieter Wachtel said, "You don't remember, you couldn't remember them all. No, But—I wonder that you don't remember one little boy. You gave him bread, Schrieber. I could never understand that about you. You beat his father to death before his eyes. His father or—near enough. You kicked him and punched him until he stopped moving. I remember. And then you gave the little boy a piece of bread out of your pocket."

He had his hand on the butt of his pistol, searching Roland Washburn's mind for knowledge of how to use it. A Luger, of course. Safety catch, aim and fire. Very simple.

"Schrieber, there must have been something human left in you. You see, that is what I find so hard to understand. I still do. I still do. That little touch of mercy, that little touch of—almost decency. Like a flaw in a tapestry of perfect evil, lest Satan himself be offended by your perfection."

Schrieber moaned. "I do not—do not understand at all. You must be sick, Führer. Upset by something. Führer. Let me get you help. I'll summon a doctor. I will have someone summon a doctor. Someone from the outer office." He started for the door.

"Stop!"

He turned around. The man behind the desk was pointing his Luger at Oskar Schrieber.

"Still, that act of mercy will have its reward. I had thought of some slow, painful death for you. Something that might begin—just begin, Schrieber, just barely begin—to balance what you did to those thousands and thousands and thousands of people.

"But the piece of bread will have its reward. No long suffering for you, Oskar Schrieber." He clicked off the safety, pointed the Luger at Schrieber's heart.

"This is—some joke, Führer? A test?"

He fired. Schrieber fell.

Pieter Wachtel stepped swiftly around the desk, looked into Schrieber's distorted face. The eyes held puzzlement and pain. "No long suffering," Pieter said again. He pointed the Luger between Schrieber's eyes, pressed its muzzle to the dying man's forehead, fired again.

He stood upright, the smoking weapon hanging limp from his hand, powder burns and spatterings of blood and brain marking his hand and his natty, silver-trimmed black sleeve.

"You killed my daddy! My daddy!" Tears rolled from his eyes. "I want back my mama! Give back my mama! Give back my daddy!" Sobs wrenched his frame. He jumped up and down beside Schrieber's corpse screaming and crying. More screams started to penetrate the inner office from the outer work area.

The door opened and a face appeared, mouth working, eyes wide with shock and terror. Pieter jumped up and down and screamed again as people hesitated in the doorway, starting forward at the sight of Schrieber's body then retreating again when they saw the pistol in Pieter's hand.

He slipped away.

He slipped into the darkness, gladly and gently, like a diver more at home beneath the warm, friendly water than above them. Someone else would have to take over now. Roland Washburn if he had the courage, or else one of the others, Buddy Satvan or Auburn Sutro. Pieter Wachtel sank into warm, comforting darkness.

19. Sravasti

PIETER Wachtel killed Schrieber?"

Renaldo Warbuckle nodded. "That's right. A Dutch boy amed Pieter Wachtel. Maybe he's a man now, maybe still a oy. I don't know. Certainly his chronological age is that of a nan. But I don't know about his experience."

Buddy Satvan frowned, shook his head until the landscape f Sravasti was little more than a chilling purple blur. "Who in God's name is Pieter Wachtel?"

Warbuckle looked concerned. Even though embodied as he Kommandant, his essential identity of Diamond Sutro nanaged to penetrate and to dominate his presence. "You are Pieter Wachtel," Warbuckle said. "So is Roland L. K. Washurn. And Auburn Sutro the mining engineer.

"Pieter Wachtel was the original personality from which ou other three descended. I suppose he is also the personaliy that will be reconstituted if you three ever get back together he way Dr. Noble St. Vincent Ettmann wishes you to. And as he Yakshis and their machines seem to think you'll have to, if ou are to stop the spaceburn from consuming the universe."

Buddy was staggered. "How do you know this? You— ou're just a figment of my imagination!"

"If so, then I suppose I have access to your mind, eh? To verything that is there. And there is enough seepage from ne personality to another—for all that you fragments try to eep yourselves isolated from each other—I suppose I just icked up the data. Is that acceptable, Satvan?"

"I—I don't know. It sounds—I don't know!"

"All right," Warbuckle said, "if you don't like that, how bout this? I used the Incomparable Value of Right Teaching o dispell the Illusion of Ego. Once that was done—by Diamond Sutro, of course, not by Kommandant Warbuckle— achieved the Consummation of Incomparable Enlight-

enment. Do you like that better? Is it more acceptable to you
mind?" Warbuckle grinned wickedly.

"Well—well, what are we going to do? I wish I had some
body here I could rely on. I can trust Tara, but she's on earth."

"Perhaps you ought to consult your other selves?" It was no
Warbuckle but Aphrité Anubis who made the suggestion.

Buddy gave her a look of gratitude. "I have a problem
getting along with Roland. And Auburn Sutro isn't here. Isn'
in Sravasti. But—I'll try it. I'll go back and see Roland
Washburn and try to figure something out."

He took a step, then turned back to face Renaldo
Warbuckle and Aphrité. "Please," Buddy said, "won't you
come along with me. Please!"

They exchanged a look, then both nodded. Together the
three of them walked toward the distant, low building. Buddy
in the center, Aphrité and Renaldo at his sides.

They entered the building, Buddy looking around to see
who was present. He found Roland L. K. Washburn in the
sitting room deeply absorbed in conversation with Auburn
Sutro.

As Buddy and the others entered the room, Auburn and
Roland looked up. The engineer grinned at Buddy. "I'm so
glad to meet you at last! All of these years sharing a body, you
know." He crossed the room and extended his hand, shook
Buddy's warmly, steered him by the elbow to a comfortable
seat that completed the triangle with himself and Roland
Washburn.

"It's really a pleasure," Auburn continued, "finally getting
to know you two fellows face-to-face. Washburn here and I
have been chatting, you know. Waiting for you to come in out
of the cold." He laughed as if he'd made a pleasant little joke,
and Buddy tried to manage a small grin.

Auburn continued again, "Rolly and I have been having a
little political dispute, you know, but he'll see the light eventually. I have faith in his basic decency. And intelligence. And
I'm so glad that you've joined us, Satvan."

Buddy was able only to make an inarticulate sound.

"Listen, Satvan"—Auburn Sutro leaned forward con-
spiratorially—"none of those shadowy Yakshi creatures
around, what do you make of this whole situation? Roland

sees it as a chance to impose his new order or whatever he calls it, on the earth. But I think we'd better apply our energies first to repairing this spaceburn business. Or there'll be no earth to set to order, nor any other world either!"

"Wait, wait," Buddy cried. "It's all too much for me. Look!" He glanced desperately from Auburn Sutro to Roland L. K. Washburn, then back to Sutro. "How did you—he—Auburn, get here? A little while ago, Roland, it was just you and me. Now there are three of us. Did the Yakshis use the machines again to summon Auburn from earth?"

"No," Washburn gritted. "It was my idea. I tried to use the machines to duplicate myself, right here. A kind of experiment. Not that I want a *lot* of Washburns on Sravasti, but I thought I could use one reliable ally.

"Instead—out came Aubnurn Sutro. Some sort of instability, I suppose. I was going to try it again, but then I decided that it would be best not to add to our ranks. That only complicates matters."

"Yes, but you see," the engineer put in, "I've been learning about this multiple personality theory of Dr. Ettmann's. I know it's old hat to you two, but it isn't to me! And it seems to me that we have an opportunity now to get things sorted out. The three of us in actual confrontation. Utterly unprecedented, of course! It will make history. We'll be in all of the literature.

"And more to the point, we should be able to sort out our problems, don't you see?"

"What *I* don't see," Washburn said, "is why we *need* to, whatever, to reintegrate. Now that we have separate bodies, I don't want any part of Buddy Satvan. Sutro, I could use some of your engineering knowledge and intellectual discipline, but I'm willing to forego that. I must preserve the integrity of my personality! It is vital to the Cause!"

"Yes, yes, the Cause, the Cause. But don't you see, Roland—and you too, Buddy—none of us is a complete man. Let us face the facts, however unpleasant. You're a nice enough fellow, Satvan, and talented to boot. But aren't you dreadfully weak? Given excessively to daydream and to drift? Wouldn't you like to regain the missing components of your personality—some strength of purpose, some dynamism?"

He looked back to Washburn. "And you, Roland—you have exactly those characteristics. But there's some stabilizing component missing from you—now, don't be angry! I'm trying to treat you with honesty! Your brand of political fanaticism hardly speaks of a balanced personality."

"Yeah?" Washburn answered angrily. He rubbed a knuckle in his eye, blinked a few times. "Oh yeah," he cried, "well, what about you, you stinky? What about you? What makes you think you're so great, you smarty?"

"I didn't say I was great." Auburn shook his head. "I don't think that I am. Look at me—cool, rational, I suppose introspective. But I have neither Buddy's creativity—despite my inventions, they're really just applications of known technology—nor your emotional force.

"What would I give to feel passion like yours, Roland! Or to know the joy of an imagination like Buddy's! If we can reintegrate ourselves, each will gain what the others have."

"No, I don't want to die!" Washburn screamed. He brushed tears from his face, then gave up and permitted them to flow. "I don't want to die! Only the Cause can save me! I must live for the sake of the holy Cause!"

Buddy Satvan reached forward, took one of Washburn's hands in his two, held the hand, trying to give comfort.

"Exactly," Auburn Sutro murmured from behind Buddy. "But you see, you will not die. None of us will. We will no longer be Auburn Sutro and Buddy Satvan and Roland Washburn, but we will still exist, all of us, as parts of the new, complete man who will emerge."

"Pieter Wachtel," Buddy whispered.

Auburn said, "Eh? Pardon, I couldn't—"

Buddy turned his face upward to where Renaldo Warbuckle stood with one arm around Aphrité Anubis. "Do you think—" Buddy started to ask the Kommandant. "—I mean—"

Warbuckle nodded. "Perhaps we three also should be present. It has never before been done, but with the power of the Vajrachedika talisman. . . ." Still holding Aphrité with one hand, he used the other to raise the glittering medallion with its brightly polished centerpiece high above his head. In the weird purplish light of Sravasti its myriad rays stood out as dazzlingly and even more mystifyingly than ever.

Parama!

The flash, the scent, the sound—and then again—

Parama!

And when the air had cleared Buddy saw Diamond Sutro, Arnaud Subhuti and Renaldo Warbuckle together for the first time. They stood side by side with Aphrité Anubis at the end of their line: Aphrité tall and dark-haired in her flame-cloak, Arnaud Subhuti trim in business suit and necktie, Diamond Sutro resplendent in his white costume with its golden trim and Vajrachedika medallion, Renaldo Warbuckle sinister in his silver-piped and blue-handed black uniform as Kommandant of the fraternal Order of the Flyfot.

"If only Arch Cantrowicz were here," Buddy muttered. "Cantrowicz and the TV people. If only they could see. . . ." Then, more loudly, he said, "You're the ones with the super powers. If this is all real—if you are real, not just something I'm hallucinating—then you must be the ones the Yakshis meant to summon. You must be the ones to settle the spaceburn."

"No." Diamond Sutro shook his head. "We are powerless. We can do nothing." He raised his arm, pointed a finger masterfully at Buddy, moved it to include the others. "We are no more capable than you are, for we are as fragmented as you. We are more images of you.

"The Perfection of Patience, the Delusion of Appearances, the Understanding of the Ultimate Principle of Reality—all of my powers are nothing but a foolish exaggeration of your own powers, the powers of the human mind. The powers of the human imagination."

"And I"—Arnaud Subhuti took over—"what am I but a parody of Auburn Sutro, as the hero is of Buddy?"

"And I," Kommandant Warbuckle snapped, "even Roland L. K. Washburn understands that I am an image of himself, *nicht wahr?*"

"Then—then—what will happen?" Buddy pleaded.

"Can't you help?"

"Can't you help?"

"Can't you help?"

"You must help yourselves!" the three men chanted in unison. Subhuti slipped his tie clip from his conservative J. Press rep. Warbuckle snapped the decorative cover from his wrought-iron belt buckle and turned it to reveal its hidden reverse. They raised the objects over their heads as Diamond Sutro lifted his jeweled medallion. In unison the three voices cried out the word of mystic power.

Parama!

Parama!

Parama!

Buddy watched, motionless, as the triplicated flash filled the room. He blinked his dazzled eyes, rubbed them to see who remained.

There was only Aphrité Anubis. She whispered something to Buddy. He leaned forward, trying to understand, but she ignored him. She flung wide her milk-white arms, spreading the flame-satin cloak like a great pair of wings. Beneath it she was nude, the splendor of her perfect form, the pale, smooth skin set off only by her vivid, perfect nipples and darkly gleaming hair.

Around her neck, hanging from a thread of spun fine gold, lay a miniature replica of the Vajrachedika. She clutched it with one hand, raised her face toward the heavens, whispered *Parama!*

She was gone.

Buddy buried his face in his hands, his body shaking with dry sobs. He looked up, hoping to see them back, but there was no Diamond Sutro, no Renaldo Warbuckle, no Arnaud Subhuti, no breathtaking Aphrité Anubis. Buddy cried, "Come back, come back!" He spoke more to himself than to the others. "Come back! *Parama!* Come back! *Parama!*"

Finally he stopped. A hand was tapping him on the knee. He looked into the serious, concerned face of Auburn Sutro. "Satvan," Auburn said, "see here, what was that stuff all about?"

Buddy drew back. "What?"

"I asked you—"

"Oh, yeah, I heard you, I mean, what stuff, specifically? Of everything that's been going on here?"

Auburn shook his head, looking puzzled. "Everything that ou've been doing, saying. You've been carrying on a whole ialogue. More. You've been leaping around, gesturing, chat- ering like an impressionist, playing every role in a drama. inally you collapsed back into your seat. Roland and I have een watching you. He wanted to stop you, make you stop."

"One good slap would have done it," Washburn put in.

"Yes, right, Roland. The old bring-him-to-his-senses-for- is-own-good business, eh?"

"Exactly!"

"Well, we didn't do that, Buddy. As long as you weren't urting anyone, we just let you run your course. But now that 's over—would you mind explaining what it was all about?"

Now Buddy looked back and forth between Roland and uburn. "You mean you—didn't see them?"

"I'm afraid not, old friend. Who are they?"

"D-Diamond Sutro. Diamond Sutro and—and the others. he Kommandant. And Arnaud Subhuti. And Aphrité nubis. She—she was wearing a satin cloak. She had—"

Roland Washburn broke in on him. "There was absolutely o one here, Satvan. It was all you. Clearly you have gone over e edge." He turned in his seat. "A madman, Auburn. That's hat he is. Nothing but a raving maniac. He's hallucinating."

"I'm not so sure." Auburn shook his head. "Those persons, uddy, that you say were here. They're all familiar names. ren't they characters from your comic strip?"

Buddy nodded silently.

"And you actually saw them here? They spoke to you? What id they say?"

"We were talking about—oh, Christ, so many things. I ean, about our problems. *Our* problems, yours and Roland's nd mine. And all that Dr. Ettmann says and all. You know."

Auburn nodded, making a vague sound of encouragement.

"And we were talking about the spaceburn, you know. All of *ur* problems seem so small, if the whole universe is im- erilled. Yet I can't feel too involved with *that* while we still ave to contend with, uh, *this.* And besides, the Yakshis say we an't solve the spaceburn until we get our own problem work- d out. The star people's computer described a mentality that as supposed to stop the spaceburn, and it wasn't any of the three of us, it was the, ah—" He fluttered his hands, trying t formulate the concept.

"Yes." Auburn Sutro supplied the words. "It has to be th integrated whole. Or perhaps I should say the *re*integrate whole, of which we three are supposedly mere fragments.'

"Check. And"—Buddy sighed, his shoulders heaving u once and then down again in a massive shrug— "and w talked about who they were. Diamond Sutro, I mean, an Aphrité and the others."

Auburn nodded vigorously. "Of course, of course. An who were they, would you say?"

"Well, ah, they were, ah"—he started naming them, tickin them off on his fingers as he recited. "They were Diamon Sutro, Aphrité Anubis, Arnaud Subhuti and Kommandar Renaldo Warbuckle."

"Come off it, Satvan!" Roland Washburn gritted angril "We all know that those are just characters in your stupi comic strip. Maybe you can make some feeble justification fo the cartoon—at least it provides your income—but you kno that your brain children aren't real!"

"Well—that's what I told them. But they said they were rea But then they disappeared. They faded away. By magic. The said *Parama* and they were gone. Even Aphrité. She isn supposed to have that power, but she had it. And—and I trie to summon them back, I said the magic word—"

"I know! We heard you!"

"—but it didn't work. They won't return."

Auburn Sutro rose from his chair and paced in a circl around the seats where Buddy and Roland still remainec Arms crossed, one hand rubbing his chin, he stopped, facin the others, and said, "Buddy, since neither of us—Roland no I—could see these people or hear them speak—"

"But *I* could, they talked to me! They were here!"

"Indeed. And precisely because you *could* see and hea them while we could not, I think we can fairly assume that the were some sort of manifestation of your mind. Your creation As Roland so aptly calls them, your brain children."

"So?" Buddy had now got to his feet and stood unhappil confronting Auburn.

"So." Sutro resumed his pacing, staring at the toes of hi

shoes, rubbing his chin with his hand. "So what they said to you is probably very important. If—to quote Dr. Ettmann—they are an externalization of some part of yourself and you have failed to come to terms with them, what they have to say can tell us a great deal about you.

"Nor am I being altruistic about you as an individual, but also according to Dr. Ettmann—as Roland has so extensively quoted him to me—*we* are all the brain children of somebody else.

"You see?" He stopped pacing, stood beside Buddy, put a hand on his shoulder. "It's a kind of hierarchy, a similarity by analogy. Am I making sense? You see, as your mind cast off Diamond Sutro and the Kommandant and the others, *our* originator cast us off. And if your characters have managed to resolve themselves, so might we be able to. And again constitute the whole individual from whom we came."

Buddy looked into Auburn's face, then away and toward Roland Washburn. "They told me that we three really have some contact in our mind. Minds. Whichever. They told me that they know I didn't kill Oskar Schrieber."

Washburn jumped angrily to his feet, pointed one finger accusingly at Buddy. Before he spoke, however, Buddy said, "And you didn't do it either, Roland! Nor—"

He turned back toward Auburn Sutro who stood coldly waiting for his statement. "Nor did you."

"Then who was it?"

Buddy shook his head. "They said it was somebody named, ah—" He heard a ringing in his ears. The room around him began to grow dim, his breath grew ragged. He put one hand to his throat. His skin was clammy, his eyes bulged. "It was—"

Two Roland L. K. Washburns faced Auburn Sutro. One said, "Did you hear that? What he was saying?"

The other said, "I heard it all. Even though I was submerged, I could hear the whole thing."

"That little pig, trying to shift the blame. Well, we're rid of him now. Rid of Buddy Satvan! Rid of the decadent panderer! We can work together now, you and I, two Washburns!"

"We can! We can carry our work forward! For the good of the Cause!"

"For the Cause!"

"And as for this other—"
"As for Auburn Sutro—"
"He has a good mind. A good technician could be useful."
"Indeed."
"He can—"
"—serve the Cause well!"
Together they turned toward the engineer. Together they asked, "Will you join us? Will you march with us to triumph?"
Auburn Sutro looked from one to the other, scanning the two identical faces and their identical expression. "I was rather inclined to believe Satvan, you know," he replied coolly. "At least—I'd like to know what he was trying to tell us. Who he was going to say did the killing.
"Emerging as you did"—he addressed the new Washburn—"was really a needless exercise in melodrama, don't you know. Really an awful lot like a scene in a grade B film of some decades ago. Very little class, I'm afraid."
"Who killed Schrieber is no longer of interest!" Washburn snapped back. "Oskar Schrieber died a martyr to the Cause. His sacred blood cries out for vengeance. I swear, a Jew will fall for every drop of blood that was shed!"
Sutro's forehead wrinkled with incredulity. "You say—now let me be certain that I have this right, eh? You say that you don't care what Buddy was trying to tell us, that it doesn't matter who killed Oskar Schrieber? Yet at the same time you are blaming the Jews?"
"Precisely. To use your favorite word, Auburn. Precisely. The question is, do you join us now—or do you regret, later, your mistake?"
Sutro laughed acidly. "May I not choose the tertium quid, Roland?"
"What?"
"The third thing. I think you are committing a logical error known as the fallacy of the excluded middle." He gestured deprecatingly.
"I don't know what you're talking about, Sutro. You're getting as jangle-headed as Satvan was. What are you trying to say?"
"I'm saying, Roland, that this ultimatum to join your Cause or, as you put it, regret it later—is a bit precipitate. There are

other courses of action to consider. Among them, I would suggest that we don three of the headbands that are used hereabouts, and try to communicate through them. Perhaps we could do that directly, or perhaps through the Yakshis' computer, You say that Dr. Ettmann is always trying to get our fragmented personalities back togeher. At the Morton Prince Institute that is very, very difficult—but here on Sravasti we have a unique means of doing that, and a unique opportunity to utilize that means!

"Will you"—he turned an inviting smile from one Roland to the other—" join me—mentally? We may achieve something remarkable. At worst, I suppose, we'll accomplish nothing. But I don't think we can lose by the attempt. What do you say?"

There was a momentary silence as the two Roland Washburns exchanged a lengthy look, the look of a man-made monster anticipating its ultimate triumph. They exchanged a smile that was unreadable to Auburn Sutro.

"Let us proceed" was the answer he received.

20. Spaceburn

INTO the machine.

Flowing through circuits, electronic analogues of protoplasmic neural networks, racing along pathways unlike those of any human brain. Locus of consciousness enters a blind maze, racing at speed-of-light, spins through conversion matrices, plunges into storage module.

Sudden experience of recorded star being's mnemotrace: drifting through white-hot lava-sea on a planet dead billions of years, encountering a fellow being, engaging in rites of exchange. A monomolecular bio-sheet floats trillions of miles from its primary, sailing the flow of solar particles. A water-planet encounters an unique Arrhenius spore, enters cystallization process, completes solidification after eons and rises to consciousness. An energy-eater nests on darkside of a small planet, extends a multimillion-mile-long flexible proboscis to such nourishment from the heart of a sun.

The full extent of the machine itself, microcircuitry packed in dense module stacks, each one cubic miles in volume. Signals flash, fragmentary thoughts collide, shatter, reform exchange.

Thought of a red ball. Recollection of a heavy blow. The odor of trapezoidal. Feel of the square root of negativity. Screaming ground slugs. Industrial leopards. Whirling gammadions.

Into the scanner. Into the spaceburn. Glowing, writhing red-orange cinders fading in annihilation.

Beyond. Beyond. Utter nothingness beyond vacuum, beyond zero, beyond negation: nothing nothing nothing.

And back, pull back: this is the scan, not a projection. Pull back, through rushing perspectives, past teeming worlds, pull back.

To Sravasti.

You—you are Roland Washburn.

You are Auburn Sutro.

Raving, racing energy entities.

Personality in electronic flux.

I am—something happened. Every electron, every particle.

I turn, I yield, I alter.

I am Buddy Satvan. You are Washburn. You are Sutro.

Yes.

Yes.

My other is gone. As well, no need.

My recollections.

The flavor of hot bread, texture of hard crust.

The color of the moon.

The feel of flesh entering flesh.

The scent of cooking flesh.

Smoke from a tall brick smokestack.

I remember the sweet smell—but we had only thin soup.

I remember the cries drowned by music.

Oom! Oom van der—

Oom Leon!

The baby! The women! The stripes black/gray/black.
Hollow cheeks. Hollow eyes.
A scarred face. A torn ear.
I remember pictures. The scarlet tights. The all-seeing eye.
Untersturmführer. Obersturmführer.
Jude!
Jude!
The cold soup. The thin soup.
Oom!
Tannie!
Oom! Tannie!
Mama!
Mama? Who said mama?
The tattered pages. The colored panels!
Reb Ottenstein to the East. To Palestine. Their own land.
Oom Leon!
Cheese shop, van der Roest, *Weissjuden.*
Mama!
The Cause! We shall triumph! Smash the degenerates!
Paps!
Who? Who calls for paps? For pa? For paps?
It's all machinery. It's all engineering. Efficiency!
He will be an ordinary man . . . well, a little unusual. . . .
The errors of the past shall be rectified!
We'll make him a scientist. A physicist. With a great house.
The laws of nature are knowable. We simply apply logic.
The Will shall triumph. The Will! Let lesser races perish!
But no one, you see, knows he was frozen beneath the South Pole.
Economic realities, they surely understand economic realities.
And those who oppose us, we will smash ruthlessly!
See, he has this magic word and an amulet, and when he. . . .
One can be safe if one simply understands the causal mechanics.
Haters?
Of course we are haters!
Hatred is our greatest strength!

Bring back my mama!

He has this enemy, of course, with a beautiful daughter, and. . . .

Where is my paps? At the bookstore?

Consider this a problem in transportation alone.

Why can't I go? Why did they take Mijnheer Rosenthal?

We do not seek softness? Don't mislead yourself!

Ja, Mijnheer van der Roest is nice. Misiz, too. But why . . . ?

Parama! Parama! Parama! Parama!

A surge of energy. The Vajrachedika amulet? The star people's machine? On Sravasti, Yakshi images quivered and swayed, swelled, divided, distorted, collapsed.

The thin film that protected the sealed atmosphere of the artificial planet cracked, shimmered, showered to the purple-tinted ground in millions of glittering, jagged shards.

Kristallennacht.

Ancient machineries disintegrated in a fleeting moment, not into broken fragments nor rusted hulks but into dust, fine dust that scattered, flowed, began a slow tidal dance to remote galaxies, traveling on a course that would take hundreds of millions of years to get well started, billions and longer to complete.

If the universe survived.

Sravasti ceased to exist. In the moment of its dissolution the final power surge through its ancient machinery sent a final traveler, a projection that sped not through dimension but through some metaphysical medium directly into the deepest heart of the blackened annihilation of the spaceburn.

Pieter Wachtel looked above him, below him, behind him.

Behind lay the rent, the seared fissure that would readmit him, if he so moved, to the universe he had left. Its rims were of turquoise blue, writhing and twisting, glowing eerily as they had in orange-red when he had seen them from within that universe.

But inside the outlines of the burning region he saw not blackness but a spectacle: suns and nebulae ablaze with light of every shade, extending far beyond the optical into both higher and lower frequencies. He was seeing, hearing, feeling the same radiances, his sensorium blended into a union of inputs. Radio emissions, X rays, cosmic rays, solar winds and intergalactic forces all rang equally on the tympanum of his sensitivity.

Time lost its meaning. Events of dazzling beauty stood crystallized at the peak moment of their efflorescense while simultaneously whole clusters of galaxies wheeled through their cycles flaring and fading in geometric majesty as they danced.

He swung his arms in wide arcs like a diver soaring from his springboard. His perspective revolved. He no longer faced back into the sidereal universe he had departed, but was instead scanning downward in the new orientation of his altered being.

Close behind him there streamed outward a great flickering cone of figures, images, ghosts. At first, a series of forms of men, one pudgy and soft, one self-possessed and intellectual, one hard and militaristic. And behind them, another ranking of caricatures, a cruel martinet, a lab-smocked researcher, a magnificent figure with streaming golden hair and cloak, a pure white garb covering his muscular form and a glittering amulet suspended about his neck by a golden chain.

Following these, others. Beautiful women in spectacular costume, scientists in laboratory clothes, dark-skinned mountain people playing carven flutes. And yet beyond these, younger men and women wearing every conceivable form of clothing, moving slowly through endless postures.

They glittered and whirled in helical ranks, spiraling away behind him, growing smaller and fainter but never disappearing; growing younger, too: children appeared in the strange march, a child version of the fiercely militaristic figure, garbed in black uniform with silver piping and decorative motif of lightning shafts and death's-heads. Another, whimpering and cringing in ragged garb of black and gray stripes. Still another, decked in miniature version of the colorful tights and boots and cape of a man farther up the long swirling line.

At last, far back, a boy dressed in loose blouse and knickers, woolen stockings and brogans; on his face, an expression of puzzlement and grief, tears running from his eyes.

They spiraled, they swung and drifted, they rose, rose, rose through the blackness.

And yet behind them, rising from some unfathomed source, the man Pieter Wachtel saw another configuration like them, at its head a figure much like himself, and behind that other Pieter a swirling pale cone of moving, wavering figures, men and women and children swaying and dancing slowly to some invisible cosmic breeze.

Almost identical, but each figure against its equivalent in Pieter's own entourage was a trifle—older. The men and women a moment more bent, more wrinkled. The children a moment larger and more mature.

And swimming again, swinging himself around, Pieter looked not beneath himself but above and saw yet another such row of bodies swinging, swirling to silent music; and beyond these, another—each a trifle younger, the men and women straighter, stronger, the children slightly smaller and less advanced.

Beneath him, older and older replications of himself and all of his followers. And over him, younger and younger. Stretching to the limit of perspective in both directions.

And around them, forming a great cylinder through which they rose, rose, rose, there lanced flame. Steaming bands of every color from red to violet and beyond: green, blue, yellow, aqua, infra, ultra, transviolet, hyperverdant, ultraxanthic, metacrimson.

And they rose, they rose, and they rose.

He could not tell what he heard—if anything. A trillion voices babbled in his ears, orchestras played, the rush of winds and roar of waters, whines and cracklings.

His senses did not become unjumbled, but he realized that he could penetrate the jumble, could assimilate the blended impressions of color and taste, odor and feel and tone.

The chimney through which he was rising grew incredibly more intense, its walls flaring in all directions until he found himself bathed in painless flames that penetrated his fiber with energies of every color imaginable and he found himself, found himself suddenly in one eternal instant out of the flame, suspended alone in a hyperuniverse of rolling eternities, endless immensities, pale grayness and slackness of force, and reflecting, he found himself gazing calmly, emotionlessly, reactionlessly, into a titanic glowering countenance.

The ears were long, the snout long, the forehead scarred. One of the ears was twisted. The eyes glittered, boring into him with a color and an intensity beyond his experience.

The face reared back, gargantuan hands appeared, wavered, fled. There was a sound that sent him crashing, spinning through metaspace, bounding and echoing off invisible obstacles, quivering and halting at last, still gazing fascinated into that gigantic countenance.

He spread himself to his greatest extent, stretching his limbs, arching back his head, shouting at the top of his voice to the giant who hovered above him.

Cease!

Cease destruction!

His voice echoed and faded, faded into remoteness. The giant seemed to turn toward him, the face revolving slightly as might a head being cocked to one side in puzzlement. The twisted ear was visible.

Who are you? You must help us! Help our people! You must save our people!

The head turned farther. One eye glittered; in it he could see a polished transparent disk. The hands came back huge and pale. They were covered with snug-fitting white gloves. One of them held a long, slim object. Pieter recognized the riding crop.

You? he shouted.

You are the Lord of the Universe?

The face seemed to nod. Down, up again, the long nose pointing beneath Pieter's feet and above his head as it moved.

Pieter screamed. *No! This must not be!*

He opened his mouth to cry the word of power, to summon another to stand for him, then ceased. Instead he drew himself taller, broader, stronger than he had been. He stood as high as the other now.

He confronted the other, their eyes on a level. Pieter could see the irises of his opponent. They were a brilliant shade.

Emerald. The other raised a hand to smite Pieter. Pieter blocked the move with his arm, drove a fist toward the other and struck him above the heart.

For a moment the other staggered backward. For a fragmentary instant Pieter glimpsed the surroundings in which they fought, then returned to the attack. His opponent raised one arm to ward off Pieter's strength. Pieter avoided the arm, managed to strike his opponent again.

Now the opponent brought a great fist roaring, sparkling at Pieter. It landed beside his head. He felt himself lifted, sent flying, whirling off his feet. High above his foe lights dazzled and danced, flashed and burst into fragments.

He tried to look around him, to see where he was, but there was too much light. Images wavered, overlapped, spun. He tumbled back toward his foe. He cried to the other: *What are you? Why are you—?*

—was struck another mighty blow.

Pieter was enveloped in blackness. He felt himself swept again from his feet, hurled away. There was a great heat pulsing in his chest, a tightness in his belly, a tingling in his limbs.

He gasped, jerked, twisted.

There was a roaring. He couldn't tell whether it was coming from outside himself or was his own voice pouring out a final inarticulation.

In the darkness he saw a vague grayish blob that resolved itself with agonizing deliberation as he himself lazily revolved. It was a vague roundness, then a cone, then a helix turning slowly, slowly, slowly. It was a helix of points of colored light. Each point became a blob. Each blob became a shape slowly turning, turning, turning in the roaring blackness.

Buddy Satvan.

Auburn Sutro.

Roland Washburn.

White and gold, jeweled and gleaming. Jeweled and gleaming Diamond Sutro.

Black and silver Renaldo Warbuckle.

Astoroth Anderson.

Glittering white-robed Crystal Knight.

Flame-cloaked, flame-eyed, flame-haired Aphrité Anubis.

Vague and purple-black, rushing and shimmering, fea-

tures mere blots of black-purple: Asoka, Kalinga, Nanda.
Tweed jacket, heavy glasses: Noble St. Vincent Ettmann.
Tara Sakti.
Willy Albertson.
Percy Dillingham/Marie Charbonnet/Boris Tuporov/P'eng Chiao-Tsu.
Tara Sakti.
Black patient Simon Timmons.
Reb. Reb. Bearded, phylacteried Red Ottenstein.
Oom Leon in gray cap and blue overcoat, cynical and thin,
Fat mustachioed Oom van der Roest.
Haggard shaven Oom van der Roest.
Soft and loving Tannie.
Tara Sakti.
M-m-a.
The golden suit, the crimson cape, the all-seeing eye.
M-m-a-m—
The whirlwind.
He was sick, his throat was tight, his mouth sour. His belly heaved.
Tara!
Paps!
Paps!
Papspapspapsss
He heaved, his head rang, he gagged.
M-m-m-m-m. . . .
A-a-a-a-a. . . .
The gray suits and the trucks.
The black suits and the train.
The chimneys and the smoke.
Mmmmmmmmm. . . .
Aaaaaaaaa. . . .
He was
He
Mamma!
He seized his opponent by the throat, frothing, grinding his teeth, tasting his own spittle and blood, letting it foam from his mouth and roll down his chin. He wanted to rip the throat with his teeth.
He squeezed.
He shook.

What—what—?

Aaah!

Are you—are you—?

God?

God?

God?

The face twisted, the features crawled, the face of the jackal.

The face of the jackal!

The scar. The misshapen ear. The glint of the eye.

The opponent raised his hands, moved them toward Pieter. He pulled his thin, bestial lips. *W-w-w-w. . . .*

Feebly he struck at Pieter's hands. Pieter looked, amazed, at the white gloves flopping before his eyes.

W-w-w-w. . . .

The sound rose into an animal howl and echoed, echoed, echoed.

The opponent opened his mouth.

Flames rushed out, roaring, searing, screaming.

He pointed to the sky, wrenching one arm from Pieter's grasp. White-gloved, he pointed.

Lightning crashed, whirlwinds howled. A hot gale swept Pieter's cheek, a wet breeze raked his face.

He threw back his head, glared at the black sky.

Huge clouds rumbled past, rolling roiling juggernauts. Green glowed through them, the emerald of eyes, flashing and grumbling.

Drops drove downward.

Splashed.

Soaked.

Smashed.

Flowed.

Pieter gazed at his hands, still loosely clutching the throat of his

of his

still clutching the throat of

They ran, they dripped, the flood of crimson, the rain of blood. He clutched tighter at his opponent.

The opponent gasped, his mouth opened and shut again

ınd again, then hung slack. Pieter felt his muscles mimicking he attitudes, his jaw falling loose, his tongue protruding. His ears ached with thumping pulses. His vision dimmed.

He strained to throw the other away. The body swung sluggishly in the rushing tide of streaming blood.

The sky was black with tints and flashes of green.

The rain splashed and spattered.

He couldn't rid himself of his foe.

The body clung, his hands clutched it. It grew heavy in his hands. It drew him down. The flood reached to his shoulders. The flood reached to his chin.

He clung to the body.

He slid forward and down, immersed, his eyes flooded with a solid wall of seething red.

He lay on a soft surface of yielding warmth.

He clutched the body to him, his arms around it, his cheek pressing to its chest, his chest pushing on its belly.

He felt its warmth, his warmth, the heat of the flood around him, the soft yielding floor.

He squeezed his eyes shut.

The body, the flood, the floor blended, merged into a single substance surrounding and supporting him. He opened his mouth and let it hang slack, the medium filling him inside and cushioning him outside, inside and outside, in and out.

Ta. . . .

Ma. . . .

a. . . .

a. . . .

a. . . .

21. New York

HE wakened screaming.

He shoved himself upright in his bed, blinking mild watery

eyes against the sharp morning glare. The sound still ringing in his ears was the echo of his own voice. He stopped the echo and the glare by rubbing a forearm across his face.

Tara sat up beside him, dark hair disarranged from the night's slumber, tumbling now over her shoulders and onto her generous breasts. "Buddy?" she said. "Buddy?"

She put her arms around him. He trembled.

"What was it? Was it a dream, Buddy? It's all right now Don't be afraid. Don't—"

He pressed his face into the soft flesh where her neck curved into her shoulder. He put his hands on her body feeling the solidity and warmth of her. He felt her hands on him, on his shoulders, on his back, pressing him tighter against her.

He shuddered once violently, then a series of diminishing after-shocks shook his body. He slipped down into her warmth, pressed his face for a moment against one breast, held in his breath then let it out again and dropped his face onto her belly, feeling the softness and warmth of her on his forehead and cheek, the roughness and comfort of her pubic brush on the side of his face. He pressed his face into her belly, shutting away all the rest of the world, till he had to draw back and take in another shuddering breath.

Her hands were still on him, kneading his flesh. Her voice was puzzled. "Buddy?" she repeated. "Is it—do you want to—?"

He pushed the heel of each hand into the mattress on either side of her hips and shoved himself erect again. He swung his legs over the edge of the bed and dropped his feet onto the carpet.

"No. No."

She slid around beside him and put her arms around his waist, clasped wrist with hand over his navel, her head pressed into his shoulder. "That's all right. You don't have to. When you want to."

He nodded and picked up her knotted hands. He pressed them to his face for a few seconds and kissed her fingers. He pulled the hands apart and put them gently away from himself. He got off the bed and walked to the bathroom, came back a few minutes later.

She smiled uncertainly. "Do you want to talk? Was it a dream?"

He pulled on his trousers and sat on the bed again, holding one of her hands. "Maybe it was. I don't—" He shrugged. "I'm all right now. Thanks. Thanks."

She moved her hands, pulled a sheet up to her throat as if suddenly modest. He managed a beginning laugh at that and she bested him. "What happened, Buddy?"

"It's all over. I need to make a phone call. No, two. No, three. Uh—" He slipped his hands around her shoulders and gave her a long kiss. She slid her hands around his neck, threaded her fingers in the back of his hair.

"Buddy, come back to bed."

He pulled away, shook his head. "Later. Tonight. First—"

She climbed out of bed and pulled the sheets into place, patted away the worst of the wrinkles. When she finished she went to the closet, then into the bathroom.

She emerged wearing casual slacks and a loose, long-sleeved blouse. Buddy was walking back and forth in the middle of the room. He watched while she buttoned her blouse.

"I don't know what—how it happened."

She pulled a wire-backed chair around, sat on it with her arms folded across the top, not speaking.

"I'm the only one here." He rubbed the side of his forefinger against his temple. "I know about the others. Auburn is still around, I know him, you see, but he's out of *here.* Roland too. He's out. And the other one. I—I've had this—like a speck, a thing, whatever. A pressure, whatever, for as long as I can remember. Like I didn't know it was there until now but it's gone. I know who that has to be. It has to be Pieter. My—I guess he was my father."

Tara moved her hand toward him; from across the room it was a gesture.

"Pieter—is gone too?"

"Gone?" Buddy looked at her. Again, "Gone? Yes. But not like Roland or Auburn. He's—*gone.* Like, not just out of my *head.*" He gestured with his hand, the palm cupped and away from his brow, moving the hand as if he were throwing something with it.

"They're just *gone,* you know, the others, are just *gone.* Bu
Pieter is *gone.*" The emphasis was completely different, as i
one statement meant gone out of the room and other, gone
out of existence.

"You mean—you've got the fragmented personalities integrated now? The way Dr. Ettmann wanted you to?"

He shook his head. "No. I'm myself. Only myself. I haven'
got the things that the others have. I'll have to work myself
back to—to whatever's missing. But the others are completely
out of my head now. I'm all myself. I'll never have blackouts
again. They'll never come back."

She almost flew to her feet. "But that's—that's marvelous
That's even better! I think. I mean—I know you were
supposed to need to get some things back from the others
from Roland and Auburn. But I didn't—

"And Pieter. If he was the original, then when you all came
back together, I was so afraid, Buddy would be gone and the
person would be Pieter. I don't—I don't even know Pieter. I'm
in love with Buddy, not with those others."

He nodded. "Yes. *I* love you. I don't know if Pieter or
Auburn would. As for Roland Washburn—" He shook his
head.

She looked at him with widened eyes. "How do you
know—?"

"About Pieter and—"

"That they're—"

"Gone?"

A whispered "Yes."

"I don't know." He shook himself all over like a dog shed-
ding water. "I don't know how I know. I just—you can *tell.* I
can just *tell.* If I could get back that—if it was a dream. Maybe I
can—it doesn't matter."

"No," she said, "it doesn't." She held his arm with both her
hands, pressed her head against his shoulder. He put both
hands on her.

They went into the kitchen and made themselves breakfast.
After they'd eaten he went to the telephone and sat down.

"Who are you going to—"

"Auburn first." He flipped the pages of the telephone book,

dialed an area code, more numbers, talked, jotted, dialed again.

She caught his eye. "Should I—?" She shrugged away toward the other room. He shook his head, no.

He talked into the telephone, listened for a long time, talked once more briefly. He doodled on the pad by the phone, a group of roughed-in faces he had never drawn before, grunted a few times into the receiver, talked some more. Finally he dropped the phone in its place and looked at Tara, smiling.

She said, "What—?"

He said, "I just talked to Auburn Sutro. I didn't know his number but fortunately his company has his name. Fortunately." He laughed.

She said, "And?"

"Same thing. Same—you know? *I'm* gone. Out of his head. The same way. He remembers me, knows who I am, everything. But we're separated now. Really."

"And the others?"

"Roland? I'll phone Ettmann. But I'm sure. As for Pieter Wachtel, I don't know where he is. Nowhere on earth, I'm sure. It's—it worked the opposite of what Ettmann was trying to do. Instead of putting Buddy and Roland and Auburn back together like pieces of a jigsaw puzzle—so Pieter would be the only one here and we others would be gone—instead Pieter is gone and we three remain. Separated like Siamese, ah, triplets."

"Is he dead?" Tara asked.

Buddy said, "No. I mean—I know he's nowhere in the—" He gestured with both hands, indicating the whole room and the whole world. "He isn't alive, I suppose, either. Not as we are. But he isn't dead."

He shook his head. "He isn't on this plane anymore." Buddy looked questioningly at Tara. "Does that make sense? Is it a lot of mystical gibberish or does it make some kind of sense?"

"No," she said. "I mean, I—think I understand."

There was a pause.

"Buddy, what do you want to do now? Today?"

"Work," he said. "Phone Ettmann in Virginia. Go to City Hall and get married. Or get hold of a rabbi to do it."

He stopped, startled. Tara looked surprised also.

"I didn't know you—"

"Neither did I! Isn't that—? Does it matter?"

"No, I—of course not."

"Or climb back in bed and f-fuck all day," he resumed. "Or go downtown and just go to the movies one after another till we can't stand any more. Eat a pound of candy. Five pounds. Ride out to Shea Stadium. Walk the whole length of Broadway. Sit on a lion in front of the library. Poke around in the cellar of an old bookstore on Fourth Avenue. I don't know, I don't know, what do *you* want to do?"

He was talking faster and faster, giggling under and between his words. Finally he tumbled back onto the bed laughing and rolling until he was out of breath.

He stood up again.

"What do you want to do?" he said.

"Anything! All of it!" she grinned.

He sat down again and used the telephone. When he had finished he smiled at Tara. "I was right," he said. "Ettmann was totally blown out. He says Roland's been claiming the same thing all morning. He had an early morning session with him. But Roland's been denying the others all along. Especially me. So Ettmann didn't believe him!"

They laughed together.

"But now he's going to have to go back to court. What a circus that's going to be!"

"Go back to court? Why?"

"Why? Because of Schrieber. Do you see what's going to—what's *got* to happen now?"

She said, "No, I don't."

He laughed. "Neither do I! I mean—maybe we can figure it out. If we can't—well, I don't suppose it's entirely our problem. Maybe not our problem at all. I'll have to get out from under that court order so we can travel and all, but I'm not suffering."

"But what *will* happen?" she pressed.

"Oh—I was, that is, the person who was found with the gun when Oskar Schrieber was shot, was committed to the Morton

Prince Institute in lieu of a murder trial, you see? Because the court ruled that there were all those people inhabiting the one body. The judge really decided that a regular criminal proceeding was out of the question.

"And Ettmann was given custody of that one body. That was before all the really strange things, the duplicating and all, started in."

Tara nodded dubiously. "What happens now?"

"Now Ettmann has to go back to the court and say that he knows which one of us killed Schrieber. That it wasn't me, or Auburn Sutro, or even Roland Washburn.

"It was Pieter Wachtel, and Ettmann has to convince the judge that Pieter is—uh, I guess,—dead. You know, gone, the way I was talking about gone, before. Out of this world. Passed on to a higher plane. It isn't what *I* mean by dead, but I guess legally it might stick.

"And the person that Ettmann has locked up, that warm body down in Virginia, that's Roland L. K. Washburn. That isn't ever going to be anybody else again, that's Roland for the rest of his life, and *he* didn't kill anybody! For all that he's a despicable fascist creep. He didn't kill Schrieber."

"Okay," Tara said. "I follow, I guess. And that should leave you in the clear too. But meanwhile, as you say, it's no great hardship sticking around New York."

She grabbed his hand and started pulling him toward the door. "Come on then, let's go eat a box of candy or something. It's too beautiful a day just to stay home. Unless you want to fuck all day!"

"It's tempting!" he laughed. "But—want to play serious secretary for a while and earn the munificent salary that I pay you?"

"What?"

"Uh—let's make a couple more calls. Tell Willy Albertson to meet us down at the syndicate office. And get hold of what's-her-name, Arch Cantrowicz's secretary. Tell her I'm coming in and I'm going to see Cantrowicz."

"You want me to ask for an appointment?"

"No." He shook his head. "Just tell her to tell him I'm coming in."

Tara grinned and reached for the phone.

They marched into the syndicate office half an hour later. Willy was sitting in Burt Bahnson's office drinking coffee. Burt was making small talk, clearly desperate to avoid any topic of personal impact.

"Buddy," Albertson and Bahnson chorused. Willy added Tara's name. Then, "Burt—do you know Tara Sakti, Buddy's secretary? She just about held the strip together all the time Buddy was, ah—"

Burt Bahnson stood up. "I know Tara, sure. How are you?"

She smiled at him.

"What's the meeting all about, Buddy?" Willy asked. "Something popping?"

"You bet. Look, would you guys just kind of hang out here while I go talk to Arch? There may be some changes made—we'll call you in if we need to, but more likely we'll just work things out and let you know afterwards."

"Thanks a lot, Mr. Satvan," Bahnson gritted.

"Sure you don't want some support?" Tara asked, amazed.

Willy offered "Maybe I should—"

"Thanks," Buddy cut him off, "I'll go in alone. Afterwards we can all go out and eat a box of candy or something. You too, Burt. Don't feel bad—I just need to go up against Cantrowicz one to one, that's all."

He left the others exchanging puzzled looks in his wake and barged into Cantrowicz's office just as Cantrowicz was completing a telephone conversation. Buddy shut the door behind himself. Cantrowicz looked up, said into the telephone, "Okay, more then later on, Stuart, sure, yes," and hung up.

"Hello, Arch!" Buddy greeted.

Cantrowicz opened a huge ebony humidor that stood on his desk, its little felt feet protecting the glass sheet from scratches. "Buddy"—he smiled—"I'm glad to see you again. Decide to take that *Big Pro* job with Walt Jensen, did you? You'll always have a home around here, I promise you that!"

Buddy thumped into the leather chair opposite Cantrowicz's desk. "No," he said, "but I've decided to take you up on your other offer."

Arch lifted a thick green cigar from the humidor and

tipped the lid down. It made a rich, positive sound as it clapped shut. Cantrowicz studied Buddy for a few seconds. "I'm pretty tied up today. You didn't let me know you were coming in."

"Do you want to talk to me?" Buddy asked.

Cantrowicz waved his cigar placatingly. "Of course. Of course. You're the creative talent, Buddy. You artists are the people this industry is all about. We business types, we're just here to get the product from the artist to the public, that's all, we're just service people."

"Bullshit."

Cantrowicz frowned. "What is it, then?"

"I'm willing to give you *Diamond Sutro.* I'll get off the strip, Willy can take it over. He doesn't even need me to ghost it, he knows the characters, he can work up his own story lines and Ivy can spell him on the inking. She's a smart kid and she'll do all right."

Cantrowicz put down his cigar with a shaking hand. "You mean that, Buddy?"

"I do."

"No strings attached?"

"I didn't say that." Now it was Buddy's turn to grin.

"Okay, you bastard. What's the price?"

"Now, now." Buddy shook a finger. "When you asked me before to get off *Diamond Sutro*—you remember your little speech about getting stale?—you said I could make some new proposals to Burt for new features."

"That's right. No guarantees we'll take 'em, of course. But you're a talented man, you have a good chance."

"Arch, what's the network deal? How much did they offer for rights to *Diamond Sutro*?"

"You are a wise bastard. That's none of your fucking business. That's between Sugarman and me and that redhead Warwick bitch. You stick to your drawing board and leave the business details to me."

Buddy shook his head. "It's not that easy. But I want to know, Arch, why do you want me off the strip so badly? That stale business is a pile of crap. And why hasn't there been an announcement on the TV deal? It's all through the trades but only rumors."

"We're still working out final details. It's going through, don't worry."

"Sure it is. Couldn't be you're worried about the Schrieber thing, could it? Or are the studio people or the network people upset?"

Cantrowicz paled. "Did Bahnson spill this to you? If that s.o.b.—"

"Don't sweat it. Burt didn't have to tell me. Anybody who can see his fingers in front of his face could figure it out. This is worth—what? Half a mill in front? Not just TV rights. Once the show starts hitting an audience every week it means, what, thirty million impressions? Forty? What're subsidiary rights worth then? What was *Batman* worth the week he made the cover of *Life*?"

"Okay," Cantrowicz growled around his still unlighted cigar. "All right, Buddy. You're a brighter boy than I figured you for. Okay, good for you. You can see what's at stake here. Well, get the fuck out of the way or you're going to get run over by a fucking steamroller. You understand that?"

"Arch, Arch, why do you think I came in? You need me quietly to step aside. No stink, no scandal. Once that happens the TV thing falls into place. The syndicate makes a bundle. You pull down a sweet bonus. Everybody gets fat and happy. Right?

"Except for. . . ." He let it hang.

Cantrowicz picked up a fresh cigar, held the two in his hands and glared at them. He put one back in the humidor, bit the end off the other and spit it into the wastebasket behind his desk. He lifted an ebony lighter and flamed the tobacco into life. He drew on the cigar, held the smoke in distended cheeks for long seconds, then blew it into the air.

"You artists are all the same, Satvan. Long as you're broke and hungry you're willing to work for peanuts, hell, you'll wash dishes for a living and give your stuff away to get it into print. Anything, anything.

"Take some punk out of the gutter and give him a job, first thing he wants to do is put a knife in your back and bite the hand that feeds him." Cantrowicz extended one hand dramatically across the desk, waiting for Buddy to bite it.

"Looks like they'll have to buy somebody else's super hero then, eh?" Buddy said.

Cantrowicz pulled his hand back and chomped down angrily on his cigar. "You'd better go home and read your fucking contract, Satvan. Take a good look at Clause Fifteen. Moral Turpitude. I'll see you back in the gutter before this is over!"

"Crap. I'm getting clear of that Schrieber business. You'll never make that stick and you know it."

"Schrieber business? What business is that? I'm talking about Clause fifteen, and that little slut you're sleeping with. We can't have people of lax morals—"

Buddy was out of his chair and across the desk, Cantrowicz's necktie bunched in his hand and the other balled into a fist. For an instant he was going to send his fist crashing into Cantrowicz's face, but the look of total astonishment and terror held him back and then he relaxed his grip, pushed himself back off the desk, the heavy humidor and ornate lighter crashing onto the floor as he stood up.

"You are too much," he finally said. "That shitty move just cost you a hundred thou, Cantrowicz. Now you listen to me. You want to fight this thing out on every TV screen and every newspaper in the country, you just go ahead and pull your stinking Clause Fifteen gimmick. What do you think *Diamond Sutro* will be worth then? You won't be able to give away the rights. You'll be cutting off your nose to spite your face."

"God damn, God damn," Cantrowicz was mumbling, "God damn, what the hell happened to you, what the hell happened to you? Casper Milquetoast in person and all of a sudden. . . ." He looked down at his ruined tie and tried to smooth it with the edge of his hand. "God damn you, Satvan, what the hell do you want?"

Buddy ticked it off on his fingers. "First, just to keep the syndicate honest and to keep me comfortable, a share of the *Diamond Sutro* subsidiaries."

"The TV rights?"

"All rights. For God's sake, Cantrowicz, don't you understand that I *created* this strip, and you're asking me to give it away?"

"You sold it to us!"

"Okay, forget it. I'm sorry I got angry." Buddy started to rise from his chair. "I'll see you in court," he added.

"No, no, wait a minute."

He sat down again.

Cantrowicz opened his cupboard drawer and pulled out a bottle and two glasses. "How big a share? You know"—he grinned feebly—"I've always said that the artist wasn't treated right, he ought to own a piece of the feature."

Buddy said, "We'll let the lawyers and accountants settle that. They're really good at that stuff. I'm just a dumb fat pencil pusher. Second, I'll do a new strip for you."

"You don't want to help poor Walt? He really needs some help with *Big Pro.* He really needs some talent there. The strip really isn't doing as well as it ought to."

"I'll do a new strip for you. I have some ideas for a good realistic strip. One that deals with contemporary problems in a realistic manner."

Cantrowicz held his head with both his hands. "Buddy, I can't *sell* that. People want escape. You know that. They want gag strips or they want adventure."

"Yeah. That's the deal."

"God damn you! All right. It just better be fucking good, that's all. How the hell come you want to do fucking contemporary realism all of a sudden?"

Buddy leaned back in his chair. "It isn't so sudden, as a matter of fact. I've been doing a lot of thinking, lately, Arch. You know, I've always done escape stuff. I think people really do need that. In our culture, anyhow. You don't automatically reach for your revolver when you hear the word 'culture,' do you?"

He didn't wait for an answer. "Most people need escape. But there has to be a market for real stuff, too. There have to be some people who are ready to face their problems instead of running away from them, don't you think? People who want to try and solve their problems?

"I mean, we offer one kind of thing for people who just can't look at themselves, at their lives. So we give them something else to think about. But can't we give something to people who are willing to look at themselves and say, hey, you know, there's something wrong here, this is really pretty shitty, you know? And do something about it? Change it?"

Cantrowicz shook his head. "You'll fall on your fat ass."

"I'll risk it. That's my deal. Let me risk it."

"And if it flops?"

"Don't sabotage me, Arch. That's got to be part of the deal too. We'll have to work some safeguards into the agreement. But if it flops I've got this other idea, something that'll put even *Diamond Sutro* so far in the shade, you won't believe it. It—never mind. It's mine. You'll hear about it when the time comes, if the time comes. Or maybe you'll just see it in the funny pages!"

"Is that all?" Cantrowicz asked grimly. He downed his drink on the end of the last word.

Buddy said, "That's all." He stood up and started for the door.

"Well, where the hell are you going, Buddy? We'll need you around here with the legal squad."

"Tomorrow, Arch. Right now I'm going to get Tara and Willy and pry your boy Bahnson loose for the rest of the day and we're going downtown and find some silly-ass movie and sit through it all day and eat stale candy till we all get sick."

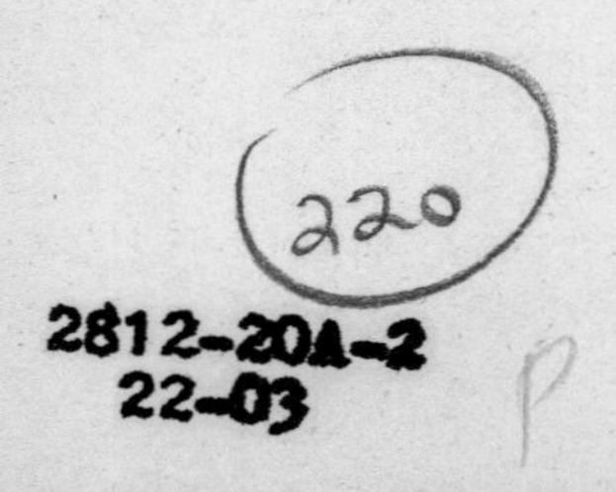
220
2812-20A-2
22-03